WILD KELTIC CAROUSELLE

DOUBLE KELTIC TRIAD 4

LIZZIE STARR

Dokopot Books

To those who love the dance;
To those who dance for joy;
And to Maggie, because.

CHAPTER
ONE

S he absolutely dreaded going back to work. Not that she disliked her job; she loved what she did and missed the camaraderie with her coworkers. What she didn't miss was the back stabbing and bitching. After nearly six weeks off, getting back to her normal routine was low on Carrie's list of priorities.

But, it was time. She'd taken the time off because she could. She'd hardly even thought about work—except to chuckle occasionally at the rumors she knew had to be flying at The Panther's Back.

Nightshade had been true to his word and hadn't contacted her about new dances or costume designs. In fact, he hadn't called her at all. Carrie leaned her chin in her hand. She missed the flamboyant exuberance of her manager—much of the world paled in comparison.

The bookstore was busy and the tiny coffee shop crowded. A moment of guilt at taking up a table when there were others who glanced meaningfully at her nearly empty mug flared through Carrie. She mentally shook herself. Why did she always have to be the one who moved aside, made way for others? She didn't—and she was staying at her miniscule table until she was ready to leave. Maybe she'd even have a second cup of cocoa.

Carrie sipped her cooling chocolate and watched shoppers browse through the myriad of colorful, slick magazines at the nearby display. A trio of women poured over the bridal magazines. It was easy for Carrie to tell which young woman was the bride-to-be. Happy, almost giddy, she pointed out dresses and giggled over honeymoon suggestions with her friends. That was as it should be, but it still made Carrie sigh with longing. There weren't many things she really wanted out of life...

A tall, pale blond man caught her attention as he crouched in front of the gardening magazines. That—the way he held himself, the intensity of his gaze, the gentle lines of his face—could be one of those things she wanted. Unable to look away from the compelling man, Carrie craned her neck to read the titles of the magazines he already held in one hand.

The slick, bland cover of an architectural digest was easy to decipher. The second magazine was gaudier, full of color. The magazines slipped in his grasp and Carrie caught a glimpse of cartoonlike drawings. Anime? She loved the Japanese style of animation. This guy became more intriguing by the second.

Carrie set her mug on the table and stared unabashedly. Certainly there must be some way to introduce herself. There were plenty of hows, the real question was how could she work up enough courage to introduce herself to a stranger. How could she be so successful in her job, yet be so hesitant to meet people when outside of her work persona? Just another one of the mysteries of her life.

All she had to do was stand up, move to the magazine racks and stand next to him. Carrie cocked her head and watched as he glanced through a magazine, shook his head slightly, and returned it to the rack. Was he looking for something specific?

Maybe she could help him look. Never mind the fact that she knew little to nothing about gardening. She'd even forget to water silk plants.

::Come, Carrie. Ye can do this. If ye really wish t' meet him, just go meet him. He'll like ye.::

Great. Carrie stared down into her empty mug. It had been a long, long time since she'd heard the voice of her imaginary childhood friend, Lottie. She didn't need to hear the odd tones and accent now; she'd long ago grown up and away from the need for an imaginary protector and friend. A low, mental sigh, then empty silence teased her mind. Had she been alone, Carrie would have called out to Lottie and begged her to return. Still, she could take the imaginary advice, even if she didn't think the guy would like her. Not after he got to know her.

Carrie took a deep breath, steadied the sudden quivering in her belly, and flattened her palms against the laminated tabletop. One last look and she'd leave. She had to pass by the magazines to reach the door. It would be a perfect time for a chance meeting. She could do this.

The man had risen and turned his back to her. From the way his head swiveled one way then another, Carrie guessed he was looking for someone. She let her eyes close in defeat. A wife probably. At least a girlfriend. Why did she even bother with daydreams?

More customers crowded into the coffee shop and Carrie could no longer justify remaining at the table. She gathered her latest purchase, tugged her purse strap over her shoulder, and turned in the chair to rise.

A pair of tiny arms wrapped around her knees prevented her from standing. A cherubic face, all wide, blue eyes over a rosebud mouth, surrounded by pale, white-blonde hair, smiled up at her.

"Mommy."

With the magazines he had been looking for tucked under his arm, Bryce rose and moved toward the children's magazines. The small, specially designed section was empty. A flare of anguish burst from the pit of his stomach. "Bree?" he whispered.

The anguish rushed to panic. Where was she? He hadn't looked away for that long—had he? She wouldn't run off; he'd drilled the dangers of such actions into her. In her four year old way, she obeyed him and limited contact with strangers. It was difficult for her. As a gregarious child, Breanna loved to talk to anyone and everyone.

Just as Bryce turned toward the front of the store where a security guard leisurely attended the entrance, he heard Bree's high giggle. "Mommy!"

Whipping his body toward the beloved sound, he scanned the area designated as the store's coffee shop. At the edge, near a low, metal divider, Bree had her arms wrapped tightly around a woman's legs.

Relief flooded through him, cooling the hot panic, and Bryce closed his eyes. Embarrassment followed and heated his face. Generally, most people accepted Bree's hijinks without a problem, but Bryce knew someday she might meet someone who didn't care to like her. It would surprise his daughter, and he dreaded the resulting loss of innocence.

Bryce rushed into the coffee shop and took a deep, shaking breath before he confronted his daughter and the woman who now spoke softly to her. The gentle tones of her voice soothed his frazzled nerves and he released his breath slowly. He looked at the woman.

And could not draw another breath.

Until she glanced up, noticed him hovering and flashed him a tentative smile. She stroked her hand over Bree's hair and gave a minute tug to the ribbon wrapped around one of her short pigtails. "Is this yours?"

"I'm sorry if she disturbed you. She knows better than to run off." Bryce crouched beside Breanna and cupped her chin with a bent finger. "Don't you?"

"It's Mommy."

"No, darlin'. This isn't Mommy. Mommy's gone, remember?"

"My new mommy." The small girl climbed into the woman's lap and wrapped her arms about the woman's neck.

Bryce squelched the insane urge to do the same thing. Well, maybe he'd hold the woman on his lap instead, but having her in his arms definitely aroused some interesting, uncomfortably pleasant sensations.

The woman gave a small sound of surprise. Before Bryce could apologize a second time, she waved at the empty chair across from her. "It's okay. Why don't you have a seat while we sort this out." She leaned back to look into Bree's face. "Do I look like your mommy?"

"Don't know. She's gone." Bree shook her head, unwrapped one arm, and patted the woman's face. "I saw you. My new mommy." With that proclamation, she snuggled into the woman's lap and tucked her thumb between her lips. "See, Daddy?" She spoke around the obstruction. "I finded her."

"Found her," Bryce corrected automatically.

"Divorced?"

"Huh?" The question in the single word startled Bryce. Was she interested in more than why Bree clung to her? He hoped so. "No, her mother died shortly after she was born. The strain of carrying a child was too great."

"How awful. You must miss her terribly."

Bryce lifted one shoulder in a casual shrug. "She was a good friend. Bree was an accident that strained our friendship." The smile reserved for his daughter stretched his lips. "A very happy accident."

"A-dent." Bree closed her eyes.

"I'm sorry. I shouldn't pry. She just surprised me. Does she often pick out strange women and call them mommy?"

"Never."

"I wonder why she chose me." The woman stroked Bree's hair.

For his own sake, and his rising interest, Bryce didn't have to wonder why. There was something about this woman. He could have picked her out of a crowd of thousands—and would, if she would give him the chance. Only once before had he felt such an instant attraction—and that to a woman who wore a mask so he couldn't even see her face.

"I'm Bryce MacAlister."

"Carrie."

"And you've met my daughter, Breanna."

Bree opened her eyes and smiled up at Carrie. "Met mommy." Then she turned her earnest gaze to Bryce and shook one chubby finger at him. "I find, you keep."

"Uh, it doesn't work that way, honey."

Bree sighed. "I know, Daddy. You'll find a way."

Bryce lifted his gaze from his daughter to Carrie's questioning expression. He shrugged again. "She's never mentioned wanting a mother."

"Not a mommy," Bree piped up. "This mommy."

A faint pink covered Carrie's cheeks and she glanced away. Bryce took the opportunity to study the woman cradling his daughter so carefully in a completely relaxed, natural embrace.

Her highlighted, golden brown hair was pulled back with a clip. Strands had escaped the confinement and trailed loosely around her face and down her neck. A tiny spot of whipped cream, a remnant from her beverage, hovered just above her upper lip. A shapely lip, poised above the lush, kissable pout of the lower.

Yep. Definitely kissable.

Her lips moved and pulled into a wide smile. Guiltily, Bryce lifted his gaze. Chocolate brown eyes twinkled as if she fought to control some hidden amusement.

He'd been caught.

"Uh, sorry for staring."

"'S okay. Actually, I'm used to it."

He could believe that.

"But, it's not usually my face being stared at." Carrie chuckled, a low throaty sound that insisted he respond. He did, in a pure, naturally male way. His gaze dropped to her breasts. She chuckled again, her body moving against the soft material of her shirt.

The Sahara Desert would seem lush and tropical in comparison to the sudden dryness in his mouth. Her breasts were—perfect. Neither overly large, nor small enough to need padding. Nope, there was no padding there. In fact, if she even wore a bra, it had to be one of those soft athletic things. He could see the tantalizing, firming peak of...

Oh, God. What was he doing?

Carrie shifted and repositioned Bree to cover her breasts.

"I... uh. Sorry." Why didn't somebody just shut him up?

To his surprise, Carrie reached over and touched the back of his hand. "Don't worry. Like I said, I'm used to it. It's all a part of my line of work."

But, it wasn't at all like to what she was accustomed. Somehow, the way he'd stared at her was—nice. There was no leer in his expression, no mental drooling. Just assessment and approval.

Carrie wanted this man's approval so there was no way she was going to tell him how she earned a living. But, with her last statement, he was sure to ask. She'd give him her stock, brush off answer and hope he fell for the lack of details.

"So, what do you do? For a living, I mean?"

He was flustered. How endearing. Now, she really couldn't tell him the truth. "I do a kind of modeling."

Bryce leaned his head one way to look at her. She canted her chin to strike a practiced pose and he grinned. "Not difficult to see why."

Part of her, some little kernel of hope, wanted her to tell him everything. A little bit of hope praying he wouldn't be disgusted or turn away when he found out the truth. Carrie bit back a sigh. She couldn't chance his rejection.

The warm bundle of child in her lap gave a sigh as deep as the one Carrie held within her. She responded by holding Breanna just a bit more tightly and stroking two fingers over her fine, straight hair. The man and his daughter were a potent combination. One that made her both jittery with anticipation and full of peaceful longing. No, she couldn't take the risk and hope he would stay. Better to be only partially honest.

And part liar.

Carrie ducked her head to hide the shame she feared grew bright in her eyes.

A masculine hand appeared in her vision and Bryce stroked his daughter's cheek. "She's asleep."

Carrie lifted her gaze and Bryce grinned at her. "It's a miracle. Bree's not the best at taking naps and sometimes she gets overly tired. I hate to admit it, but she's not a joy to be around when she's cranky. Hopefully I can get her to the car without totally waking her."

"Why don't you go pay for those."

"Huh?"

Carrie nodded toward the magazines stacked at the edge of the table. "Your reading material. I can carry Bree out to your car. The fewer times she's moved, the less chance of her waking up." That way she'd get to hold the warm, sweet smelling child a short while longer. Holding Bree was suddenly the most important thing she could do. Besides, it would keep her close to Bryce as well.

Nodding once, Bryce rose, slid the magazines from the table and left the coffee shop. Carrie stared at his back as he walked toward the cash register. Nice. More than nice. She swallowed heavily. She'd have to do whatever she could to keep this man.

Keep him? How could she keep what she didn't have?

::*Yet.*::

"Shut up, Lottie," Carrie murmured under her breath. Great, more comments from her imagination. Yet, those thoughts merely echoed her own, reinforcing her unconscious decision to do just that—make Bryce MacAlister hers.

Rising carefully, she watched Breanna's face as she tried to juggle a child who was heavier than she looked, her sack of books, and the eel-like movement of her purse strap. She frowned at the large white mug still sitting on the table with a wadded paper napkin popping from the top. She hated leaving a mess for someone else to clean up, but there was no way she could add the cup to her burden.

An elderly woman touched her elbow softly. "Are you leaving, dear?"

"Yes. You're welcome to the table. I'll get my mess out of the way—somehow."

"Oh, don't worry about it. I'll take your cup back with mine later. I wouldn't want you to disturb your sleeping angel. Go on now, take your baby home and love her."

"But, she's not—"

"An angel? I'm sure she is, dear. Run along now. The longer you delay, the cooler my cappuccino is getting." The woman's wrinkled face burst into a sunny smile. She shooed Carrie away from the table and sat in the recently vacated chair.

"Thank you. Enjoy your cappuccino."

"Double mocha. Of course I'll enjoy it. Give that angel a kiss for me." The woman lifted her mug, inhaled deeply, and took a careful sip. She waved one hand then turned her attention to a book she pulled from her purse.

Carrie hurried toward the front of the store where Bryce waited. She tried to read his expression, but distance hid any nuances from her. By the time she stood at his side, his expression was guarded and his smile tentative. Was he regretting letting her help him with his daughter?

He rested his hand at the small of her back as they exited the bookstore and used easy pressure to guide her through the parking area to his car.

Carrie bit at her lip to stop a nervous giggle. His four-door, white sedan was parked right next to her small SUV. If she believed in fate, this would be a prime example that they were meant to meet. But, there was no fate, no luck. Nothing directing her life except her own decisions.

Silent, she watched Bryce unlock his vehicle then open the rear door and ready the child seat. He nodded back at her and stood to the side to allow her to place the still sleeping girl in the seat. Before she backed out of the car, Bree opened one eye. "Bye, Mommy, see you soon." Bree's eyelid slipped closed and she tucked her thumb back into her mouth.

Carrie chewed on her lower lip. Only minutes ago this child broke into her life and changed it. How could she let the small girl go? She shook her head. It wasn't up to her—or was it? Straightening, she angled to face Bryce.

"I'd really like—"

"Would it be okay if I—"

They chuckled together at their simultaneous speech.

"Daddy first." The soft instructions came from inside the car, but when Carrie bent over to peek in at Bree, the girl had curled slightly to one side with her cheek resting against a soft, stuffed hippo. Carrie glanced up at Bryce and he shrugged.

"Would it be okay if I called you sometime?" A faint ruddiness colored the fair skin over his cheekbones.

Yes! Her heart screamed the word. She barely kept the single syllable from slipping from her lips but was unable to contain a silly grin. "I was going to say I'd really like to see you—and Breanna—again sometime. So, of course. Yes. Call me."

"I will. Your number?"

"Oh." The nervous giggle returned to tickle her throat. "I guess that would make it easier, huh?"

"Much." Bryce held out the paper sack with his magazines. "Write it on here."

Carrie dug a pen from her bag, lay the sack on the hood of his car, and carefully printed out her phone number. She paused a moment, then wrote a second number. "I'll give you my cell number, too. Sometimes that's the only way to reach me."

She seldom gave anyone the number to her cell phone. There were too many crazy people who would harass her mercilessly if they could reach her. "And the other number is unlisted."

"You're a very private person, Carrie."

"I have to be." She handed the sack to him and inched toward her vehicle. She didn't want to leave, but she couldn't stand around a parking lot all day either. He'd call. She was positive he would do as he said he would. She'd hear from him soon. Now, all she had to do was convince herself he hadn't asked out of politeness or because he thought she expected the request.

The keys rattled loudly when she pulled them from her purse and juggled them to find the right key for the door lock. Bryce covered her hand with his. "Let me." He took the keys from her hand, easily found the proper key, unlocked and opened the door for her. He kept her keys in his hand until she slid behind the steering wheel. When Bryce placed the keys into her waiting, open palm, she tingled from the brief touch of his long fingers. Oh, he had to call.

"Well, uh, bye. Thanks for your help with Bree."

"It was my pleasure, Bryce." Saying the word pleasure and connecting it with his name increased the tingles.

Bryce stood in the open door; his fingertips lingering against Carrie's palm. Reluctant to let her go, even though he had her phone number, he simply looked at her. She returned his gaze with frank, honest interest. There was no way she was leading him on, pretending to be interested. Her hand trembled.

How soon could he call her? With his free hand he touched the plastic lump of his own cell phone. As soon as she left the parking lot? No, not while she was driving. How long would it take her to get home? No, that would make him seem desperate. Tomorrow. He would call her tomorrow. Maybe she would be free tomorrow night.

Bryce smiled and Carrie returned the grin as she curled her fingers around the keys and moved her hand. Cold settled over Bryce. Had her touch warmed him that much?

"I'll look forward to your call." Pink rushed to cover her face and Bryce wondered at the reaction.

"Me, too."

"Daddy, home. I'm sleepy."

"There's a new one. My daughter admitting she's sleepy. Will wonders never cease? Carrie, thanks again. I will call."

"I... I know."

Bryce stepped back and shut the car door. She gave a jaunty wave after starting the vehicle, checking behind her, and backing from the parking stall. Bryce stuffed his hands into his pockets and watched as she drove away. He still watched the street for long moments after her distinctive purple vehicle disappeared from sight.

He turned back to his car and ducked into the back to secure Bree in her car seat. Her bright, blue-green eyes glittered at him. "Do you like my new mommy?"

Bryce kissed the top of his daughter's head. "Yes, honey, I think I do."

C arrie's gaze hovered at the rear view mirror's reflection, watching the tall, slender figure standing next to her vacated parking slot grow steadily further away. Until a driver in the next lane held his hand on his horn longer than was necessary. Carrie jerked the steering wheel sharply to return her vehicle to a single lane. She waved an apology to the man who returned a one-fingered salute and raced down the busy street.

"Creep." The sleek, silver sports car zoomed over the crest of a short hill and disappeared. Carrie stopped gratefully at a red light, brushed a few strands of hair from her forehead, then leaned her elbow against the window and pressed her palm to her temple. A quick glance in the rear view mirror showed her only the vehicle filled street; the bookstore parking lot was out of sight. She blew out a long, shaking breath.

What was she doing? She'd almost caused an accident—and with a driver who looked to be primed for a case of road rage.

What *was* she doing—watching a man instead of the road? Normally a cautious driver, one who didn't even answer her cell phone while driving, she couldn't believe the irresponsibility of her actions.

Thankfully, she pulled into her apartment complex a short

time later. Shaking, she fumbled with the key for the entry door. As often as she told herself differently, it wasn't the near accident making her shake so much. It was her reaction to Mr. MacAlister. And his adorable daughter.

Once inside her building a short jog up two flights of stairs got her to her apartment. At the door, she easily found the correct key, let herself in, then leaned back to close the door.

She glanced at the clock. How long would it be until he called? She shook her head and took another step into her apartment. He might not even call. She could call him though. He didn't give her his number, but she knew his name. Carrie stared at the phone. When would he call?

"Oh, my gosh," Carrie spoke out loud to the silence of her apartment. "I'm acting like a love-struck teenager!" Not becoming behavior for someone well past her teen years. But then, not much of what she did was 'age appropriate'. Certainly a majority of those in her profession were younger.

How old was Bryce? She'd never been good at guessing ages so she no longer tried. Carrie tossed her purse and books to one end of the couch, plopped down on the other end and, after kicking off her shoes, curled her legs to the side and rested her cheek against the high, overstuffed arm. Her eyes drifted closed and she retreated into a world of imagination—a practiced world of safety in daydreams.

A tall, female figure strode toward her. Disappointed, Carrie attempted to change the direction of her daydream. She wanted Bryce.

The figure remained unchanged. Carrie sighed. ::*Lottie?*::

::*Aye, m'friend.*::

::*Why have you come back? I'm too old for you now.*::

::*Ne're too aged fer a friend, Carrie. An' ye may be needin' me, fer I have been called again to ye.*::

::*Lottie, don't be angry. I'm just surprised.*::

::*Nae more than m'self.*::

::*I wonder what it means.*::

Lottie merely shook her head, her long golden braid swinging casually over one shoulder. She fingered the hilt of a long, thin sword worn low on her hip.

Carrie opened her eyes and frowned. When she was young, Lottie had protected her from the nightmares her father's preaching had caused a young, innocent girl. Lottie had kept her company through long hours locked in a small, dark closet in punishment for her evil ways.

But, never before had she seen Lottie with a weapon.

Before she could reason out the puzzling reappearance, the shrill ring of the phone startled her to a straight-backed, upright position. Bryce? Was he calling already?

Her heart accomplished amazing flip-flops, pounding in her chest as she scrambled to her feet and tripped on her way to the bar separating the kitchen from her living room and snatched up the handset just before the fourth ring.

"Hello?" Carrie closed her eyes and winced at the airy, breathless tone of her voice.

Laughter, deep and slightly mocking came through the earpiece. "Dare I hope to have interrupted something... interesting?"

"Nightshade," Carrie sighed. "No, only a daydream."

"Damn. I so hoped for you, girlfriend."

If only her manager knew the amazing hopes coursing through her at the moment. She might actually surprise the flamboyant man. "Keep hoping. What's up?"

"Are you ready, Carouselle? Ready to come back to work? Your regulars are getting restless."

"My regulars?" Carrie laughed. "You mean old Mr. Wells?"

"Carouselle, darling, he won't even sit near the stage without you up there. Let alone tip any of the other girls." Nightshade's voice dropped to a conspiratorial whisper. "And you know how unhappy that makes them—especially Ivie."

"Ivie Promises? That b—"

"Carrie! Didn't your folks teach you better than that?" Nightshade chuckled, and Carrie imagined him studying his well-kept nails. "Not that she isn't a bitch. With a capital B. Honey, she's threatening to take your spotlight. To talk Bill into making her the headliner. You need to get back to work, girl. And soon."

"I know. It's time. Besides, I know you miss your cut."

"Cut? Carrie you wound me. I must admit, though, I make more managing you than any of my other girls. Even in combination. And, have I got an idea for you. I'll only give it to you, Carrie, for only Carouselle could do this justice."

"Is it as good as the Zydeco number I did at the N B Tween?"

"Better." There was a slight pause. "Oh, there was someone there—a gentleman of my acquaintance... who wants to meet you."

"Your acquaintance?" Carrie chuckled. Nightshade's friends were—interesting. But not anyone she would be interested in beyond friendship.

"No, honey, you misunderstand. Not *that* kind of acquaintance. A man more to your tastes. I think you'd like him, Carrie. Trust me. He's a keeper."

A keeper? But, she'd just met someone who fit that designation completely. "Oh, I don't know, Nightshade."

"Think about it. I'll have to tell him when you dance again anyway. I must uphold my honor and my position as matchmaker for my straight friends."

"Matchmaker?" Carrie laughed out loud. "I've missed you. Do you have any supper plans?"

"Well, darling, it's your fault if you missed me. You were the one who set up the rules for your time off. No communication, remember? I waited as long as I could. But, no, no plans. Do you have potatoes? I haven't had one of your stuffed potatoes is such a long time." Nightshade's voice ended in a plaintive whine.

Carrie circled the counter and pulled open the drawer where she kept potatoes and onions. Two large bakers occupied the drawer. "You're in luck. I just happen to have two of the fattest potatoes just waiting for someone like you to join me for supper."

"I'll be over in about an hour. But, honey, I can't stay too long. I have to meet... an acquaintance later this evening."

"An acquaintance, huh? You'll have to tell me all about him."

"Maybe later. For now, tonight will have to be a business meal. With a little matchmaking thrown in with the bacon bits. You do have real bacon, don't you?"

Carrie shook her head at his audacity. "Of course. Would I offer you anything but the best? I'll get the taters started. How about—"

"Wine? No problem, honey. I just happen to have a bottle of honey mead from that local winery you like so well. Hang up now, honey. I've got to primp so I look proper."

"A proper what?"

They laughed together before disconnecting the call. Carrie grinned and hummed to herself as she washed the potatoes and stuck them in the oven. Even though she had wanted to totally get away from her life at The Panther's Back, she should never have included Nightshade in that deal. He was much too good a friend. And she realized now how much she had missed him over the last six weeks.

T he triple knock at her door made Carrie smile. Nightshade always knocked the same way, so she knew it was him. A nice, caring touch and she appreciated his concern for her safety. The knock sounded again and she lurched into action, wiping her hands against the thighs of her jeans.

The smile on the man's face when she opened the door was familiar, but the figure was strangely dressed. Carrie took a step back to view the full effect.

"Who are you and what did you do with Nightshade?"

He turned in a slow pirouette. "I told you I was meeting someone."

"But this... this is so... not you."

Nightshade froze and, eyes wide, stared down at himself. Arms akimbo, he glanced back at Carrie and grinned. "It must be me, for no one else would dare assume to pretend to be Nightshade. I will admit these clothes feel strange. May I come in?" He waved a brown bag containing a wine bottle. "Honey, we don't want the wine to warm so it's undrinkable."

Nightshade casually swung the bottle as he sauntered into her apartment. Carrie watched with amazement. She'd never seen her manager in street clothes other than tight jeans and a flowing, wide-sleeved shirt. And he certainly never dressed like this on those rare occasions he consented to appear onstage.

Khaki slacks hugged his trim, well-shaped buttocks and hung to a tiny cuff just at the top of his Birkenstocks. At least that wasn't different; Carrie didn't think he owned any other type of shoes. The shirt made her shake her head in wonder and disbelief. Nightshade—in a knit polo? It was almost too much for her to comprehend. "What in the world happened while I was on vacation?"

Nightshade shrugged, pulled the wine from the sack, and reached into an upper cupboard for glasses. "Got a call from someone I knew long ago—in another lifetime."

"You must really like this guy."

A faint ruddy blush touched Nightshade's high cheekbones. She'd hit the clothing nail on the head. "I'm happy for you, Nightshade, it's about time."

"Darling, don't you know it. I've pretty much given up hope. But, such is not the case this time. Just someone I used to... work with. This is how he expects me to look."

Ignoring the rest of his statement, she latched onto a single word. "There's always hope, Nightshade." Deep in her heart, hope called a name. A name she hardly dared pin her hopes on.

"And for you? What is that hope I see in your eyes?" He handed her a glass with pale, golden wine. "Shall I say it's about time as well?"

She longed to confide in Nightshade, but she wasn't even sure what there was to confide. She'd met a man, a man who said he'd call her. There wasn't much more to tell.

::Breanna.::

Yes, Breanna. The tiny girl who stole her way so smoothly into her heart. When Carrie felt Nightshade at her side and glanced up into his face she met a soft smile.

"I see. So tell, girlfriend. Who is this guy that puts such a dreamy look on your normally oh so serious face?"

"Well…" She took a sip of wine. Ah, as smooth and wonderful as she remembered. The wine hit her empty stomach and she sighed. That would never do. "First we eat. You know that if I drink even part of this glass without eating anything I won't be worth anything to anybody."

"My darling Carouselle. I want information, not foolishness. I can wait until we eat. So, how long do I have to wait?"

"Five minutes?"

"I suppose it will have to do." Nightshade gazed high into the corner of the wall and sighed dramatically before turning a wicked grin to her. "Anything I can do to hurry this process along?"

"Nope, all I have to do is slip the potatoes under the broiler to melt the cheese. Your timing is impeccable. As usual."

Although she was reluctant to tell Nightshade about Breanna and Bryce, Carrie hurried to set the meal on the table. Nightshade found his seat, watched her with a bemused smile and carefully swirled the wine in his glass. Uncomfortable under his intense scrutiny, Carrie fumbled with the salad until he rose and took the wooden bowls from her.

"Sit, Carrie. You know I'll only pry a little."

"Yeah." She chuckled. "Only a little more than I want." Carrie hefted two huge, stuffed potatoes and brought them to the table.

Nightshade adopted a wounded expression. "You know me too well. Eat first, then I'll grill you until I have to leave."

"I think I'd enjoy raking you over the curiosity coals instead."

"This is just a meeting of friends. I doubt you'd find him worthy of your interest. There aren't, and won't be, any of those juicy details you're expecting. This meeting is… well… almost business."

"What kind of business?"

Unable to answer around the full bite of potato he'd taken, Nightshade shrugged. Carrie was curious about his evasive attitude but shrugged herself. He didn't corner the market on evasiveness.

They ate in silence for a few minutes then Nightshade laid his fork to one side, refilled their glasses and rested his chin on his palm. "So—give."

"I met a man at the bookstore today."

"Uh hum." Nightshade returned to his meal. "Go on."

"Well—it was a strange meeting. I was watching him look at magazines when a little girl came up and grabbed me."

When she paused, he cocked his head to the side. "And?" he drawled.

"And, the guy I was watching is this little girl's father."

"And?"

"We met, we talked. I helped him get his daughter to his car." Was that really all there was? She pinned such big hopes on so little. "I gave him my phone numbers."

Nightshade's eyebrows rose.

"And now, I'm waiting to see if he calls."

"Be a fool not to, darling."

"So you say."

"So I do. And you know what Nightshade says becomes real. Got a special source for fairy dust you know. Make a wish, honey, and Nightshade will do his best to make your dreams come true."

Carrie took a deep breath and let the air out slowly. She could make many wishes, dream many dreams where Bryce was concerned. Where would she start? She wished he'd call.

"So, favorite dancer of mine, does this delectable fellow have a name?" Nightshade chased a bit of potato skin around his plate.

"His daughter's name—"

"I asked his name, not his kid's." Nightshade pointed the tines of his fork at her in mock ferocity, but his expression was a study in tightly controlled laughter.

"Is Breanna."

Nightshade's brows drew together over his bright gray eyes. "The guy?"

"Bryce MacAlister."

Intensely interested in the movement of food upon his plate, Nightshade stared down at the remnants of his potato. "That so?" Lacking the normal, smooth tones, his voice sounded...strained.

"What's wrong?"

Nightshade lifted one arm and glanced at his watch without raising his head. "Oops, I've got to run. I can't be late." He rose, carried his dinnerware to the sink and stared at the tile covered backsplash for a moment. His shoulders shook. He turned to face her, chewing on his lower lip.

"Listen, I think we have a lot to talk about. They really do want you back at the Panther soon. Tomorrow. Can you meet me tomorrow?"

"Sure, but—"

"You know that little Mexican place down on Dawson?"

"The fast food place?" Mexican fast food? Nightshade despised fast food.

"Meet me there at six." He wiped his hands on a dishtowel and handed the damp terrycloth to her. "Sorry to leave you with the dishes. I owe you, darling."

"But—"

"Just meet me. We'll get business taken care of then. Gotta run."

Carrie followed him to the door and shut it firmly behind him. The muffled sound of laughter rang through the wood and she almost opened the door to chase after Nightshade and force him to tell her why he acted so strangely.

Acting strangely? She chuckled and returned to her small galley kitchen. She'd really never been able to tell when Nightshade acted more strangely than usual. He liked keeping the people around him off balance. Still, he was the best manager she could imagine—and a good friend. She was glad to put up with his eccentricities in order to have him in her life.

She kept Bryce from her thoughts for as long as it took to load the few dishes into the dishwasher.

• • •

Bryce tugged his watch from the small pocket in his slacks, flipped open the cover, and stared at the numbers. Almost twenty-four hours. Was it too soon?

With Bree visiting her cousins he'd had a quiet afternoon and should have been able to nearly complete the landscape design for a proposed office complex. But all he'd done was doodle the shapes of a few trees on scraps of paper. Until he talked to Carrie, he wasn't sure he'd get anything done. And he'd already scheduled a meeting to discuss the basic designs at Logan and Associates the next morning.

He reached for the phone and dragged the handset toward him. Even if it was too soon to call, he was going to take the plunge. Next, he searched through the mess on his desk for the sack where she'd written her numbers.

No sack.

Bryce shoved papers from one side of the desk to the other. He would not panic. A second search of the desktop reveled nothing except notes on current and future projects. Scooting his chair sideways across the plastic floor mat, he attacked the drafting table. Nothing. The floor received a thorough search with Bryce crawling on his hands and knees under the desk after a suspicious sack that turned out to be nothing more than one of Bree's artistic renderings of—something. He sat on the floor and stared at the colorful swipes of crayon. What was it she said this was?

After carefully smoothing the slightly crumpled drawing, Bryce rose, tacked the page to the corkboard that covered half of one wall, stood back and grinned. Bree had made him quite a display, both here and on the refrigerator.

Losing the grin, he cast a despondent gaze about the room. The trash can. Bryce rushed toward the wooden container and peered into the dark recesses.

Empty.

Frustration rose like a tidal wave threatening to overthrow Bryce's common sense. The sack couldn't have gotten up and walked away by itself. The magazines were on a low side table. He lifted each one, peered beneath it, then slapped the stack back onto the table with a low growl. What did he do with Carrie's phone number?

The front door slammed. The sound of rapid, short footsteps sounded down the hall. With physical effort Bryce reigned in his frustration, took a quick breath, and turned to meet the exuberance of his daughter's advance.

"Lookit what Auntie Lara teached me."

"Taught me." Bryce crouched and a crumpled paper square dropped into his open palm. He lifted the lightweight square and examined the misshapen box from all sides. "It looks great, honey." His heart lurched. The square looked to be made from—a paper sack. From the bookstore. Bryce stared closely at the square until Bree snatched her treasure from his hand and skipped from the office.

He reached toward her but the words died before he could call her back. Lara leaned against the doorframe, arms crossed, a ripped piece of paper sack dangling from her fingers. She grinned. "Looking for this?"

Bryce let his hand drop to his side. Lara straightened and held the ripped portion of the sack to display clearly written telephone numbers. "Bree had this sack when Iain picked her up. She wouldn't give this part up until I showed her how to fold the rest into a simple box. I thought the numbers might be important. So, what's up, Bryce?"

Taunting him, she waved the paper slowly back and forth until Bryce lunged forward and snatched the sack from her. He glanced down to confirm the numbers were there, folded the bit carefully, and stuck it in his shirt pocket.

"Just numbers for someone I met yesterday."

Lara cast him an appraising look and he shifted uncomfortably. "Bree said these were her mommy's phone numbers."

Hearing Breanna moving a chair in the kitchen, Bryce eased past Lara. Maybe if he ignored the question...

"Walking away won't stop me, Bryce. You know that. I'm curious as to why Bree would say such a thing."

In the kitchen, Bryce lifted Bree to her chair and poured a bit of chocolate milk into a plastic mug. Bree thanked him and drank noisily while Bryce hesitated at the open refrigerator door. "Yesterday we met a woman at the bookstore."

"Yep, met Mommy. More milk, Daddy?" Bree shifted in the chair to watch him.

Bryce shook his head. "Not now. I've got to go to the restaurant tonight."

"Ooh. Can I come?"

"Not tonight, darlin'. You're going to visit your granda tonight."

"Will Pop Pop be there, too?"

Bryce ruffled her hair. "Do you think he'd miss your visit?"

"Nope. Go now?"

Lara sat next to Bree and took the child's chubby fingers in her hand. "How about if I drop you off on my way home."

"Yea!" Bree turned back to Bryce with a slight pout to her pink lips. "Okay, Daddy?"

Bryce held back a grin and leaned his head to one side, waiting.

Bree took a deep breath. "Can I go with Auntie Lara?"

"May I."

"Please, Daddy, may I?"

How could he resist the imp in cherub's clothing? Besides, it was getting late and he needed to call Carrie before he left. He knelt by Bree's chair. "Of course. And know what?"

Blue-green eyes wide, Bree shook her head.

"Granda asked if you could stay all night." He grinned at the expectant light filling her sparkling eyes. "I said yes."

"Yippee!" Bree threw herself from the chair and wrapped Bryce's neck in a chokehold. Lara's chuckle was a low, comfortable counterpoint as the father and daughter exchanged noisy, loving kisses.

THREE

Unbelievably, she'd let Nightshade talk her into this meeting. The faux adobe building with neon signs in the windows certainly wasn't his style. But—Carrie shrugged before she exited her car—she used to eat frequently in places like this. The time could turn into an unexpected blast from the past.

A marquee above the door advertised the day's specials. Carrie winced. It was Tuesday—kid's night. What had possessed Nightshade? He had a fairly low tolerance for children's antics, and a crowd of young people playing around while he was trying to conduct business would undoubtedly disturb him.

With a second shrug, Carrie pulled open the double, glass-paneled door. A faint scent of chili pepper and grease wafted from the kitchen area. A signboard announced the evening's entertainment. A magician.

That might be interesting. Carrie had been intrigued by magic ever since the first grade when she saw a television special on a rare visit to a friend's house. Her parents would never have let her watch secular programs. The echo of her father's voice pounded through her mind. Illusion was a trick of the devil and to be avoided—no matter the cost.

Carrie snorted to herself and peered up at the menu posted over the cash register. Her parents had been successful in teaching her intolerance and avoidance. Now, she had no tolerance for their 'god-fearing' ways and avoided them as much as possible. Not that they ever tried to contact her either.

The specter of the past would not spoil her evening. Determined to avoid thought of her parents, Carrie ordered a southwestern style salad and turned to find a table in the crowded dining area. If she sat where she could watch the magician, maybe she could catch how he tricked his audience.

A table, set against a back wall, was draped by a length of black cloth with pale silver stars stenciled at the edges. Supported by wires attached to the drop ceiling, the cloth created a darkened cave where the magician sat. But, when Carrie took a seat at the last available table, she could see only the magician's hands.

Amazing hands. Long fingered, slender, graceful in swift, deceptively simple movements. The rumble of the magician's voice, while he spoke in soft, modulated tones to the crowd of children before him, carried to her. She could discern no words, but the pleasant rise and fall of the voice soothed her.

Carrie listened and studied the magician's hands while she picked through her salad. Would the rest of the magician match the beauty of his hands?

Rising to refill her soda, Carrie glanced at the clock placed prominently on one wall. It was nearly seven? Where was Nightshade? He'd said he would meet her an hour ago. A kernel of anger twisted into a knot in her stomach. Then, the anger dissipated as she began to worry. Nightshade had never been irresponsible about attending meetings. What if there had been an accident?

She returned to her seat and reached for her cell phone. A sound of disappointment rose from the children. Carrie paused with her phone clutched tight in one hand.

"I'm sorry. My time's up—for tonight." The magician's voice was louder and—familiar. Carrie leaned to the side trying to catch a glimpse of the voice's owner.

"See?" The long fingers wiggled slowly and a small girl giggled. "The magic is gone from my hands. Next week... next week the magic will have returned. And so will I. Perhaps with new magic to amaze you."

The children turned away and returned to their tables and forgotten meals. The magician's hands rested, palms down, on the cloth-covered tabletop for a moment. Then one hand moved away and reappeared with a small case. The accoutrements of magic were quickly packed away and the case locked. The curtains rustled.

Carrie held her breath. The material swirled back from the side of the table and the magician appeared. Dressed all in black and surrounded by the black curtains, only his pale blond hair gave off brightness in the artificial light. The expression on his face was calm and noncommittal.

His green eyes met hers. A slow, incredulous smile highlighted his face.

Carrie tried to shake off the physical impact of meeting his gaze. The thrill caused by his smile filled her, then quivered along her skin when Bryce moved toward her like a sleek, stalking panther. Only the light strands of his hair and his pale eyes dispelled the rise of a hidden memory. Then he stood before her, and there was no time to question the memory.

Bryce gestured to an empty chair. "May I?"

"I'd like that." Carrie twisted in her seat to face him as he set his case between his feet. She took a long sip of her soda to calm her raging emotions. When she pulled her mouth away a dribble of soda ran down her chin. She caught it with her finger and sucked the sweet liquid back into her mouth. Mortified heat filled her face, and she tried to hide behind the paper napkin she then used to dry her chin. She couldn't seem to stop acting like a love-struck teenager.

Bryce chuckled. Instead of mocking her, the sound made her lower her napkin and laugh in response. Comfortable. This became a comfortable moment.

Bryce leaned his head to one side before he spoke. "I'm

surprised to see you here. This doesn't seem like the kind of place you'd frequent."

"I don't. I haven't been to a fast food place for—oh, a long time. I was supposed to meet my manager here. Why he picked this place, though, is beyond me. It's even less his style." She shrugged. "He's late. I haven't heard from him and I'm starting to worry."

"Call him."

Carrie slapped her forehead. She'd been so consumed with the odd impression she must be making, she'd forgotten about the phone she'd dropped to the seat when Bryce emerged from the magician's material draped cave. "Oh. Where's my brain tonight?"

"I tried calling you earlier."

The simple statement, made in an even, unassuming tone, told her much. He'd called her. Beyond that, she didn't care about any lingering doubts. "I wasn't home."

"I know."

"Oh. Of course. Didn't I give you my cell phone number?"

"Do you have the phone turned off?" He grinned and Carrie melted. Sparkles. His eyes actually sparkled. "Huh?"

"Is your phone turned on? I left a voice mail."

The few moments before Carrie tore her gaze from Bryce's face stretched into delightful infinity. Then, she blinked and reached blindly for the phone. The hard plastic was an anchor to the real world. But, did she want that real world— or the fantasies that persisted in elevating her hormone level?

Bryce leaned his elbows on the table and crossed his arms. "Maybe your manager called while the phone was off."

"Of course. That must be it. I'll check." Carrie fumbled with the phone, finally punching the right combination of buttons to activate the phone and receive her voice mail. She listened to the first message.

The lines of her face softened into what she realized must be a dreamy smile. How could one man's voice do that to her? This was the stuff of fantasy—of fairy tales. She liked it.

Bryce leaned closer. His pupils had expanded to deep, dark circles, filling his eyes. "I hope that's my message making you smile so... so beautifully."

"Yes. And yes, I'd like to see you again. Soon."

"How about—"

Carrie held up one hand to silence him as the phone signaled a second message.

Bryce waited patiently, happy to be simply watching her, watching emotions flow across her face. A changeable face, a face he could watch forever. Even after an eternity he wasn't sure he would have seen all her expressions nor understood what each one meant. Her eyes grew wide and she stared at him. Then her eyelids closed, hiding her soft brown eyes. Eyes as changeable as her expression. As if in disbelief her head moved from side to side.

"What is it? Is something wrong?"

Her eyes opened. "No, nothing wrong. The message is from my manager, Nightshade."

"Nightshade? I thought he only managed—dancers."

Carrie rolled her eyes and Bryce realized how stupid his statement had been. She softened her words with a smile. "I think you need to listen to this."

Bryce took the phone and held it facing her so she could poke at the buttons. Then he placed the hard, warm plastic against his ear.

"Carrie, darling." Yep, Nightshade, all right. "Sorry I didn't make it to our meeting. But, I hope you met someone else there. Remember I told you about the man who wanted to meet you, the one who saw you dance at the N B Tween? This is him, sweetness. The man you gushed over last night. Gawd, I could barely eat." Nightshade laughed. "Seriously, Carrie, I'm glad you met Bryce all on your own. Saves me a lot of trouble." There was a short pause. "And Bryce—I'm sure Carrie's sharing this message with you— this is Carouselle. The one who bewitched you with her spell even before Korin's delightful dance loosed the magic that night." He laughed again. "Now, it's up to the two of you. If you have any troubles, don't hesitate to call little ol' matchmaker Nightshade.

Bye now. Not to sound overly trite, but don't do anything I wouldn't do."

Nightshade's deep laugher sounded as the call disconnected. Bryce pulled the phone away from his ear and stared at the small silver rectangle. In his roundabout way, Nightshade was trying to tell him something.

Carrie touched his hand and took the phone. "Nightshade's my manager. I'm a dancer at The Panther's Back. About six weeks ago I did an exhibition dance at the N B Tween. Nightshade told me that one of his friends saw me dance and wanted to meet me. But, because of his own rules for his dancers' safety, he couldn't tell that man anything about me. I went on vacation and had asked him not to call me. He didn't."

She set the phone on the table and touched his still extended hand. "Bryce, was that man really you?"

Slow, so slow. The world around him moved in slow motion. The words he'd just heard echoed through his head, but Bryce wasn't sure he understood them. This woman—the one his daughter had been drawn to—was the same as the dancer. The woman he'd ached for and dreamed about for forty nights—until he met Carrie at the bookstore and dreamed about her instead.

He lifted his gaze. Carrie's eyes were worried, the brown swirling in chocolate confusion and tentative hope. He could take that worry from her. All he had to do was speak a single word. A word hovering behind his lips. A word that escaped when he smiled.

"Yes."

FOUR

Titus stood at the sink in his opulent, chrome and marble bathroom and stared into the clear mirror. Leaning forward, he peered into his own light blue eyes. Then he pulled the hair back from his forehead and grimaced at the light blond regrowth glinting against the black he'd last used to color his hair. His mouth twisted. It was time to change.

The catering venture had been moderately successful, but had done little to damage Zeroun's reputation or disrupt their business. Damn them, they were more successful than ever. And the extended Zeroun family kept slipping through his fingers.

After easily disposing of the defunct catering business, he had decided it was time for a new identity. A new appearance. A new plan.

Titus straightened and rolled his shoulders to ease the tension tight at the base of his neck. Too much time passed. He needed action—results.

He turned his head to the side and strained to see his profile in the mirror. He was tired of the darkness—the black hair and dark eyes. If only he could return to his true appearance. That was impossible now, but soon, he felt the assurance deep in his bones and in the pit of his stomach. Not long, and his plans of revenge would come to fruition.

The thought made him smile and he turned to face the mirror. Perhaps light brown. Then, if his helpers could create a moustache it might be enough, and he wouldn't have to wear the uncomfortable contacts to change his eye color.

What else would succumb to this rash of changes? The apartment would continue to be his base of operations, but he needed to alter his way of dressing. And his transportation.

Titus shook his head. He would not give up his sleek Pantera, but he could change its appearance as well. Moving swiftly to his dark, wood paneled office, he snatched the telephone directory. It took only a few minutes to schedule two appointments—one to change the color of his hair, the other to change the color of his car. That would do.

With a satisfied sigh, Titus leaned his chair back, thumped his feet to the desk, and crossed his ankles. Now, for his plan.

The direct attack had not the desired effects. Perhaps, this time, an indirect approach would bring him closer to his goal—the utter destruction of Jaye Zeroun, along with everything and everyone he loved.

FIVE

C arrie peered through the twilight at Bryce's taillights as she followed him to his house. So much of what had happened the past two days was totally unbelievable. Bryce had seen her dance and had immediately wanted to meet her. They'd met by accident at the bookstore. Then at the restaurant by arranged accident. Bless Nightshade—she could just strangle him.

If only she hadn't been so stubborn about wanting to totally avoid anything to do with her career during her weeks off, she might have met Bryce sooner. There was so much to discover, so much she needed to know about him right now. And she wanted to cram those six weeks of knowledge into one evening. But not at a fast food restaurant crowded with children.

So, she had agreed to follow him home.

Part of her mind urged caution. Weirdoes and serial killers looked just like everyone else. She could be walking into a dangerous trap. But, if she disappeared, at least Nightshade would be able to contact the police with information.

Carrie gave her head a violent shake. What the heck was she thinking? Being an exotic dancer had helped hone her senses, and she rarely read a person wrong. All she sensed from Bryce was—oh, he felt so good to her mind and soul.

She followed his car into an older neighborhood. Glancing at the houses lining the street across from City Park, she took a deep breath. There had long been a dream hidden inside her. A dream to own one of these small Victorians and restore the house to its original glory. Although not as grand as the homes along the Boulevard, these smaller houses were a testament to the tenacity of their owners past and present.

When Bryce turned the vehicle into a narrow, high-curbed driveway, she bit at her lower lip. He couldn't live here? Could he?

Bryce leapt his car the instant she pulled next to the curb. Carrie stared openmouthed at the small Queen Anne, and even after Bryce knocked softly then opened her door, she was unable to move. Not only was the house immaculate in the subtle blending of colors, the front gardens flowed from the house to the sidewalk in a similar profusion of shades, textures, and just plain beauty.

"It's just a house." Bryce's breath tickled the side of her face. She turned her head. His face was only inches from hers as he leaned into the car.

"Oh, no." Breathless and airy, her words were hushed and awed. "It's a dream. How?"

Chuckling, Bryce took her hand to help her from her vehicle, led her across the street to stand at the edge of the park and turned her to face his house. He pointed to another small Victorian three doors away. Painted in similar colors but with a different base color on the body of the house, the small structure glowed in the fading light.

"I don't understand."

"My aunt Allyn owns that house. She's been in this neighborhood a long time, and was the first to begin rehabilitating the houses along the street. She's an artist."

"I have no doubt of that. What about the next house?" It, too, had a similar color scheme and a front garden filled with butterflies and hummingbirds.

"My folks live there. As the houses on this block come up for sale, someone in the family purchases them. See the house on this corner, next to my house? Allyn's sister-in-law and her new husband just bought that one. We're making this a true family neighborhood."

Amazed that a family could be emotionally close enough to live next door to each other, Carrie remained silent. Although her parents lived across town, she didn't want to even be in the same city as her family, let alone on the same block. She turned her thoughts back to the houses. "Your aunt must be extremely talented."

"Ah, very much so. I think you might like some of the interior touches she's created."

"Did she do the gardens? The plantings are beyond anything I've seen around town."

Bryce took her hand and led her back across the street. He didn't speak until they were at his front walk. "No. I did the gardens."

"My god, Bryce. Your talent is amazing."

He shrugged away the compliment. "It's something I enjoy. Luckily, it's how I earn a living as well."

"Do you own your own company? You should."

He plucked a blossom from a tall plant she didn't recognized with her limited botanical knowledge and handed the fragrant, pale lavender bloom to her. "Between raising Bree and helping with the family business, I don't have time to devote to opening a business of my own. Besides, I get enough work from one of the local architectural firms. It keeps me plenty busy."

"Family business? You live close together and work together? I can't... I just don't understand, I guess. What business? Have I heard of it?"

Bryce chuckled. "Possibly. Zeroun's, the event planner."

"Oh." Carrie nodded. One of the most successful businesses in the city, there were few who hadn't at least heard of Zeroun's.

A car roared around the corner and squealed down the street. Bryce stared after the plain black vehicle. "Idiot. With the park right here, you'd think people would be on the look-out for pedestrians and kids. Drivers like that..." He took a deep breath. "Would you like to come inside?"

"Yes. Uh, where's Breanna?"

"Just down the street. She's spending the night with my folks."

Time alone with Bryce. Although she wanted to learn more about his beautiful child, the chance to spend adult time with Bryce stole her breath. Adult time. That could mean so much. Before going inside she should decide and should understand what that meant to her, but at the moment, she didn't care. All she could see were peaceful moments, long moments spent learning about this man.

Bryce forced himself to breathe naturally. Would Carrie change her mind about coming in now that she knew Breanna wasn't home? Knowing that she'd be alone with him? The ache to learn more about Carrie was a physical presence inside Bryce, a presence promising more than desire, more than wanting, more than his numbed, useless brain imagined. He wanted, no, he needed to know everything about this woman. And in time, to let her know about him.

A nugget of shame bounced against the ache. If he cared for Carrie as he thought he did, there should be no secrets between them. Strangely, he wasn't concerned about the family connection with the Faerie Otherworld, somehow he seemed to know she would accept and understand. But eventually he would have to introduce her to his parents.

The last woman he'd brought home to meet his folks immediately turned around and silently left. Left the room, left the building, left his life. He hadn't really missed her after she'd gone, but the experience left him hesitant to jump right into introductions. He loved his folks, only so many people didn't understand.

The curiosity in her gaze sank past his troubled thoughts and he looked into her eyes. She was nearly as tall as he. It would be no problem to inch forward and brush his lips against hers. Her lithe body would fit against his, soft against hard, in all the right places. Thought fled as instinct pushed him to...

Bryce blinked and took an involuntary step back. Carrie's brows drew together for a brief moment, then returned to their normal, smooth arch. She smiled. "I could use something to drink."

Mentally berating himself, Bryce cupped her elbow and escorted her up three steps to the wide porch. "As you wish. We'll get something to drink, I'll give you the dime tour if you'd like, then we can talk."

"Good."

Bryce led the way to the kitchen and opened the refrigerator. "I have water, of course, some soda, wine, I could make tea or coffee."

"Is that chocolate milk I see?" Carrie leaned over his shoulder, her body pressed lightly against his back.

Biting back a groan, Bryce angled the upper half of his body to look at her. Her eyes were wide with delight and she licked her lips. His body tightened uncomfortably.

"It's been ages since I had chocolate milk."

SIX

As soon as he'd turned the corner, he recognized her. Titus wrenched the wheel of his rental sedan and skidded into a parking area at City Park. He leaned eagerly over the steering wheel and stared at the couple standing in front of the second house from the corner.

Adjusting the material of his slacks, he let a half-smile touch his lips. Oh, yes, he remembered her. Interesting. And now she was with one of Zeroun's extended family, with one who could be a part of the revenge he craved like a man lost in a desert craved water. Perhaps this discovery would work to his advantage.

After the couple entered the house, Titus sat back and closed his eyes. While the memory of his encounter with the dancer hovered close, he backed away from the pleasure and searched his mind for ways to use her instead. He touched the radio controls on the steering wheel and swiftly searched through the local stations. He remembered a talk program, filled with people and ideologies he could use.

A low, calm, almost seductive voice oozed from the speakers. Ah, this was what he wanted. Titus grinned at the speech; he had used similar tactics himself.

That was before the usurper appeared; before he was torn

from his place of honor. Before Zeroun. Teeth clenched, Titus fought the anger. His lack of control had brought him to this place. He would not allow it now to take his advantage. Anger would not return him to his rightful place. Only the calm destruction of Jaye Zeroun and his family would bring Titus any peace.

There, the voice on the radio changed slightly. What this man spoke of—this would underscore his plan and personal success. Now he knew the people he could use, the people he needed to convince. Calm, Titus shifted the car into reverse and exited the parking area. As he passed the colorful house he let an evil chuckle fill the interior of the car and waved one finger at the closed door.

SEVEN

Carrie tried for a nonchalant glance over the rim of her glass. Bryce gave her a tentative smile and lifted his coffee mug in salute. He'd offered her wine, and she was drinking chocolate milk. Not exactly a romantic drink. But when she'd seen the plastic gallon jug filled with the chocolaty brown liquid, she'd been unable to resist. Never allowed such a treat when she was younger, chocolate milk always touched upon her sense of childhood longing and the thrill of the forbidden.

That sense of the forbidden enfolded her now, becoming a deep longing in her chest, a thrill that traveled to the tips of her breasts and coursed low in her belly. She cast away the vague possibility that Bryce was forbidden to her with a blink of her eyes. He was thrilling. Exciting, too, was the idea that she'd only met him a few days ago and here she was, sitting in his kitchen, drinking chocolate milk. Like she belonged there. With him.

A dark voice in her mind, one sounding almost like a memory, hinted that she should not be there. There was danger in being alone with a man she barely knew. She would become one of those sad, missing women—whose disappearances filled the airwaves of the myriad of police and forensic shows.

Remember, the voice whispered, and fear.

Before she could consciously banish the voice, another, softer voice chased away the sudden chill. *::Be gone.::*

Carrie sat her glass on the table and frowned down into the remaining drops at the bottom. Lottie had chased the hint of danger from her mind, a danger she should know, understand, face. Danger from a memory?

"Carrie? Is something wrong?"

Bryce's concern cut through the seconds of her musing, and the near memory dissipated. "Uh, no," she managed to stammer. "Just thinking about the chocolate milk."

The concern in Bryce's light, jade-colored eyes faded behind a flash of humor. Oh, Lord. It wasn't her imagination. His eyes did sparkle as though stars had been sprinkled through them. She didn't wish to look anywhere else, couldn't if she tried. As she returned his steady gaze, the sparkles changed, the color deepened. The tiny smile lines at the corners of his eyes softened.

A movement at the edge of her vision caught her attention for a fraction of a second. Not long enough to draw her gaze from Bryce's face, but enough so she didn't yelp and jump away when Bryce touched one of his thumbs to the corner of her mouth then swept it softly over her upper lip.

He grinned. "Milk moustache." The brilliant green eyes softened further when Carrie leaned into his outstretched hand. The gentle touch of the pad of his thumb brushed along the fullness of her lower lip. Carrie fought both to contain a sigh and to keep from capturing his thumb between her teeth. The second battle she won, and unknowing regret flitted through Bryce's expression. The first battle lost, she closed her eyes, sighed and whispered, "Thank you."

"For what?" A rough, vibrating undertone laced Bryce's simple words. His pupils darkened, filled the jade orbs and glistened with unspoken promise.

Ah, the sparkles. If she didn't say something to change the mood... oh, but did she want to? Carrie let another deep sigh fill then escape her lungs before she returned his grin and answered.

"I'd hate to go through the rest of the night with a chocolate milk moustache."

"Anytime." Hidden by the tabletop, Bryce rubbed his palm against his thigh. Tingles lingered at his fingertips. If a small touch created such a reaction, what would it be like if he kissed her? To press his body to hers? To feel the length of her skin, intimate against his? Part of his body twitched to life. He squirmed and tried to think of something else—anything to pull his mind from the erotic pathways it, and his body, seemed determined to take.

His success was negligible.

Silent, Bryce watched Carrie and she returned his gaze with a steadiness that surprised and delighted him. When he had first seen her dance, she had captivated him, although he would be hard pressed to describe the music, her costume or the appearance of her skin as she removed parts of the costume. It hadn't been a purely sexual attraction that had caused his unsuccessful search for her, not lust that had him badgering Nightshade mercilessly until only two weeks ago when he'd forced himself to give up on his search. He'd never be able to put the instant attraction into words.

Now that he'd met the woman behind the dancer, he knew the truth of his instincts and felt the rightness deep, clear down to his toes. But words? The mere concept failed him.

Carrie cocked her head to one side and with sudden insight he realized the silence had gone on too long. Reluctant to lose the warmth of her regard he tore his gaze from her face, cleared his throat and asked the first question that popped into his mind.

"Does it bother you that I know?"

A thin wrinkle marred the smooth plane of her forehead. "Know what?"

Bryce caught his lower lip between his teeth. Do not pass go... place foot directly into mouth. Unable to think of any other subject, he exhaled a sharp breath and took a chance with his original thought. "Does it bother you that I found out what you do for a living? That you're a... stripper?"

Carrie's softly arched, brown eyebrows lifted as if surprised by his question.

"I mean—you did tell me you were a model. The only reason I know otherwise now is because Nightshade's a family friend."

She leaned forward and touched his upper arm. Bryce held his breath. "It's not really a secret." Carrie's shoulders rose and fell in a quick shrug. "I don't, however, always get a positive reaction when someone finds out. I was afraid—knowing it could chase you away—that you would despise me even before knowing me. Many people consider me nothing more than a 'woman for hire' and not want me near their children."

"You're not..."

"No, I'm not. Though some dancers do... sell favors." Bright pink flushed to red over her cheeks and Carrie ducked her head.

Corresponding heat filled the back of Bryce's neck. He'd made it sound as if he doubted her. He didn't. Taking a sudden change of tact, he pressed a slightly shaking hand over hers. Even with the tremors in his palm, he felt her shaking as well. She was afraid—afraid he'd turn his back on her, force her to leave. Such thoughts were the furthest thing from his mind.

"Carrie, what other people think isn't important." Bryce winced inwardly at his words. Too many times he should have listened to those words, and didn't. He shook the thought away. "I know who you are—"

"Do you? Do you really, Bryce? Are you sure?"

"Very sure." He curled his fingers around hers, lifted her hand and planted a kiss on the side of her tightly curled thumb. "How about we take a tour of the house now?"

Doubt flashed through her eyes but she must have conquered the feeling for her hand relaxed and a tentative smile eased the tension in her face. "That sounds great."

· · ·

B ryce and Carrie talked late into the night, speaking of inconsequential things, of their hopes and dreams, of beliefs and sorrows. Together they learned of each other.

Ending up in the office at the end of the tour, Carrie stared in open mouthed astonishment at the wall of floor to ceiling books. She scanned the eclectic assortment of volumes and paused at a long shelf devoted to Edmund Spenser. She twisted to look back over her shoulder. Bryce sat behind his desk, leaning forward on crossed arms to watch her.

"Spenser? I tried to read *The Faerie Queene* in college, but never got very far. In either the book or college. I've often thought about trying again. The book, I mean. I love stories with fairies and this seems like the ultimate tale."

Bryce's eyes brightened and he took a breath as if to speak. Then a strange expression, a melding of hope and regret, flashed across his face. He turned his head to the side. When he looked at her again, his expression was composed. She'd missed something in his changing expressions and felt the loss in a wave of odd disappointment.

"I happen to know a bit about Spenser, should you ever wish to try again." Bryce pointed to an adjacent shelf. "My family actually has a 'thing' for Shakespeare. Specifically *A Midsummer Night's Dream*. So, I guess you could say we enjoy fairy tales as well."

Carrie turned back to the shelves and gently touched the spine of an obviously ancient, leather-bound volume. Bryce had avoided her questions about his parents and, except for Breanna, hadn't said much about his family. But then, neither had she. Now she spoke quickly to cover the confused silence. The tone, the slight emphasis when Bryce had said 'fairy,' was as strange as his earlier expression. What caused the odd catch in his voice, the tonal change she doubted many would notice?

"Spenser and Shakespeare. Deep reading for a landscape architect." She faced him and rubbed her hands up and down her arms.

Ruddy color crept across Bryce's cheekbones. Oops. She shouldn't have said something like that so early in their relationship? Ready to leap into an apology, Carrie's words died on her lips when Bryce chuckled.

"Actually, the horticulture and design classes were only minor interests in college. I—umm—have a Masters degree. In Spenserian literature. *The Faerie Queene* to be precise."

"You're kidding."

Bryce rose and stared down, indicating the length of his body with a sweep of one hand. "Don't I look like a scholar? Truth be known, all I have left is a thesis and I can add a Doctorate to my collection of useless certificates."

"Then why...?"

Bryce shrugged. "I don't have any interest in teaching. However, I love the art of designing landscapes and gardens. I seem to be good at it."

"If the gardens up and down this street are any indication, you're a verifiable genius."

Scuffing the toe of his shoe along the thick area rug, Bryce mumbled, "Aw, you'll make me blush." He lifted a twinkling gaze to her.

Her knees turned to jelly and Carrie's insides melted. Ever since she discovered old Gene Kelly movies she'd been a sucker for sparkling eyes. She wondered if Bryce could dance, then blinked and shook her head. It was late and she was getting loopy.

"I think I should be going. I haven't kept my usual hours since I went on vacation and I'm not used to being up so late."

Bryce moved to stand before her. He rested his hands on her shoulders and traced tiny circles with his fingertips. She really didn't want to go, and when Bryce angled his head toward hers, she tilted her chin and accepted the soft brush of his lips across hers.

"I'm sorry," he whispered against her cheek. "I should have watched the clock." Bryce's fingers twitched and she leaned closer.

"I've really enjoyed being here tonight." Carrie lifted her

hands until they brushed Bryce's waist and lingered, her palms pressed against his sides.

With another soft, lingering touch, he kissed her again. It was... not enough. Bold, she touched the tip of her tongue to the seam of his lips.

For a fraction of a moment, Bryce froze. Then his lips parted and she drew her tongue along the softer inner lip and across the hard planes of his teeth. The contrast sent shivers trembling through her. Jolts of electricity followed when his tongue danced against hers. Carrie slid her hands around his waist and twined her fingers together to hold him close.

A silent groan vibrated where their bodies touched and Bryce speared his fingers through her hair to cup the back of her head in his palms. Pressing his lips firmly over hers, he deepened the kiss. Carrie welcomed the sensations and arched against his body, pulling him closer.

Dark laughter crowded the pleasure filling her mind. The almost-memory returned, mocking her.

::Remember. Know how it could be, what you refused to give. Remember.::

Carrie fought the voice; opened her eyes to force the unwanted intrusion from her.

::I said, remember.::

Holding tightly to Bryce, Carrie tried to ignore the voice. Fearful of what the memory might expose, Carrie struggled to clear her mind. She would not remember, not now. No. Not now. Her eyelids drifted closed under the sensuous assault Bryce made on her lips.

The words in her head disappeared, but were replaced by vivid images of a dark street. A tall man, slender, made nearly invisible by his black clothing, hovered at the edge of her inner vision. The only light was the glint of his perfect, straight teeth when his lips pulled into a feral grin. He moved forward and Carrie tried to take a step back.

Hands in her hair held her in place. Bryce's hands, she told herself, not the dark stranger's. It was Bryce who held her, kissed her, wanted her.

The feral grin widened to a predatory smile. "No," she whispered.

Bryce inched his lips from hers and took a series of rapid breaths. "Carrie?"

She struggled but couldn't open her eyes. The dark man held her captive with his fathomless gaze. Denying the vision, Carrie shook her head. Bryce held her. Blond, green-eyed Bryce.

::*None but I.*::

"No!"

"Carrie? What's wrong? What have I done?" The agony in Bryce's voice drew her attention from the vision of the dark man. Laughing, he shrugged back into the shadows.

::*Remember. I am always here. Waiting.*::

"No."

"Carrie?" Bryce moved his hands to her upper arms and gave her a shake. "What's going on?"

Carrie blinked once, twice, then a third time. She shrugged off Bryce's hands and backed away. "I... can't. Not now. I have... to go."

"Carrie?"

She slammed one hand against Bryce's chest to stop his advance. His outstretched hands slapped back to his sides. "Tell me what's wrong? Was it too soon, too much? Carrie, I—"

"Hush. It's not you. It's not me. It's—I don't know. Bryce, I have to go." Laughter echoed through her mind and she fought the urge to cover her ears with her hands. "Am I going crazy?"

"You're not crazy, Carrie."

The meaning of his words seeped into her. Oh, Lord. She'd said the words out loud. He'd think she was nuts. Was she? First her childhood imaginary friend returned, and now this dark, evil man. Why didn't Lottie chase him away? Carrie bent double, lowered her head to her hands and covered her face. Lottie was part of her imagination. So was the man. Bryce was real. Why didn't she hold on to him—and never let go? Somehow, she understood Bryce could chase the stranger from her mind. If she allowed him to...

::No! You shall not.::

Carrie cried out at the intensity of hate and anger tearing through her mind.

Gentle hands covered hers and eased them from her face. Bryce held her fingers loosely in his palms, led her to a chair and pressed carefully on her shoulder to encourage her to sit. She perched on the edge of the seat and stared up at him. Crouching before her, Bryce stroked her fingers.

"Do you need me to drive you home?"

No. She couldn't do that. He'd find out where she lived. She shook her head. "I'll be okay. I must be more tired than I thought. Forgive me? I'm not normally so weird."

The smile Bryce tried was honest yet filled with confusion and concern. "I know. It has been a strange day. May I call you later? Better yet, will you call me when you get home? So I know you're safe?"

Safe? Would she ever be safe with the dark man hovering in her consciousness? Who was he? Why wouldn't he leave her alone? The questions fought each other for prominence while Bryce watched her and waited silently.

The sparkles disappeared from his eyes and Carrie grew sad. He shouldn't worry about her. There was no reason. He barely knew her.

Tugging one of her hands from his gentle hold, she touched her lips. He had kissed her with gentle passion. A passion that lingered in the sensitized skin of her body and the way the breath caught in the back of her throat when she looked at him. She stared into his eyes for many long breaths before she answered.

"I'll call. It should only take me about fifteen minutes to get home." Carrie slid her other hand from under Bryce's and touched his cheek. "Don't worry. I'll be fine. Thank you for a wonderful evening." She rose and although he followed her from the room, through the house and onto the porch, she did not turn back, look behind her or acknowledge the warmth of his presence.

EIGHT

Titus eased into a hard, wooden bench at the rear of the hall. Parishioners crowded the pews, transfixed by the weaving movements of the man who stood, dead center, in front of the altar leading the song. Titus nodded once, dragged a thick songbook from the holder before him and opened it to a random page. Instead of joining in the hymn, he watched silently.

Like a snake rising from a basket, the man swayed with the music. His arms lifted high above his head, his face angled toward the ceiling. Titus noted with satisfaction how a single, small spotlight highlighted the man's upturned face to give him a radiant glow. The man was a master, and therefore worthy of Titus's notice. Titus bit back a chuckle. Good as this man was, he could still benefit from Titus's experience. Perhaps he would pass on a few...secrets.

One by one at first, then in groups, the people rose from their seats, swaying with the leader. Hands waved back and forth in praise. The leader tilted his head slightly and scanned the congregation. A tiny twist of his lips showed satisfaction.

Titus let his lips twist in a similar manner. He missed the control, the way others hung on his words, followed his lead with blind devotion. He ached for a return of that power. But, in this world, at this time, it was more difficult to gain a position of such power and control. Unless... He closed the hymnal and tapped the edge of the binding with an index finger. Unless he could somehow insinuate himself into this organization. The minister's politics would support his needs, and when the time came, he could easily dispose of the man.

Titus leaned back in the pew. The song rang to silence and the congregation returned to their seats. Having no interest in any form of religious ceremony, he let his mind wander to his own plans. Why worship another when he was the one who should be the focus of worship and adoration?

He would have that worship again. Soon. Those who had assisted his transition to this world continued to counsel patience and waiting. Titus tired of waiting. He would have his revenge. And with the satisfaction would come also the return of his power and glory.

The low rumble of the minister's voice curled through him, demanding attention and allegiance. Yes, the man was good. Titus listened for a few moments, then imagined his message given through those lips. He closed his eyes to savor the moment of delightful imaginings.

"We have a prayer request, Reverend Templeton."

Titus's eyes opened slowly and he glanced around for the speaker. There. A tall, gray haired man tugged a woman to her feet beside him. He wrapped his arm about her shoulder in a show of support that made Titus's stomach roil in disgust. He was about to turn his thoughts inward again when the man spoke a name that insisted Titus listen intently.

"It's our daughter, Carrie. She still follows evil, dancing in one of those downtown clubs. We have prayed long and hard for her to see the light and return to the flock. We need your help, the help of every prayer to turn her back to the light."

Dancer? Carrie? Titus grabbed the edge of the pew to keep from leaping to his feet in exultation. His mind's eye focused on one dancer out of many. Could they be talking about the dancer called Carouselle? He stared at the mousy woman shivering before the congregation. Yes, it could be—the shape of the lips was the same. And the shine of fear in the woman's eyes. Yes. Their daughter Carrie and Carouselle must be one in the same. If so… Titus loosened his grip on the pew and rubbed his hands together. Better and better.

With a suddenness nearly exploding from him in a gasp of breath, an idea developed with complete clarity. An idea that brought a wide smile to his lips. An idea to well serve his myriad purposes. An idea to hasten his return to power. An idea…

Titus slipped from the hall as the minister began a loud plea to his God. The seemingly sincere words echoed from the high ceiling and chased Titus from the building. Titus leaned against the hood of his car and turned back to watch the doorway. When the older couple exited, he would speak with them and show his honest concern for the wellbeing of their daughter. Offer to help them save her from depravity. Convince them that he was the answer… to their prayers.

CHAPTER
NINE

C arrie curled on her side with her fist wrapped in the sheet and pressed to her chin. Tucked under her comforter, completely covered except for a small hole for her face, she sought the familiar safety burrowing in her covers had brought her as a child.

Wrapped tightly in her bedding, she didn't feel like a child. She felt like a woman. An unfulfilled woman. With great care and deliberation, she flexed her tight fingers and touched the tips to her lips. Why had she been compelled to run from him when the pleasure of Bryce's kisses was so great?

The black hole in her memory, the darkness that frightened her when Bryce held her had returned to a tiny pinpoint as she had driven home. Now, the terror was manageable and, in the safety of her bed, Carrie tried to analyze her fear. If she could get past the blackness, she could deal with the feelings and put them where they belonged. Somewhere far from here, not in her life, that was for sure.

The memory remained hidden as frustrated tears pooled in her eyes, caught momentarily on her lashes then rolled down her cheeks to stain her pillow. Why couldn't she remember?

When she had remained aloof, uninvolved with a man, there'd been no darkness. Why now? Why, when she finally met a man she thought she could care for deeply, a man she could... love?

Carrie flopped to her back and stared at the ceiling. Dim light from the streets filtered through her blinds to highlight the swirls of texture above her. Lord, she hated textured ceilings. Smooth plaster, something one could paint a different color, or leave a clean, flat white—that's what she wanted. Like the ceilings in Bryce's house.

She let her imagination travel through his house following the path he'd taken when he'd given her the tour. Happily, she relived the closeness she'd felt to the man, and let the comfort of his home fill her. There were nicks and crannies in the small Victorian, architectural and decorative features she longed to study. Especially the intricate border around the top of his bedroom. The vining, interwoven pattern intrigued her. He'd said it was a Celtic design, done by his aunt.

Keeping the image in her mind, Carrie imagined the design knotting around her. There was magic woven into the design, magic to keep her safe. Sleep finally touched her mind and with a sigh, Carrie relaxed into her pillow and loosened her tight grip on the bedding.

Beyond the safety of sleep, Lottie smiled at her and nodded. ::'Tis a guid thing.::

"Lottie?"

::Aye, young one. I am here fer ye.::

"Why am I afraid?" Carrie mumbled as sleep softened her voice and the images in her mind.

::Dream, Carrie. Mayhaps the meanin's there. I shall protect ye. Dinna fear, young one. I am here.::

"Night, Lottie. I missed you." The words slurred with sleep.

The guardian of Carrie's dreams, her imaginary childhood friend, sat cross-legged with a long sword laid across her thighs. The veil between worlds muted her view of Carrie, as though she peered through thick gauze. She fingered the sword's simple, unadorned hilt.

The child she had protected from the pain of Carrie's early life was now a woman grown. The guardian shook her head in contemplation and her long thick braid swung against her back. She grinned at the feeling but the brightness in her expression faded quickly.

There had been much danger lately for those she guarded. Rubbing her fingers lightly over the finely honed edge of her sword, the guardian shivered. The creature, recently loosed in her plane of existence, and recently destroyed, still haunted her. Evil forces continued to gather to harm her loved ones.

And now, she had been called inexplicably back to Carrie. The power and innate evil of Carrie's hidden memory frightened her and touched deep within her own long memories. If she had been with Carrie at the time, mayhaps there would be no need for such memories. The guardian sighed. This hidden darkness built upon the strong foundation of humiliation the woman had suffered as a child. Humiliation the guardian had not been able to prevent, but could only diffuse. This failure fought the guardian's true purpose.

The guardian rose in a fluid motion and swung her sword in a soft, low arc. Failure she could not pierce with her blade, failure she could only live with and move beyond. The sword swished through the air once before she returned the blade to the scabbard at her side. She would not need a sword for Carrie's dreams this night.

Concentrating deeply, the guardian cast a silver light about herself then expanded the light to surround Carrie's sleeping form. Reaffirming what needed to be done, she closed her eyes. In order to help her charge, in order to fight for Carrie, she needed to understand what they fought. ::*Ye must remember. I am sorry, young one, but ye must. 'Tis time, fer us both.*::

. . .

The night had gone well, and she had a thick wad of bills tucked into her purse. She was tired, and there were still three weeks until her vacation. An eternity. She glanced up to the sky. Overcast and thick with clouds, the dark sky pressed down upon her. A door slammed, the sound echoing through the dimly lit parking lot.

Startled, she whirled to face the sound. A tall figure, dressed in black like a movie villain, face shrouded by shadows, stood between her and... everything.

Sliding to one side, she tried to dodge the figure but it moved with a grace she'd never seen to block her way. It was the same when she moved the opposite direction. She took a step back, then another, and another until her back pressed against a brick wall. Cold and unyielding, the wall, and her rising fear, held her frozen in place. The figure advanced, sleek, catlike. She couldn't see, but felt the predatory smile directed at her.

The guardian leaned forward trying to see clearly through the gray veil separating her from Carrie. Before she could see the man's face, the dream abruptly changed directions.

Shrinking within herself, she cowered against the wall. She knew how to fight, but had no will. When long, pale fingers reached toward her, she closed her eyes. Her mouth moved in a silent plea.

Her father's hands shook her, dragged her from the warm safety of her bed. She'd cocooned herself in the bedding, keeping only a small space open so she could breathe, but the protection hadn't helped. Once she was standing by the bed, he shook her again.

"It's time, girl. Into your robe."

She stood on a narrow dais, surrounded by a swirl of robed and hooded figures moving around her, coming ever closer. The robe disappeared and her child's body stood naked, exposed to the leers from beneath the heavy hoods of the surrounding figures. Closer. Closer the circle closed. A hand brushed her stomach and she flinched away.

And crashed to the dais, the print of her father's hand red and burning on her cheek. She was pulled to her feet, shaken, and made to

stand as others touched her. Nothing but touches. Nothing but humili-
ation. Punishment because she did not act as her father said she must.

The burning of shame filled her young body and her mind cried out
for comfort, for a release from the pain of what was done to her.

She tried to cover herself with her small hands but they were
slapped away. She tried to crouch, but was jerked to her feet and made
to endure.

When her young mind could take no more...

The guardian sighed and reached toward the sleeping woman, but the veil would not part before her. That was when she first came to Carrie. Had it been her presence that blocked the child—now the woman—from remembering? Who was the dark figure at the beginning of the dream?

The hand gripping her shoulder lifted her effortlessly and pulled
her close to a hard, cold body. Slipping down her body, the man's hand
—for man he was—cupped her bottom and pressed her against the
firm ridge at his groin. She opened her mouth to scream. His mouth
slammed down on hers, stealing the scream, smiling as he ground his
hips into hers. He was going to...

A silent scream tore Carrie from the dream. She lay panting for a second then jerked to sitting and fought to throw off the binding of bedding. She rose, wrapped a chenille throw around her shoulders and padded from the bedroom. It was only a dream. The images weren't real.

Were they?

Her father couldn't have—wouldn't have—allowed her to be treated that way? Carrie sank onto the couch and curled her feet under her. Yes, he was capable. In his blind faith, he would do anything Templeton asked. Including disowning her all those years ago.

Who was the other figure? Had she been attacked, molested, and she didn't remember? How could that be? She couldn't forget something that painful.

The rosy light from the rising sun touched her face hours later. Still unable to understand or fully remember, her eyes dry, she remained motionless and stared out the window.

. . .

Bryce opened his eyes when light invaded his restless sleep. The rumble of a garbage truck roared past the house. His muscles ached, and he massaged his neck. Straightening, he rubbed a hand over his face, wincing when he discovered the long, pencil shaped indentation in his cheek. He'd fallen asleep at his drafting table.

Rising slowly to let the kinks and creaks work themselves from his stiff body, he scrubbed his hands through his hair. A quick glance down verified that he had completed the designs needed for his meeting with Logan and Associates in—he glanced at a small clock on the bookshelf—forty-five minutes.

Forty-five minutes! It took nearly that long to cross town at this time of day. An expletive burst from his lips and he sprinted to the shower. With no time to allow the hot water to rise from the water heater, the blast of icy wetness froze the last bits of sleep from him. His teeth chattered as he dried, shaved, combed and dressed.

Bryce took no time for a final check of his drawings, just rolled them carefully and slipped them into a thick cardboard tube. Thankful Breanna spent the night at his folks, he zipped through the kitchen.

A glass with a ring of dried chocolate milk at the bottom, jerked him to a full stop. He stared at the clear cylinder as if waiting for it to speak.

Carrie. He'd meant to call her first thing this morning. He lifted his hand and messed his carefully combed hair. There was no time if he had any chance of making it to the meeting. And he dared not be late. The client, a prominent businessman, was reputed to have little patience and fired many consultants for lesser reasons than a late appearance.

Taking a long, slow breath, Bryce eyed the glass then ruthlessly turned and strode from the house. He tossed the landscape plans onto the seat next to him, roared the car to life, and backed from the drive. Mentally, he checked to make sure he had his wallet and other essentials, including his cell phone.

He could call Carrie while on the way. Bryce reached for the tiny, plastic rectangle tucked in his pocket. A squeal of tires from a side street made him grip his steering wheel with both hands. His heart pounded as if trying to explode from his chest. What was he doing—considering breaking one of his personal rules? Never use the phone while driving.

Never. But, there wasn't time to pull over and call Carrie. The worry keeping him awake long into the night, the concern he somehow focused into the energy to complete his detailed designs, flowed back into him with a rush of adrenaline. Rules were meant to be broken in an emergency, weren't they?

He glanced in the rearview mirror, caught sight of Bree's car seat and relaxed the tension between his shoulders. He couldn't. If he broke the rule once, it would be easier to break it again. Then again. He tried to ignore the siren's call of instant communication. He'd do nothing to endanger his daughter. Or anyone else's daughter or loved one.

Easing onto an expressway, Bryce gave a rueful thought to how easily he had become attached to his cell phone—once he'd been finally persuaded to get one. Tempted once again to cancel the contract and let others reach him as they could over regular phone lines and email, he shook his head. As an independent contractor, he needed the phone for business.

He needed to talk to Carrie. She'd been so distracted, almost afraid when she'd run from his home. From his arms. For the thousandth time, Bryce replayed the kisses in his mind, wondering what he might have done to frighten her. For the thousandth time, he fought his physical response to the memory of Carrie's soft, yielding body against his.

By the time he pulled into the parking lot, his brain had regained control of his hormones. A quick glance around the lot as he drew a deep breath, clutched the tube of drawings and started for the door, showed no unknown vehicles. Bryce released the breath. The client hadn't yet arrived. An antique, gothic clock placed above the building's entrance let him know he had three minutes to spare.

Not enough time to call Carrie, but enough to compose himself for the meeting. *I'll call you soon. Promise.*

CHAPTER
TEN

Except for a few minor decorating differences, the restaurant was the same as every other facility in the chain. Titus lounged in a booth in a far corner and watched the entrance. He shook his head as a waitress offered him more thick, offensive coffee and shuddered at the smell of eggs and grease rising from the kitchen. How could they eat this crap?

An elderly couple entered and paused by the cash register to peer around the crowded restaurant. Titus straightened and lifted one hand in a casual, yet imperative wave. The man noticed, took his wife's elbow, and moved through the maze of tables to the booth.

Titus rose and extended his hand. "I'm glad you decided to join me, Mr. Newcomb."

Titus resisted the urge to wipe the residue from the man's clammy palm against his tailored slacks. He turned his attention to the woman, who took his fingers between hers and gave a tiny squeeze. "Mrs. Newcomb. Won't you sit down?"

Titus waited until they slid into the booth, then returned to his seat and signaled the harried waitress. As she neared the table he turned to his guests. "Coffee?"

At their affirmative nods, Titus gave the order and turned his attention to the fidgeting couple across from him. They were nervous, and afraid. The scent rose as strong as the coffee fumes from the cups placed before them. Titus restrained a smile, fighting to maintain a concerned, serious expression. They feared him. Good.

"I was touched by your plea at the service two nights past."

The man nodded. "The Reverend Templeton spoke with us after you contacted him. How do you think you can help us save our daughter? I fear she is lost to evil."

Titus let silence draw out after the question before he posed one of his own. "I understand your daughter has been an exotic dancer for quite some time. Why have you waited so long to save her?"

A pink blush infused the woman's face. "We... we didn't know what to do. When she first left home we had hopes she would continue in the church and become a blessing to us all. When she turned to her evil ways, we disowned her. The church banished her. That was six years ago.

"Through all this time, we have had no contact with Caroline —Carrie. But we pray for her daily. Pray for her to see the light and turn from the darkness of her ways."

Titus nodded sagely, then took a sip of coffee to cover his reaction. There was a hint of darkness within their daughter, undoubtedly more since he had taken the first taste and left her with a deep suggested memory. While he had no true desire for the woman, he savored the darkness. Now, she had stepped unknowing into his plans to create a trap he would use for ultimate satisfaction.

The urge to leap to his feet and dance in the power of sheer joy trembled through his leg muscles. How long had it been since he had felt such satisfaction with the flow of events under his control?

"Mr. Avery? Is anything wrong? We will be able to save her, won't we?" The woman sniffed and surprised, Titus glanced at her. The foolish creature cried?

He patted the hand that rested against the tabletop. "We shall most certainly bring her back, Mrs. Newcomb."

The man took his wife's hand from under Titus's and held it tightly. "What must we do?"

"If you truly wish the return of your daughter—"

"We do," Mr. Newcomb affirmed with a sharp nod of his head.

"If you so wish it, then you must be prepared to do as I request, without question. My methods may seem a bit— unorthodox. But, I assure you, I have achieved remarkable results. You shall see the return of your daughter. And we shall save other souls as well, thus assuring your place in heaven."

Titus took another sip of coffee and watched the couple over the rim of the thick mug. The mention of saving other souls brought a fanatic light to the man's eyes. The woman was not so convinced, but Titus knew she would follow her husband's lead. There was a beaten down, submissiveness tight about her eyes.

He turned his attention to the man, leaned forward and spoke just loud enough so the couple had to lean toward him to hear. "There is something I must show you. I fear the corruption of your daughter goes far beyond her lewd parading before men. There is a darker danger to her soul. A corruption that must be excised. Will you meet me again, at the east parking lot in City Park?"

"That's across town from Carrie's apartment."

"I know. Mr. Newcomb. If I am to assist you in saving the souls of a number of lost sheep, you must trust me."

The man looked at his wife who nodded slowly. Then his steely gaze returned to Titus. "We'll do as you say. Nothing is more important than saving a soul from degradation and hell."

The couple rose silently and left the restaurant. Titus watched through the window as they moved slowly toward an ancient, rusty sedan. He could almost hear their animated conversation and feel the excitement emanating from the man.

Ignoring the speculative, inviting look from the waitress, he tossed a few bills on the table and sauntered to his freshly painted, dark blue Pantera. Titus leaned back in the soft leather seat, closed his eyes and allowed a smile of intense anticipation to touch his lips.

ELEVEN

A knock sounded on Carrie's door, soft and tentative, as if the caller really didn't want his presence known. Not that Carrie planned on answering any summons, either at the door or on the phone. Her occasional bouts of tears had long ago dried, and the coffee she'd forced herself to make had cooled to a dark, oily brew in her cup.

The murmur of two voices, male and female, caught her attention. Vaguely familiar, the voices nearly drew her from the cocoon she'd made from a crocheted afghan. But before she moved there was another single, light tap on the door and the voices faded away.

Curiosity wove its way through her numb mind and she crawled off the couch. Shaking off the clutching fringe, Carrie let the afghan slip to the floor as she stood and crossed to the window facing the street side of her apartment building. A large, dark pickup and a rusty sedan parked on the street. She thought the truck belonged to the property manager, so she watched the sedan.

Moments later, a couple exited the building and moved slowly toward the car. The woman turned to stare up at the window.

Carrie gasped and leapt back, bumped into a footstool, and

swung her arms for balance. No. It couldn't be. Holding her breath, she angled her body to one side of the window, cowering behind the lace curtains she'd hung despite the lease's stipulations against holes in the walls. After letting her breath out in a slow, even stream, Carrie hooked one finger at the edge of the curtain and lifted it an inch from the window. She could see the car and the couple who paused in conversation before the man opened the door for the woman and waited until she was safely seated before pacing to the driver's side.

The vehicle emitted a puff of dark smoke, then pulled away from the curb.

How had her parents found her? Carrie leaned back against the wall. What were they doing here? She glanced around the small living room. She liked this place, had felt safe here, and didn't want to move yet again.

Unless someone... someone like Bryce... wanted to share space with her.

Bryce. Her mind whispered the name and the burning of tears filled Carrie's eyes. How could she imagine, dare hope he would want her now... now that she remembered? Now, when she was nothing more than damaged goods?

He'd told her he had been abandoned as a baby—left to die in a chemical toilet. So, perhaps he would understand the psychological abuse at the hands of her ultra-religious parents. Maybe he would understand those memories and forgive her for them.

Carrie shook her head fiercely and returned to the corner of the couch, tugged the afghan up to her chin, and leaned her forehead against the arm of the overstuffed furniture. No, he wouldn't need to forgive her; the abuse was not her fault.

Her head knew the facts, but her heart still heard the words, heard her father scream that every problem within the family was her fault. Because she was a bad girl.

Bad. Carrie punched the couch.

Bad. She curled into a ball with her forehead on her knees. "No. I'm not bad."

::Nay, ye are no bad, Carrie.:: A cool, invisible touch stroked

across Carrie's shoulders. She sighed and wished, as she had never wished in her childhood, that Lottie were real.

::I am real, sweet child.::

Child? "I'm not a child anymore. I shouldn't need protecting. I've taken care of myself for a long time now."

::Aye, ye have. An' done a fine job.::

"Oh, no. My job." Carrie straightened her back and mechanically folded the throw. Her vacation over, she was scheduled to dance that night, returning to the headlining spot.

But was she ready to return? What about the dark figure, the man who attacked her? That had been outside the club—what if he were there tonight, watching her? Waiting.

A deep breath cleared some of the fear from her mind, although her body shook with sporadic shivers. She couldn't hide from her memories, and she certainly couldn't hide from the real world. There were no fairy tale happy endings. The best she could hope for was Bryce's acceptance and his friendship. How could she hope for more now?

Tossing the folded throw to the far end of the couch, she glanced at the clock. She'd need some extra time to prepare for her first set, and the afternoon was nearly gone. Carrie blanked her mind, using the strains of music she and Nightshade had chosen for the specialty number to push the memories—and her hopes—to the far recesses of her mind.

L ight, happy steps carried Bryce from the conference room and back to his car. He turned toward the building and grinned. Logan and Associates had prospered since he first contracted his service to the architects. This new building, far different from Garr's original cramped office, was a delight to the eye.

And the landscaping wasn't too bad either.

Bryce took a few moments to appreciate his own work before climbing into his car. The designs for the new contract had been wholeheartedly approved by both Garr and the client. After the client left, Garr had led him to an empty office.

Confused by the silence of the man beside him, Bryce had commented favorably on the wide expanse of windows overlooking the plantings at the rear of the building.

"It's yours," Garr said. "If you want it."

Bryce grinned into the rearview mirror, replaying his mumbled surprise and continued confusion. Garr had chuckled and clasped his shoulder. "I'm offering you a partnership with Logan and Associates, Bryce."

A partnership! With one of the premier architectural firms in the area. When the offer had completely registered through the numbness in his brain, he had easily accepted. Now, only the legal formalities remained.

Bryce pounded the steering wheel and let out a whoop. No more independent contracting, wondering when and if a new job would come in time to pay the bills. Logan and Associates proved to be extremely generous in their offer of compensation and a benefits package. Now he could stop constantly stressing over money and job security.

He needed to celebrate—to tell someone. To share the moment with Carrie. He'd wait until the next day, after the meeting with the attorney and the papers were signed, to tell anyone else. The superstitious part of him didn't want to jinx the future.

Using his cell phone, he called both Carrie's home and her cell phone and left messages at both. Then he called Nightshade. If anyone knew where Carrie might be, it was her flamboyant manager.

"Shades of the night."

"Nightshade. I've got a bone to pick with you." Bryce was barely able to withhold the happy tone in his voice as he tried to tease his lifelong friend.

"Bryce?"

The faint overtones of worry broke Bryce's reserve and he

chuckled. "Why didn't you send Carrie to the restaurant sooner? You know how much I wanted to meet her."

"So, my dear boy, things went well last night?"

"Well enough."

"Do tell."

"You're incorrigible."

Nightshade laughed. "Of course I am, and you love me for it. But, honey, where would you be without me?"

Putting the banter aside, Bryce grew serious. "Thanks, my friend."

"Not a bit of a problem. You two had already found each other anyway. My tiny matchmaking just sped things along."

"Um... do you know where Carrie is?"

"Now? What am I—my favorite dancer's keeper?"

"I need to talk to her." At times Nightshade could get downright irritating. "I'd really like to see her again. Tonight."

"That good, huh? Well, dear heart. If you want to see Carrie tonight, you'll have to come down to the Panther. She's scheduled back from vacation tonight and will be up on stage. Actually, she should be here soon." There was a dramatic pause. "Unless you don't want to see that much of her." Laughter rang through the connection.

Bryce remained silent. He knew she was an exotic dancer, but now that he knew *her*, he wasn't so sure he liked the thought of those other men ogling his Carrie.

"Bryce, you there?"

"Uh, sure."

"Honey, it's okay for you to feel that way. That's why it's the Panther's policy not to allow boyfriends or significant others in the establishment when a girl's working."

"What way? What are you talking about?"

"You're all bristly and protective. You don't want anyone else watching Carrie strip. Admit it, or I won't bend the rules for you tonight."

Bryce shrugged, but didn't dignify Nightshade's delighted

laughter with a response. From the tight knot in his belly, he knew he would have a difficult time with Carrie's profession if he continued to see her. The situation could get complicated—more complicated than the knot designs his aunt created. Was he up to the challenge?

Nightshade hummed tunelessly, creating a soothing background for Bryce's rapid thoughts. This was definitely a challenge he would face, a challenge he would overcome. Although he had known Carrie only a short time, she was worth any effort.

"I'll be there. What time is she scheduled to... dance?"

"Good for you, Bryce. I knew you wouldn't let me down. Carouselle's first set is at seven forty-five. You might want to get here early, dear heart. Many customers have been anticipating Carouselle's return."

"I understand."

"Ta, Bryce. Just keep that wonderfully open mind of yours and you and Carrie will be fine. Listen to your old uncle Nightshade."

Bryce chuckled and he cut the connection. First, he'd stop by his folks and see if they'd keep Breanna another night. There would be plenty of time for him to spend with his daughter before he needed to shower and head for The Panther's Back. Then, he'd wait until Carrie was done—dancing—and take her out for a late snack.

Yeah, that would work. He could deal with her employment at the strip club, as long as she came home to him. And only him. He shook his head at himself, revved the engine and tore from Logan and Associates' parking lot. He had no idea he could feel so— bristly and possessive.

Nervous energy and adrenaline mixed until Carrie could barely sit still long enough to paint the exaggerated makeup onto her face. Why had she decided to dance as the Harlequin? She should have started out with one of her simpler, less artsy sets. Definitely less makeup would have made her return so much easier.

The other girls were thrilled with her return. Well, Carrie

grimaced at the mirror, probably not with the fact that she was back, but the announcement of the end of her vacation saw the return of a number of regulars to the bar. From what she could see as the dancers left the stage, tips were good. Other than the extra bills clutched in their fists or tucked into what remained of their costumes, Carrie knew most of the younger dancers had little use for her.

She sighed and traced a wide black line across her white pancake makeup. Maybe it *was* time for her to retire. She was already older than most of the dancers, although she didn't think it showed in her body. Nightshade would tell her if she let herself go, like he had suggested the time she had a large mole removed from her back.

Standing and turning toward the full-length mirror, Carrie smoothed her red and black costume. Nope. If anything, she was more toned and muscled than when she began dancing years ago.

After adjusting the meager bits of Lycra and sequins, Carrie nodded in satisfaction. As she stared into the mirror her reflection wavered and blurred. Over one shoulder the disapproving faces of her parents hovered like vultures over a dying man. If only they could have understood the success she finally made of her life. If only they could have loved her. If only... she had been good enough.

A vicious shake of her head tossed a sequined headpiece to the floor but wouldn't dispel the disproving apparitions.

Sparkling green eyes appeared over her other shoulder. Bryce's eyes. He hadn't seemed disapproving when he realized where she worked. But when the realization really sank in, his response could change and he might condemn her as her parents did. He might never want to see her again. Or worse yet, he could he only see her as the stripper, a body used to entertain men. What would he want from her then?

Carrie closed her eyes and shivered at the darkness surrounding her. Once he thought about her dancing, he might want only what that other man wanted. To take from her, no matter how she fought him. Carrie sank to her chair and rested her forehead against her palms.

She had to say the word she'd been avoiding the entire day. She had to admit what happened to her. Say it. Say the word. Make it real and move on.

A calm presence surrounded her. Her imaginary friend was with her. At that moment, Carrie didn't care that imaginary friends were only for children. She accepted the comfort, stared at the mirror and filled her lungs. Released the air slowly through pursed lips. Casting her gaze about the reflected dressing room, she made certain she was totally alone. Another deep breath. It so hard to force her lips to form the word.

"I..." she whispered. She swallowed around the hard lump in her throat. "I... was raped."

Carrie held her breath until her lungs burned with the need for oxygen. As she exhaled, she whispered again. "I was raped."

A flash of anger, brilliant as an atomic blast blinded her. She had been raped. A man took by force what she had been saving. Her virginity was no longer hers to give to the one she chose. She slammed her fists on the table scattering the makeup, snatched up a box of loose powder, and threw it across the room.

As the arc of powder settled, so did the anger. Sorrow followed close on its heels and the sting of tears burned her eyes. "Oh, Bryce. I'm so sorry."

Startled, she stared into the mirror. Why did she need to apologize to Bryce?

"Carouselle," a voice rose from beyond the curtain sectioning off parts of the dressing room. "You've got about four minutes."

"I'll... I'll be right there." How she made her voice sound normal was beyond her comprehension. But now she understood the apology. It was Bryce to whom she wanted to give her virginity. All these years, waiting, knowing none of the men she dated were him. All that she'd saved, gone in a few minutes of pain, fear, and degradation.

There was no getting back what was lost. No, what was stolen from her. She had to move forward. She'd read enough self-help books, watched too many talk shows not to know the routine. Perhaps, now that she remembered...

"One minute."

Automatically, Carrie stood, adjusted her costume, and bent slightly to peer at her makeup. She looked—normal. At least she had some time before she saw Bryce again. After running from him the night before, she wasn't sure he'd be so anxious to see her again any time soon.

She waited behind a panel of drapery hung to barely hide the door back to the dressing room. The lights dimmed and the faint sounds of the intro to the Harlequin set rumbled through the speakers set high on the walls. She grimaced at the tinny sound. The bar really needed a new sound system. She shrugged. The patrons didn't come for the music. They came for the dancers.

"... Carouselle!"

Carrie let her mind go blank, focused on the music and danced into the bright lights.

TWELVE

Two dark corners edged the bar, and the furthest one was already occupied. Titus glared at an old drunk in the corner nearest the entrance until the man frowned and moved closer to the stage. Easing back into the shadows, Titus smoothed the front of his black shirt and scooted the chair back into the deepest shadows of the corner. A swift jerk pulled the tiny table toward him, helping to hide him from other patrons. He could observe the width of the establishment, but not the front door. It was a small concession for the anonymity of the darkness.

Once the barely clad waitress took his drink order, he scanned the crowded room. Nothing but the usual types who frequented strip clubs. His gaze froze at the table at the other corner—his preferred seating. Startled by the two men, he narrowed his eyes to squint through the haze of cigarette smoke, darkness, and ineffective colored lighting.

So. His thoughts darkened and Titus scowled. Even when the young woman returned with his club soda and brushed suggestively against his arm, he merely grunted, tossed her a bill, and shook his head at the offer of change. His scowl deepened until she moved from his line of vision and he could watch the other table.

"... Carouselle!"

The crackling of the sound system and the announcement of the next dancer drew his attention from the men who turned toward the stage. Titus followed their example and let a small smile tug the frown from his face. This woman was why he was here.

A crescendo of music accompanied the dancer to the stage. The already dim lights lowered further, and a spotlight highlighted the red and black costume. Sparkling as she moved, Carouselle eased into her dance, playing the part of a Harlequin. She was superb.

Yes, she was. Titus lifted his glass in mock salute and let the undulations of her body return him to the night he'd discovered just how superb. Then he sighed. But, she never would be again.

When he'd taken her in the darkness of the alley, he had been surprised to find his way blocked by the evidence of virginity. He'd not believed one such as she could be anything but a whore. When he thrust past the barrier, he'd experienced a rush of power such as he had not known in years. He took a long sip of his drink and treasured the memory. If only he could get that feeling back. That power. It was as if... somehow... his stolen power returned to him. Each glorious thrust, each time her fist pummeled against him, each cry increased the sensation.

Titus shifted, both to ease the pressure at the front of his slacks and to rub the soft material against himself. Perhaps there was truth to the legends of virgin sacrifice. Having her again would ease his baser needs, but his use for her was done.

Never again would she offer a virgin's power.

Titus laughed softly and glanced at the far table. Let that one have her; it would suit his plans more fully. He needed to contain his impatience and let her parents appear to make the decisions he had chosen for them.

After gulping the last of the club soda, Titus rose and, even before Carouselle had removed any of her costume, eased out the door.

THIRTEEN

Bryce clutched a short, thick glass. His mouth was dry, but the vodka concoction Nightshade ordered for him would do nothing to ease the dryness. Not as long as Carrie was on stage. Taking off her clothes.

He tried recalling when he had seen her dance at the N B Tween only a month and a half ago. It hadn't bothered him that she bared parts of her body to everyone then. It was just that then, he was just a part of the audience, one out of many every-ones. It hadn't been just her sensuous dance that attracted him and made him want to see more of her. There had been some-thing else, a dip in his chest then a rise in the area of his heart. He'd spent all those weeks looking for her, only to have his daughter discover her at the bookstore.

Even though others in his family believed strongly, and even advocated love at first sight, he'd never thought the concept possible. Yet, when Carrie danced that night, a part of him flew to her, raced to be with her, ached for her to return to him.

Without taking his eyes from the stage, Bryce shook his head. That wasn't love, was it?

The music changed, the rapid beats of the initial piece slowed to a smoky jazz ballad. Carrie dropped more of her costume to the stage. Carrie bared her breasts. To the eyes of every man there. His hand shook and the ice rattled in the glass.

A warm hand covered his, pushed the glass to the table, and held it there. Nightshade leaned close to his ear to speak over the god-awful music. "This is why boyfriends—"

"I know."

"Bryce. This is what she does. How she earns the money she needs to live. It's what she's good at."

"I know."

"And it's okay for you to feel this way. Like I said, it comes with the territory, honey."

Yes, he did feel bristly and possessive. He ground his teeth together, wanting to rip the eyes from every skull in the room. In a minute he'd leap on the stage and cover Carrie's body. Somehow he'd make her understand...

"Calm down, Bryce. The number's almost over. Then Carrie will change and come out to mingle with the customers. Though," Nightshade chuckled softly, "I don't think she'll get past this table."

The muscles in Bryce's arms and shoulders quivered with suppressed tension. If another man offered her money, and she bent over them that way to take it in her teeth, he'd toss the table across the room.

"They can't touch her, Bryce. See, there's no physical contact when they tip her. It's the law here, just like the fact she must always be wearing a g-string. No total nudity in this city."

"Thank God."

Nightshade patted Bryce's hand and sat back.

The music rose to a clashing crescendo then faded into silence. Carrie posed in the center of the long, narrow stage, one leg wrapped around a pole set into the stage, her back arched and her arms lifted. She smiled at the accolades of the crowd, waved, and blew a few kisses. A handful of bills folded lengthwise were tossed to the stage. Bending backwards, she picked one bill up with her teeth.

The cheering rang in Bryce's ears until he ached to shout his anger and frustration. This was insane. He shouldn't be here. She shouldn't be here. With his new partnership at Logan and Associates, he'd have enough so she'd never have to do this again. He'd never have to sit through another night imagining dirty old men ogling her. He pressed his palms against the table to rise.

Nightshade's hand was heavy on his shoulder and amazingly strong holding Bryce in his seat. Nightshade shook his head, his eyes sad with understanding. "Now's not the time. Don't make me regret I bent the rules. She'll be back and you can talk. I'll arrange it so she doesn't have another set tonight."

Reluctantly, Bryce nodded, but remained rigid in his seat. Nightshade gave him a wry grin, shook his head, and left his chair. The movement barely registered as Bryce watched Carrie glide toward the curtain, gracefully gathering bits of her costume as she went.

Carrie turned back to the crowd for a final wave. It felt good to dance again, but she feared some of her muscles had grown a bit slack during her weeks off. She wasn't as toned as she thought. Scanning the crowd one last time, she gave a final wave to a few of the regulars, then glanced toward the table Nightshade often occupied when she danced.

He wasn't there.

But Bryce was. Her knees turned watery. Hidden by the curtain, she clutched the doorframe. He looked... furious. With her? He knew this was her job. She swallowed heavily and knew behind her white pancake makeup her own skin had to be just as pale. Everything, her color, her emotions, her hopes and dreams, drained from her in a rush.

Backing from the stage, Carrie held back tears until she reached the bathroom. Dry, wracking sobs, held nearly silent by the hand she pressed over her mouth, shook her, chilled her, froze her soul.

She had to face him. Carrie stared at herself in the cracked vanity mirror. She'd faced too many things today, yet still ignored too many emotions, leaving her empty and unsure. If she wanted to try a relationship with Bryce, she had to face him. Face his anger. And tell him the truth.

Behind her closed eyelids, a pair of eyes formed. Not the bright green of Bryce's eyes, but the somber, calm blue eyes she associated with Lottie.

"How am I going to do this?" she asked herself and her childhood imaginary friend.

The somber lights left Lottie's eyes and Carrie felt her smile. She took comfort from the change of expression and found a bit of hope. If it was meant to, it would work out—whatever it was.

Heaving a sigh, Carrie left the bathroom and returned to the dressing room, quickly cleaned the white makeup from her face, and dressed in a baby doll tee shirt and jeans. No sparkles for this confrontation. She didn't even apply new makeup and barely ran a brush through her sweat-damp hair. Now or never.

And never would never, ever do.

By the time Carrie eased around the bar, the rigidity had disappeared from Bryce's posture. Drink cradled between his palms, he slumped forward. His profile was partially hidden by shadows so she was unable to read his expression.

The announcer introduced a dancer and music blared from the huge speaker suspended above the bar. She couldn't talk to Bryce with this noise. Since she'd made the decision to tell him about what happened to her, there was no question of waiting. If she waited, she'd chicken out and that secret would always hover between them.

Bryce's shoulders hunched up as if he shrugged, then relaxed. His posture straightened. He glanced at the dancer, watched for about three seconds, then stared down into his drink.

A flare of jealousy burned in Carrie's chest. Just as quickly the emotion dissipated. He didn't seem interested in Ivie Promises.

A tall body stepped in front of her, blocking Bryce from her sight. When she tried to move around the human obstacle, hands rested lightly on her shoulders. Ready to give the man a few choice words, she looked up at her manager. Nightshade's gray eyes were gentle, his expression caring and worried. Was he worried about her—or about Bryce?

He leaned to speak directly into her ear. "Go to him, honey. We've done some rescheduling to give you the rest of the night off. Go someplace quiet with your man. I think you two have things to work out."

"Is he... does he...?"

"It's up to him to tell you what he feels, dearest."

Carrie shook her head. Maybe she'd never have to tell him about... about that. Maybe after tonight watching her at work, maybe he'd never want to see her again. Nightshade cupped his finger under her chin and gently forced her to look at him.

In the silent communication between good friends, she nodded. He gave her a sad smile and stepped aside. Carrie took a deep breath.

Just as she stepped forward, Bryce angled in his chair to face them. Their gazes locked and nothing remained in the room. No blaring music, no Nightshade, no pulsing strobe lights. He rose, faced her, and held out one hand.

Frozen in place by warring hope and indecision, Carrie felt the press of Nightshade's hand against the small of her back. "Go on, Carrie. It'll be fine. I know. Honey, listen to Nightshade."

She took a step, then another, a slow motion advance toward a future she couldn't see and didn't dare imagine. Bryce met her after five paces, took her hand, and led her toward the restrooms at the rear of the bar. The music was only slightly less pounding there.

She looked at their hands, then into Bryce's face. His expression remained closed giving her no indication what he was thinking. She licked her dry lips. "Nightshade said I have the rest of the night off."

"He said he'd try and arrange it."

"We should talk."

A mocking half grin tilted Bryce's mouth. "That we should."

"Can we go somewhere else?"

"Are you hungry?"

Had she eaten anything that day? Nothing but coffee that cooled in her cup as she tried to sort through the onslaught of memories and the odd visit from her parents. She shook her head. She couldn't eat anything; the food would stick painfully low in her throat.

"Can we...?"

"Yes, Carrie?"

She cleared her throat. This was a chance, but there was only one place where she thought she might feel safe. "Can we go to your house? I can follow you in my car."

"I didn't drive, Nightshade brought me."

Despite the worry, she couldn't help smiling. "Wanna ride, mister?"

"Okay, I know what I want to talk about. But, it can wait. What do you want to say to me, Carrie?"

Carrie sat cross-legged and tucked her feet into a lotus position at the end of a deeply cushioned couch. She held a fine, blown crystal goblet. Afraid her nervous fingers would snap the slender stem, she cradled the bowl in her palms. Where to start? She stared into the distance past Bryce's shoulder. Should she start with her parents' emotional abuse, or with what happened not that long ago?

Bryce knelt beside her, and she looked into eyes so full of concern her heart lurched. "Carrie, why did you run away from me last night?"

He shook his head. "No, that's not important. There are so many questions I want to ask—I don't know why I asked that one."

By asking that question, he'd given her an answer to her own. Until the dream had opened a floodgate of memory, she wouldn't have been able to give him an answer. But now... now she could. She really hated that knowledge.

Carrie took a long, slow breath. "It is important. Very important. I didn't understand why myself, not until I had a dream last night. No, not really a dream, more like a memory. One I truly wish I didn't have." She had to pause to force back tears and to let the knot in her throat loosen so she could speak again.

In the silence Bryce rose, took her glass and set it aside, then sat facing her. He took her hands. "Take your time, sweetheart. I'll wait."

"Oh, Bryce. I wanted to wait. Planned to wait. Was waiting. But now it doesn't matter."

"I don't understand."

She had to make him understand and erase the stressed lines from his forehead and around his dulled eyes. Somehow, she had to make the sparkles return. "Last night, when I ran away, I was scared. Frightened beyond reason. And... I didn't understand why. All I knew was that despite how your kisses made me feel, despite how much I wanted to continue... to do... more..."

"I would never pressure you."

"I know." Carrie held tightly to Bryce's hands and found strength and comfort in his touch. A hint of cool, pleasant affection filled her and she sighed. With both Bryce and Lottie encouraging her, she could speak the words and make the confession that might cleanse her of the terror. She glanced at Bryce from under her lashes. His eyebrows were raised slightly, his expression calm yet curious. He waited.

"All the way home I tried to figure out why I acted the way I had. I lay awake a long time, afraid of what I didn't understand. Oh, and so afraid you'd never want to see me again." She hung her head and closed her eyes. "You still might not."

"No, Carrie, never. I searched too long for you. I can't imagine anything you might tell me that would change my mind—or my heart—about you." Bryce lifted one of her hands and touched his lips to the backs of her knuckles. Then he lowered her hand and gave a wry chuckle. "Though, I admit I don't know if I can ever see you when you're at work again."

She lifted her gaze to stare at him.

"After tonight it'll be difficult enough just imagining how those men leer at you and fantasize about you. How they long to touch you." His grip grew painfully tight, yet Carrie welcomed the intensity of his physical reaction. It gave her the strength to speak.

"I think...one of them did."

Confusion drew Bryce's brows low over his eyes. A double line of worry indented the smooth skin of his forehead. "What do you mean, sweetheart?"

"It was one of the memories I found last night. One I'd tried to bury so deep I'd never find it again. One that your kiss brought to the surface."

"My kiss was that terrible?" The hurt behind the question was softened by a tiny, sad smile.

"Oh, no. Your kiss was wonderful. More than I deserve."

Bryce's eyebrows lifted and his fingers tightened around hers.

"Carrie, tell me. Tell me."

"Please, don't hate me."

"Carrie, sweetheart—"

"Listen, Bryce. It's not pretty. I don't want to know these things, and I don't want to admit them to you. You'll think of me... like my parents always told me I was. A harlot. A whore."

"I know that's how a lot of people think of exotic dancers. But I don't. I never have."

"You might now."

His fingers tightened painfully around hers and once again Carrie welcomed the intensity. The pressure allowed her to concentrate on the words she needed to say. "One night, shortly before my vacation, when I was leaving The Panther's Back, a man was waiting for me. He was dressed in black, had black hair, and stayed in the shadows. He grabbed me and pulled me into those shadows."

Bryce rose and paced the width of the room. He stood frozen for a moment then turned back to face Carrie. His fists clenched at his sides and he leaned forward on his toes in a posture of pure anger.

"What did that bastard do to you?"

"I..." Carrie stared down at her hands. Now he would order her to leave his house. To leave his life. It was what she feared, and there was nothing she could do now.

He strode back to her and knelt beside the couch to cup her cheeks in his hands and lift her gaze to his. Anger still flashed in the intense green of his eyes, but was tempered by jade depths of sorrow. His lips were soft with concern, but a muscle ticked tightly along his jaw. "Tell me." The intensity of his voice made her wince and try to draw away from his touch. Bryce's hands slid to her shoulders. "I'm sorry, Carrie. I think I understand. You don't have to say anything." Soft and sad, his tone wrapped tight bands of pain around her already wounded heart.

"But, I do, Bryce. I have to say it to make it real."

He nodded and stroked her cheek with the back of his finger. "I'll listen. I'm here. Tell me."

There was nothing else to do. She had to say the words. Carrie took a deep breath. "When he pulled me into the shadows, he ripped my clothing. He was rough, like he needed my pain along with the... penetration."

The rise of Bryce's chest indicated he was about to speak. Carrie pressed her fingertips to his lips and shook her head. "I have to finish. I remember the feel of the gravel against my back and the weight of him on me. He... he... laughed. And when he... he stole my virginity—"

"Carrie!" Shaking with suppressed emotion, Bryce gathered her into his arms. Now she couldn't see his face and couldn't tell his thoughts. He must not hate her—yet. Maybe her words and the meaning hadn't registered.

"Bryce," she whispered against his neck, then struggled to pull away enough to look into his face. "I was raped. And when he ripped into me, he laughed again and mumbled something about power. He took my virginity. The gift I would have given—to you."

There, the words were out. Both admissions. Either of which could turn Bryce from her in an instant.

Silent, he stared at her, his eyes wide and unreadable. Carrie chewed on her lower lip, held her breath and waited. So much was riding on his reaction, so much she hadn't even considered. Her future, her life. She loved this man.

Unbelievable as it was, in just a few short days, she had fallen in love. Now her heart would be broken in the same short period of time. She hoped it wouldn't be long until he rejected her as tarnished goods, she couldn't stand the waiting. Then she'd gather what was left of her dignity and leave.

Why didn't he say something?

While Bryce struggled to absorb her words, he watched emotions cross Carrie's face, linger in her expressive brown eyes, then flitter away. Raging inwardly at the bastard who raped her, who forced himself upon an innocent woman, he thought he knew what she was thinking. But he couldn't find the words to convince her that it didn't matter.

Innocent? Carrie's final statement eased past the rage and settled heavily around his heart. She wanted him to be the first? God, how could he take that pain away? Now she was frightened...of him...of his reaction to her admission.

His teeth clenched, tightening the already tense muscles of his jaw and neck. If he had tried harder to find her maybe this wouldn't have happened. If Nightshade would have told him... Bryce closed his eyes, shook his head and tried to draw a deep breath. This was no one's fault... except the man who attacked Carrie.

Carrie drew away from him. Why, when she so desperately needed comfort, would she? He understood. She thought he rejected her. Bryce's eyes popped open to the abject sorrow and pain of Carrie's expression. Her throat worked as she struggled against the tears welling in her eyes.

Bryce let a shallow, hopefully comforting grin pull his lips. "Carrie, I understand. Don't run away again. We can work through this, I know we can."

Confusion replaced some of the pain swirling in Carrie's eyes. A single tear escaped and trailed down one cheek. She shook her head.

"Yes, sweetheart. We can. Did you report the attack?"

"How... how could I? I didn't remember it... until last night."

"We should still report it. Anything you remember might save another woman from attack."

A hopeful, determined light shone through the tears. "Tomorrow. I'll go tomorrow."

"I'll go with you." Appealing to her sense of responsibility had redirected her focus. He let his grin widen slightly. Pride for her strength and resiliency flowed through him.

"You... don't have to. You don't have to be around me—"

Bryce shook her gently. "Don't say that. I choose to be around you. I choose to love you."

"Love? But, you can't."

"Carrie, shh." He'd said too much, too soon. She looked frightened as a rabbit caught in a beam of light. Her lips trembled and he couldn't help himself. Bryce leaned forward and carefully touched his lips to hers, tasting the salt of her tears. The agony of her pain washed through him.

Angling back, he stroked the hair back from her face, tucking the strands behind her ears. Her body shook as she fought to control her tears. To cleanse herself of some of the pain she needed to cry. So, he eased beside her on the couch, tucked her against his side and rubbed one hand slowly up and down her back.

Carrie turned her face to his chest, wrapped the material of his shirt in her fist and sobbed. He held her as tightly as he dared and let her cry until the tears dried and only the occasional wracking sob shook her body.

When she pulled back and looked up at him her eyes were puffy, her nose was red, and her cheeks glistened with wetness. She was the most beautiful creature he'd ever seen.

"I'm afraid to go home." He barely heard her whisper.

"You can stay in the guest room."

"I don't want to be alone. I'm afraid of the dreams."

Bryce took a long breath. Using the hem of his shirt he dried her face and spoke softly, unwilling to frighten her further. "Do you want me to stay with you?"

"Yes."

FOURTEEN

"What do you want?"

Carrie couldn't answer, not really. Not when she ached for him in her bed. That's all she wanted. So, when someone passed by the open door carrying a musical instrument, she gave a different answer.

"A musical serenade with a live oboist."

He laughed, eased himself down at the end of the narrow bed and leaned against the footboard to watch her. So close. So far away. Did he sense the loneliness, or did it show in her eyes?

He rose, a bare movement against the mattress, and crawled to stretch his body beside hers. "How's this?"

His face was near to hers. Close enough that all she had to do was turn her head and let her lips brush his. A faint touch, barely enough to register in her nerve endings, yet it did. And sent jolts of longing, sharp shards of fear, the heavy heat of desire, chasing each other through her body.

A puff of air passed his lips and blew across hers. So kissable. So... oh, God. She wanted him to kiss her.

Easing more fully to his side, he grinned as he leaned toward her, closing the barest distance between them. His lips almost touched hers before he pulled away. Angling his face, he barely pressed his mouth *against hers. And again, at yet another, delightful angle. His bottom lip grazed hers, their top lips not meeting. He tilted his head to graze her lip again.*

She wanted to let loose the wild longing, to moan at his kiss, to hold him close. But, she was afraid, even as his soft, oh so soft, kisses tickled her lips.

Finally, with infinite care, he let his lips linger against hers, moving slowly, gently, still barely brushing her sensitized skin. He made a sound low in his throat, increased the pressure, and touched the tip of his tongue to the fullness of her bottom lip.

Carrie jerked awake at banging somewhere outside and immediately closed her eyes, trying to recapture the wonderful sensations of the dream. Her lips tingled. She touched the pads of her fingers to her bottom lip and shuddered at the waves of response washing over her body. Her mouth felt pouty, as if she had been kissed so delightfully. By Bryce. The sparkling, delightful green of his eyes broke into rainbows behind her closed lids.

Then shattered to darkness when she remembered where she was—alone in the bed in Bryce's guestroom. He'd lead her there and, after waiting outside the bathroom door as she'd washed her face, tucked her into the bed. He'd pulled a chair close and held her hand as she fell asleep.

How could he have done those things after what she'd admitted to him? Maybe, maybe he did care. He couldn't—no, no one could love her now. Not like she loved him.

Carrie turned her head and opened one eye. The chair was empty. Just as she suspected, he'd probably left her as soon as she'd fallen asleep. Now, all she had to do was find her clothes and sneak from the house. A tiny portion of her mind wondered if she could keep the soft, worn tee shirt he'd given her to wear. The material smelled of him and she could almost—almost—imagine him caressing her.

There was a dip in the mattress at her side, a bare movement that she rolled to face. Bryce lay on his side, his bent arm propping his head watching her. It was her dream come to life.

"Good morning, sweetheart."

"Bryce?" He'd slipped out of his clothes and wore only boxers and a tee shirt. His hair was mussed and his eyes heavy lidded as if he'd just awoken.

"What do you want?"

It was her dream. And like in the dream, all she wanted was him. In her bed. His bed. This bed. It was time to chase away the demon dreams.

In her silence, he inched closer. "How's this?"

All she had to do was turn her face just a tiny bit and her lips would brush his. She did. Jolts of longing, desire, and fear chased each other through her body. Would she prove to him that she was a whore?

Bryce angled his face and barely grazed his lips across hers. Again, at another angle. And a third time. Her breath caught in her throat. She prayed this was real, that she hadn't fallen back to sleep and reentered the dream.

Bryce's lips lingered against hers, moving slowly, gently, still barely brushing her sensitized skin. He made a growling sound, low in his throat, increased the pressure, and touched the tip of his tongue to the fullness of her bottom lip.

This was no dream. She wanted him, and if he wanted her... "Bryce, I want..."

"Are you sure, sweetheart? No pressure."

"I do. Only..."

"Only what, Carrie?" Bryce kissed the tip of her nose and leaned back. She immediately missed the warmth of his presence. Her world was cold without him.

"I'm so sorry. I can't give you—"

He stopped her words with a firm, insistent kiss. "No apologies. Let me show you how... this is our first." Another kiss stole her breath. When her lips parted, he stroked his tongue over the tender, sensitive skin of her inner lip.

She found the breath to whisper, "Show me."

"You're sure?"

At her nod, Bryce rained kisses over her face and neck, slowly drew the comforter down, and snuggled close to her side. The kisses continued until her senses reeled and her body was afire with longing. Only when her breaths came in harsh gasps and she clutched at his shoulders did he begin to touch her through the soft material of the tee shirt.

Determined to make this the memory of her first time at loving a man, Bryce hoped that with slow precision, he'd wipe away the other memories. Pausing in his exploration of her body, he gazed down at her closed eyes and swollen, parted lips. No, he couldn't erase what that bastard had done to her, but maybe he could help her past the fear.

Even though she moaned at his touch, her body remained tight, her muscles quivering and tense. She was frightened. Taking firm control over his body's needs, Bryce slowed his pace. Breanna's mother had taught him well in the ways of Faerie seduction, so he rolled to his back and curled Carrie against his side.

Perhaps if she felt she had the power and the control she would not be so frightened. Attacks such as she suffered were not about the sex, but about control. And power over another being. He fought the return of the furious anger against the rapist. Now was not the time for anger. Now was the time for gentleness and love.

At Carrie's questioning look, Bryce lifted his head from the pillow and took possession of her soft lips. She followed as he lay back, partially covering his chest with her body. Then, without speaking, Bryce took her hands and guided them over his body, silently teaching her to give him pleasure. She found the place at the base of his spine that sent shivers coursing over his body; she lifted his shirt, touched her tongue to his nipples and wet-hot jolts of lightning surged through him.

The fearful tension left her body, replaced by a delightful tension quivering her skin under his touch. Only then did Bryce lay her back and strip the clothing from her body. She tugged at the waist of his boxers and he helped her push them past the strength of his impatient erection.

Skin touching skin, Bryce slid against her, but still resisted the need to settle himself in the cradle of her thighs. He kissed, nipped, sucked at her exposed skin until she was covered with a rosy blush of need. He whispered Fey words of seduction against her skin, words that had no human translation, and gauged her body's response.

Carrie's lips moved against his chest and he ached with need of her. She heard his words and repeated them back to him. Writhing against each other, the sweet friction of their damp skin burned with unbearable pleasure.

"Bryce," Carrie whispered on a moan.

"In the nightstand..." Bryce gasped to slow his breathing. Confusion filling her eyes, she reached into the small drawer. The tiny package she held in her hand made her frown. Bryce pressed a kiss to her temple then whispered, "We'll talk about children when we're ready, sweetheart."

Carrie's eyebrows shot upward and for the briefest of moments Bryce thought she might still reject him. Instead, she fumbled with the condom, growling low in her throat with frustration at the bit of foil packaging.

After tugging the packet from her fingers, Bryce made short work of releasing the condom and protecting them. Carrie's body surged against his, encouraging, welcoming, and she moaned his name.

He rose above her, slipped one hand under her buttocks, and encouraged her to lift her hips. Positioned against the welcome of her wet heat, he paused.

"Bryce." An agony of waiting filled her voice. He entered her but stopped when he'd buried himself but a bare inch.

Hovering over her, Bryce traced his tongue along the shell of her ear. "First, sweetheart. *I* am the first." In one swift arch of his hips, he fully embedded himself in the slick, tight essence of Carrie's body. Waiting for her to adjust to his presence, he held himself still on stiff arms.

Carrie's inner muscles clenched rhythmically around him, her sharp cry and wide eyes made him smile. But the needs of his body did not allow her to recover from the intensity of her orgasm. He withdrew and thrust into her in long, slow strokes.

The flash of feeling, so wonderful—so different from... that time—lifted Carrie once more to an impossibly high place. The movement of Bryce's body over and in hers, kept her perched at the edge of an amazing precipice. Aching to leap again into the void, but held back by the remnants of fear, Carrie lifted her hips to meet his thrusts, threw back her head, and gave into the vocalization of her pleasure. Bryce drew his lips from hers and whispered against her cheek. His words were strange combinations of syllables she didn't understand, yet she knew deep within her skin, somehow they tightened the intensity of their joining.

She'd never thought such feelings were possible. And she'd never feel this with another—only with Bryce. The slick friction within her, the stroke of his hands over her body, the insistent press of his lips, the heat of his tongue...

"Oh! Oh!"

"Let it happen, Carrie." He threw back his head, increased the tempo of his thrusts, then paused to smile down on her. Sweat covered his forehead; his entire body glowed in the early morning light.

Carrie arched her hips to meet his and ran her fingertips over the place low on his spine that delighted him so. When her fingers lingered there, his jaws clenched. Tight cords of muscle stood out on his neck and he forced her hips deep into the mattress. As he shook with his release, she let go her hold on the tight, brittle nerves and her body exploded. They cried out one after the other.

Carrie sat propped against the headboard, the sheet tucked tightly under her arms to keep herself covered. She listened to the sounds of water from the bathroom where Bryce showered, and grinned at the closed door separating the rooms.

This time with Bryce really had been like she'd dreamed her

first time making love would be. There was no sadness or disappointment, but still... a lingering doubt marred the tingly happiness surrounding her body.

Now that they'd had sex, it was still possible Bryce would turn from her? The brow-beatings her parents had given her when she was young, the lectures she'd been forced to suffer, all told how a man would spurn her if she gave herself to him without the institution of marriage.

Marriage? What good had that done her parents? Neither was happy and they had taken that unhappiness out on her. As an adult she could see their actions and words for what they were. But, as a child, she had wholeheartedly believed what they'd told her, what they'd done to her. A child was always supposed to trust their parents' words.

She reached for the discarded scrap of foil nearly hidden in the messed bed covers. Toying with the tiny package, she stared at the bathroom door.

He had the condom easily available and hadn't hesitated to use it. Was Bryce afraid of catching some disease from her? In spite of his pretty words, did he really consider her a whore? The foil crinkled in her fingers and she twisted and crumpled the bit into a tight ball.

The door rattled and Bryce, wrapped in a short robe, stood in the steamy opening. He ran his fingers through his hair, then wiped his palms against his sides. In three steps he was at her side and leaned over the bed to plant a kiss against her lips. He pulled back with a look of surprise when she didn't respond to the soft caress.

"What's wrong, sweetheart?"

"Nothing." Carrie hid the destroyed condom wrapper in her palm and shook her head. "Nothing."

"For some reason, Carrie. I don't believe you." Bryce sat beside her and carefully pried open her clenched fingers. ""What's this?"

"The package from—"

"Was it the wrong kind of condom?" Bryce grinned and tossed the wrapper into a small trashcan.

"No, of course not. Don't be silly."

Then, why does it worry you?"

"I'm afraid you had to use it because..."

"Hmm?" He stroked one finger up and down the inside of her arm, treating her to a remarkable trail of liquid fire from wrist to elbow. Her words would make her sound like a fool—or perhaps the harlot he must surely think her to be. Carrie swallowed heavily. "That you thought I might have some STD or something."

Bryce stopped tracing her arm, lowered his gaze, then glanced at her from under his lashes. "I was protecting you—us—from the chance of a child before we're ready. Carrie, I haven't been with a woman since Bree's mother, so I'm clean. If you were a virgin..."

Carrie jerked from his touch and scooted to the far side of the bed, dragging the bedding with her. If. He said if. He didn't believe her.

"Carrie, no. I know you were innocent—"

"No, Bryce, I wasn't. Inexperienced maybe, but not innocent. Somehow, you made me feel that way. Then you made me feel, oh, so wonderful. I can't believe it. But now..."

Bryce stood slowly and paced from the bed. He kept his back to her. "I don't mean to hurt you. I never want to. Why do you think the worst of me? Didn't I show you—?"

"That I'm a whore? Just like my parents said?"

Jerking to face her, his eyes went wide. "Is that what...? You believe I think that? Carrie."

He turned away and, after standing frozen for a moment, left the room.

How could he walk away like that? Carrie moaned to herself. Now she really had chased him away. Damn her insecurities. Struggling to stand on weak legs, she tugged the sheet from the bed, wrapped it around herself, and rushed after him. "Bryce."

"Yes?" He peeked around the doorframe and grinned. "I accept your apology."

"My apology?" Carrie slammed her fists against her hips and glared at him.

"Yep. For not believing how much I care for you. For not realizing how none of your past matters to me. All we need to concern ourselves with is the here and now."

"It's hard to believe."

"Then, I'll have to show you." Bryce entered the room and swept her into his embrace. Kissing her possessively, he backed her toward the bed. But as he bent to lay her down, he glanced at the clock.

"Shit."

"Bryce? What?"

"I have a meeting in just over an hour. I can't miss this one." He sighed dramatically, kissed her mouth, then sighed again. "There's no time to show you properly."

The doubt and confusion fled Carrie's mind and a sudden sense of freedom and belonging filled her. She stroked the side of Bryce's freshly shaven jaw. "How long will the meeting last?"

"Too long." He crushed her against his chest and liquid fire trailed after his moist, open-mouthed kisses along the column of her throat. "Much too long." He groaned and stepped back. "Then I have to pick up my daughter. I've imposed on my folks enough for a few days."

"I'd love to go with you when you get Breanna. I'd enjoy meeting your folks." Just as long as he didn't ask to meet hers.

Bryce paused for a long moment. He formed the words slowly as though hesitant to agree. "That would be fine. Maybe we can invite ourselves to lunch." A moment later his expression relaxed and he gave her an honest smile. "Sorry. The last time I took a woman home to meet the folks didn't turn out to be such a happy occasion."

"I won't go if you don't want me to."

"Of course I do. They'll love you, sweetheart. But I wanted to go with you to the police station this morning."

"Oh," She had forgotten her promise to report her attack. An attempt at a fortifying breath was marginally successful. "I'll be okay by myself. Don't worry about me."

"I will."

She shook her head and lifted to her toes to kiss his forehead. "Thank you. You go take care of your meeting, and I'll talk to the police. We can meet back here and go find your daughter. I'm looking forward to seeing her again. She's such a doll."

"Hmm. At times." He grinned. "I'm off to my room to dress. Take your time here. There's a spare house key in the clay pot on top of the fridge." He turned, paused, then stepped back, opened the nightstand drawer and pulled out a handful of condoms. "For later. I don't have any of these things in my room." His eyebrows lifted and he winked one eye slowly. "Haven't needed them— until now. I laid in this supply when I had a couple of rowdy guests."

"Rowdy?"

"Oh, yeah." Bryce eased back to face Carrie and stroked his palm over her breast. "Maybe sometime I'll show you how loud they got."

Carrie tucked her hand under the short hem of his robe and lightly ran a fingernail along his lower spine. "Sounds interesting."

Bryce swallowed heavily. "I... I've got to go. Now." With a quick kiss, he sprinted from the room. Carrie laughed at his speedy exit, then set about preparing herself for the ordeal at the police station. For all her brave words, she was petrified.

FIFTEEN

"Bryce, This is Randall Corley, my attorney. Rand, Bryce MacAlister."

The men shook hands and settled into chairs around the large conference table. Garr Logan, of the architectural firm of Logan and Associates, handed Bryce a thick document and shrugged apologetically. "Looks imposing, but counsel here said we need all the legal gobbledygook to make your partnership binding and official. I'll have Annie bring us some coffee while you take a look."

Bryce stared at the formal document for a moment. A favorite family story was how Jaye had offered Pop a partnership in Zeroun's. Now Bryce understood the elation in his father's voice at each retelling. This was amazing. He still couldn't believe it. After scanning the first page, he settled in to read the meat of the document.

He glanced once at the attorney who sat with his hands folded, looking out the window, then returned to the agreement.

When he turned over the last page, the attorney angled his chair to face Bryce squarely. "I know there must be questions."

"Mr. Corley—"

He lifted one hand. "My association with Garr is informal. Please, call me Rand."

"Uh, sure. I'm not understanding the gobbledygook as Garr calls it, on the sixth page." Bryce shuffled through the pages and double-checked the section that was unclear to him. "Um, section twenty-one."

A slight frown marred Rand's forehead. "Would you read that section to me? Sometimes hearing it will help clear up the confusion—for both of us." He smiled and canted his head to one side.

Bryce read the paragraph. When he finished he nodded. "Okay, that makes sense now."

"I find that method often works. I depend a great deal on my hearing."

Garr chuckled, then composed his expression when Bryce turned to him. "So, Bryce. Any other questions? Can Logan and Associates list you as a partner on the letterhead?"

"This offer is even more generous than I expected. I don't know if I can live up—"

"Bryce, you know how particular I can be about my projects. If your work wasn't up to my standards, you would never have been asked back after the first assignment. And certainly, you would not be here now. Your landscaping style complements my firm's architecture. We want to offer our clients a complete package. And, we want to keep you with us." There was no doubt in Bryce's mind that he wanted to remain with this firm. Being offered a partnership—not just employment, a partnership!—out of the blue was amazing. He turned his attention back to the documents and shuffled through the pages. With a show of precision, he stacked the papers with the signature page on top. "Looks like I'll need new business cards."

Garr rose and held out his hand. "Welcome to Logan and Associates, Bryce. There's a company dinner in a few weeks—catered by your family, I believe." He grinned. "Can we save the official announcement until then?"

"Not a problem." Bryce turned his attention to the attorney. "How many copies of this do I have to sign?"

The men laughed together. Rand pulled a slim case from his briefcase. "Call me superstitious, but for agreements such as this, a new pen is called for." He opened the case to expose a thick silver and mahogany pen. "And, you'll remember this agreement each time you use this pen, Bryce."

Rand reached again into the briefcase and pulled out the additional documents. Garr took the stack, sorted through them, and began slashing his signature across the appropriate pages.

Bryce fingered the smooth pen, took a deep breath, and found the first signature line marked with a bright red arrow sticker. After signing his name and dating the line, he sat back and stared at his signature. Not bad for a kid abandoned and left to die in a portable toilet.

The signing was completed rapidly and Rand gathered the papers to tuck back into the briefcase. "Your copies will be delivered to you after this is filed appropriately." He rose to shake Bryce's hand. "You're part of a great company now."

"I know. Thank you, Rand."

"That's my job." He nodded to Garr. "Cricket."

A rustle of movement sounded from under the table. Startled by the presence of the pale, golden Labrador that moved to Rand's side, Bryce could only stare when the attorney bent slightly to the side to find the harness at the dog's shoulders. "Forward, Cricket." Rand and his dog moved surely around the table and toward the door. The attorney chuckled.

Garr joined in the laughter and clasped Bryce's shoulder. "Welcome to Logan and Associates, Bryce."

T he uniform-clad woman closed the file folder and gave Carrie a brief smile. "I'll process this information. Will you be available if I have any further questions?"

"Of course. I'll do anything I can to help catch this guy."

"We appreciate that, Ms. Newcomb". Carrie turned toward the deep voice coming from the doorway. A tall man in a slightly rumpled suit nodded as the officer left the room. Carrie wondered irreverently if the man's appearance was common for a detective.

He held out one hand to her. "I'm detective Roger Corley. I have just a couple more questions for you."

Carrie sighed. She'd been over the rape time and again, both with the officer and with a counselor. What more was there to say?

"Yours was not the first attack, Ms Newcomb. I understand your memory isn't clear to the exact date of your attack, but there have been two dancers assaulted in the past four weeks. Only one woman came in right after the attack, so we have DNA samples. The descriptions of the perp are similar in each case. However, the other two women had something in common that I see is different in you."

"We're all dancers?"

A ruddy flush touched the detective's high cheekbones. "Yes. However, the other girls dance at—shall we say—less desirable clubs. They do, however, both have violet eyes. And both mentioned their attacker commenting on their eye color."

Carrie twisted her fingers together. "All he said with me was something about power."

"Um." The detective paged through a small notebook. "Is there anything else you can remember, something that may seem insignificant now?"

Gnawing on her bottom lip, Carrie thought about the detective's question for a long moment as he casually tapped his pen against the pad, then shook her head. "I've only just regained the memory. Maybe later more details will come to me."

"That's possible. Here, take my card. If you remember anything, call me as soon as you can."

Carrie glanced at the plain, white business card before tucking it into her purse. "I will, Detective Corley."

After a few inane pleasantries, she left the tiny room and stepped into a day bright, sunny, and full of life. The sun on her face warmed her entire body, leeching the chill of her memories from her. Now, instead of another day of unknown fear, this was a day of new beginnings. Beginnings she could have with Bryce.

She glanced at her watch, then she checked her cell phone. No messages, so Bryce must still be in his meeting. She'd drive back to his house and wait in the park across the street for him to return.

First, though, she punched a key for an automatic dial.

"This best be important, Carrie."

"How'd you know—oh, caller ID. Nightshade, I have something important to tell you. Wake up and listen."

"About you and my boy, Bryce?"

"Yes—no—maybe later on that one. No, this is more important."

"More important than the happiness of two of my favorite people? Wait, I'll sit up for this."

"I'm serious, Nightshade. I'm at the police station."

"Carrie, honey, what?"

"I was raped." There. The words were out... again.

"What! Bryce—"

"Of course not. The attack happened some time ago, I'm not sure exactly when. Bryce knows about it. I told him last night."

"Good gods, baby girl, I'm so sorry. What do you need me to do? Meet you there?"

Carrie allowed herself a tiny smile. Although he'd deny it when confronted, Nightshade had a protective streak a mile long. "No. I'm okay. But a detective told me there's been other attacks, all on dancers. We need to do something to protect ourselves. At all the clubs."

The rustle of bedding and a soft grunt indicated her manager was in motion. "Have no fear, Nightshade is on duty. I'll contact the club owners and have them make sure all the girls are escorted to their cars when they leave."

"That's a good start. I think we need to tell the dancers about these attacks, too, so they're aware of what's happening around them."

"Done as well, Carrie. You need to talk, you know where I am."

"I know, Nightshade. Thank you."

"Carrie?"

"Yes."

"Be careful, honey. Keep trusting Bryce."

Carrie glanced around the parking lot, trying to follow her own advice about being aware of her surroundings. "I do. Thanks for being here for me, Nightshade."

He gave a somber chuckle. "Seems like I should have done something more."

"I'm okay. Really. I'll be with Bryce for the rest of the day."

"Forget working tonight. I'll get a replacement."

"Oh, no. I couldn't let you do that."

"I can and I will. Honey, I don't want you in any danger. And, right now, I believe you are. Listen to me, Carrie. And do this for Nightshade."

Relief washed through her and weakened her knees. She hadn't realized how much she dreaded going to the club and dancing, not knowing if her attacker was there, watching. Planning to molest her again. She let her sigh travel through the phone. "You're right, of course. But, if you need me to—"

"I need you to recover. Even if the... it happened some time ago, if you just now remembered it, there's a great deal of internal work you'll need to be doing." He paused. "Bryce can help."

Carrie grinned. "Pushy, aren't we, Nightshade?"

"*Moi?*"

"Don't worry. He will. He has already."

"That's my girl. Now, go find that young man and I'll talk to you both later. I've got work to do. Kisses."

The phone went dead and Carrie peered at the tiny device before she shook her head and tucked it back in her purse. Nightshade was an enigma, and as long as she'd known him, she still couldn't gage his reactions or rapidly shifting emotions. Serious one moment and literally flittering about the next, he was an expert at keeping everyone off balance. Chameleon might be a better name for the man.

. . .

S itting at a picnic table left Carrie feeling too open and exposed, and when a sleek, dark blue sports car drove past for the third time, she hurried across the street to wait in the shadows of Bryce's wide front porch. Cocooned in the cool darkness cast by thick vines with clusters of fragrant flowers, she felt marginally safer.

The vehicle drove by a fourth time, and she peered through the vines, attempting to see the driver. The tinted windows hid any occupants; still she shivered knowing the driver could see her. The shape of the car was strange, foreign, and evil looking with a sharply pointed front end and finlike angles at the rear. The engine roared. The car squealed away leaving the faint odor of rubber on the air.

Belatedly she realized she should have looked at the license plate. Just in case. Or, was she now being suspicious of everything? Carrie hoped not. She didn't want to live that way—fearful and suspicious. It would make her adult life too much like her childhood.

Before she had a chance to sink into the unwelcome memories of her youth, Bryce's sedan pulled into the driveway and, looking around, he quickly exited the car. Carrie moved from the shadows and a wide smile brightened his face. He leapt over the small plants edging the driveway, crossed the immaculate lawn, and swept her into his arms.

Gentle and questioning, his gaze softened. Then his eyes filled with a blaze of desire and he lowered his mouth to cover hers. The intensity of the short kiss startled her and she clutched his arms to remain upright.

"Are you alright, sweetheart?"

"I—I. Oh, now I am."

"Good." Masculine satisfaction shown in his half-smile before his lips flattened to a thin line. "Things go okay at the police station?"

"They told me there've been other attacks and they think the assaults were done by the same man."

Bryce clasped her shoulders and leaned close to her face, holding her gaze with his. "I don't think you should go back to work until they catch him."

A faintly hysterical giggle surprised her and she covered her mouth with her fingers. Bryce canted his head to one side and waited. She found some self-control and said, "That's what Nightshade decided, too."

"Smart man. I'd hate to have to fight with him on this issue."

"Is it really such an issue, Bryce?" Even as she asked the question, she knew the answer. It was etched in the deep worry lines around Bryce's eyes and the tight set of his firm lips. She answered for herself. "It is. But, you shouldn't worry about me so much. I'll be fine." *I always am.*

A heavy breath filled Bryce's chest before he gave a sharp nod. "I called Pop earlier and invited us over for lunch. We've got a few minutes before we need to be there." His expression changed suddenly, reminding Carrie of Nightshade's chameleon-like moods. "I've got something great to tell you. Let's go inside."

She held back against the pressure of his hand guiding her toward the door. "Can't we talk out here? It's such a beautiful day."

It wasn't that she didn't want to be inside—alone—with Bryce. It was... oh, she didn't know. Her indecision and insecurity must have shown on her face, for questions filled Bryce's eyes before his expression cleared and he nodded. "Sure thing," he said and led her back to the glider.

"So, what are the cops doing about these attacks?"

"They didn't let me in on their procedures." Carrie chuckled. She didn't want to know what they did, or how they did it, she only wanted them to catch the man before he raped another woman. "I talked to a policewoman, then a counselor and a detective. He gave me his card in case I remember anything else." She dug the card from her purse and handed it to Bryce.

He scanned the small rectangle and frowned. "Corley? I met an attorney named Corley this morning." He shrugged and handed the card back to Carrie. "Wonder if they're related."

"An attorney? Is anything wrong?"

"Wrong? No, sweetheart. Suddenly, so much is right I can hardly believe it. You know I've been doing landscape design as an independent contractor." He waited for her nod then continued. "Granted, most of my work has been for one architectural firm, but the life of an independent isn't very secure. I never knew when the next contract would come my way. I've had some lean times between jobs and if it weren't for Pop's catering business..."

He took Carrie's hands and rubbed his thumbs over the backs of her knuckles. "But that's over with. Today I became *the* landscape designer for Logan and Associates. Complete with a corner office with windows."

"I've heard of them. Didn't they do the new entertainment complex?"

"Yep. And, get this, I'm not just on staff—I'm a partner in the firm."

"Partner?"

"I can't believe it. This is an amazing opportunity for me, Carrie. It means—well, we can talk about all that later." Bryce chewed on the inside of his cheek. He'd nearly said more than he intended.

Carrie leaned forward, curled her fingers under his chin, and kissed his cheek. "I'm so happy for you. Being a single parent, it had to have been especially hard not knowing if there was going to be a paycheck coming in."

Inches from his, her lips invited another kiss. He accepted the invitation, but denied his body's insistence he drag Carrie close and kiss her until she clung to him. He kept cool air between them, but teased her mouth with feathery touches of his lips. Sweet heavens, it was torture and ecstasy at once.

Carrie made a soft sound deep in her throat and he reacted without thought, inching her closer. One of his hands slipped into her hair to cup the back of her head. The seam of her lips parted at the barest touch of his tongue. To taste, to explore the depths of her mouth, demanded more time than he had to give, so he minutely increased the pressure against her lips, then reluctantly pulled away.

At the frown she gave him, he used his index finger to push up the corners of her lips. "Later, sweetheart." He glanced at his watch. "Time to go."

She touched her lips and her smile turned dreamy. A starburst of male satisfaction shot through him. He put that look on her face. And he'd do so again. And again. Forever, if she'd let him. He swallowed and forced out the words. "Time to visit my folks and find that daughter of mine."

Carrie's eyes lost their soft, dreamy expression. "Why are you nervous about me meeting your family?"

"My family is—unusual."

"Isn't everyone's, in one way or another? Does this have something to do with that last time you introduced a woman to them?"

"Partially. She turned around after meeting my folks, stormed from the house, and never looked back. Never spoke to me again either." He'd realized it hadn't been that much of a loss after all, but now, if Carrie reacted the same way, he wouldn't recover from the rejection. Sure, she was friends with Nightshade, but this was different.

"Come on, 'fraidy cat. I want to know the people who raised such a good man."

"So, now I'm a good man?"

"Uh huh." Faint pink blushed over her cheeks, and he couldn't resist a quick kiss after he pulled her to her feet.

"Off we go then." Keeping hold of her hand, Bryce led Carrie to the sidewalk, turned left, and walked with her two houses to the south. "Here we are."

"Must be difficult living so far away from your parents."

Bryce chuckled at the easy sarcasm in her voice. "Horrible. It's difficult to arrange family gatherings with the great distance." He pointed to the next house. "Especially when Jaye and Allyn live next door."

"Jaye and Allyn?"

"Pop's business partner, Jaye Zeroun, and his wife. Even though we're not blood relations, Jaye's an uncle to me, and their kids are like my brother and sister. It gets really confusing when you add in Bree and Lara's kids. To them all the adults are their aunts and uncles. Luckily, you won't have to meet the whole clan today."

Carrie agreed, although she thought she might enjoy the experience of a large clan. As an only child, with no extended family, there had been too many times when she was younger she had been so terribly lonely. If not for her imaginary friend, she had no idea how she would have survived.

"I'll look forward to meeting them later. Every single one of them."

"Just remember, I warned you. It's a family full of characters."

"Good. Now..." She dragged him up the sidewalk. "Let's start with your folks."

Bryce knocked on the door and waited a few moments before opening it and hollering into the dim entryway. "We're here."

"Hold on, just a minute. I'll be right there." The shouted words rumbled down a narrow stairway as they entered a spacious living room. Soon the owner of the voice followed, unsuccessfully trying to tuck in his shirt and smooth his ruffled hair at the same time.

"Sorry. You're a bit earlier than we expected."

"Traffic was light, Pop." Bryce chuckled and drew Carrie forward. "Pop, I'd like you to meet Carrie Newcomb. Carrie, this is my pop, Tom MacAlister."

Bryce's father took her hand and held it tightly. "So, you're the one he mooned over for so long. Glad to see you finally found each other. And, Carrie, no one calls me Tom." He gave his son a reproachful look. "I'm Tommy. Now, have a seat."

Bryce glanced around before he sat. "Where's Bree?"

"Lara has her kids next door to visit their grampa. So of course, when she heard the commotion, Bree had to visit, too. They'll bring her back in a bit. Now, Carrie, what do you think of my beautiful granddaughter?"

Carrie studied the man. He didn't look old enough to be Bryce's father. His face remained unlined but for a few smile crinkles at the corners of his eyes. His hair was light brown, cut short, yet stylishly wavy. Not at all what she expected—except for the love and pride emanating from the man when he looked at his son. Somehow, she'd known love would abound in this house.

And why shouldn't he appear young? Not everyone looked their age. Nightshade was ageless, and would never admit to anything that might enable another to guess at how old he was. And her parents—Carrie stifled an irreverent giggle. She'd always thought they must have looked old and tired when they were teenagers.

She was about to answer when Bryce tensed, his sudden stillness transferring to her through the couch where they sat. She followed his gaze to the stairway.

Impeccable in khaki slacks and a Polo shirt, a tall, blond man descended. Long hair pulled back with a strip of leather highlighted the sharp angles of his cheeks and jawline. He was a breathtaking, sensual man and when he flashed a bright, white smile, the sense she knew him flowed through Carrie. Strangely, she felt she'd known him a long time.

"Aye, an' I see our guest has arrived."

Bryce stared at her face. So, this was what he was concerned about—he had two fathers. She touched his hand and smiled in gentle reassurance. "I'm not leaving, Bryce. Introduce us."

Tommy shook his head and muttered, "How does he do that? I look like... and he..." At Carrie's words he turned an unbelieving expression to Bryce. "You didn't tell her?"

Bryce stood and tucked his hands behind his back. "Carrie, this is my Da, Derrik. Da, this is Carrie."

"'Tis a pleasure to meet ye at last."

"I'm glad to meet you as well." His accent, the sparkle in his blue eyes, and the shape of his lips were so familiar. She struggled to think when she may have met him.

Bryce touched her shoulder. "Carrie, sweetheart, I should have told you."

"Yes, you should have. How could you think it would make a difference to me? Isn't Nightshade my friend, my manager?"

"Friends can be different than parents."

"If these two men raised you to be the responsible, loving man that you are, then you're the lucky one. I'd trade my folks in a minute for even a small portion of the love I feel in this room." Oh, Lord. Had she really said that? She hung her head in shame.

A large hand appeared in her lowered vision and a soft touch to her cheek lifted her head. Derrik smiled. "Ye are welcome here, Carrie. Dinna be embarrassed at yer past, or yer feelin's. Come, I'm thinkin' it may be time fer lunch, is that nae so, my Tommy?"

"Just need to set the finishing touches on the table."

"Is there aught amiss, Carrie?" Derrik peered into her face. Confused by a sudden realization, she shook her head, then found her voice. "No, it's just that you look so much like... and sound like... oh, this is going to sound silly."

Giving her silent encouragement, Bryce took her hand.

"I had a friend when I was little, an imaginary friend." No need to admit Lottie was again an active part of her life. "You look, and sound, quite a bit like her."

"Oh, aye? I dinna ken quite how to take that. A compliment?" The bright smile flashed. Yes, it was nearly identical to Lottie's happy expression.

"Compliment—yes, of course. She was my friend when there was no one else. She helped me get through tough times."

"Aye, many children have need of a friend such as yers." With a look of devilment in his sparkling eyes, Derrik leaned toward Bryce. His stage whisper carried through the silence. "Ye were a bit early, ye ken?"

A bronze flush tinted Tommy's cheeks and he turned toward the back of the house. "I... I've got to check on lunch."

Carrie lowered her head and grinned to herself. She was right. Love abounded in this house. And, as Bryce held her hand, she accepted the loving gift being with this family gave her.

Tommy called from the dining room inviting them to come to

the table. Derrik held out his crooked arm to her. "An' did yer friend have a name?"

"When I was little I couldn't pronounce her name, and I'm afraid I've forgotten it. But, I call her Lottie."

The tall man at her side paused for a fraction of a moment. "Searlait," he muttered.

"Yes." Carrie drew out the word while she searched her memory. "That could be it. Searlait. How did you guess?"

He shrugged and although he smiled, sadness and pain swirled deep in his eyes. Unwilling to pursue the sadness, Carrie turned her attention to the table.

Bryce chuckled at her open-mouthed admiration. "I told you Pop is an event planner."

While she examined the tablescape and the artfully filled plates, she noticed how Tommy hurried to Derrik's side. The two men stood intimately close as they spoke together, Tommy's hand resting on Derrik's shoulder. The love and affection of the simple act made a lump rise to her throat. Her parents had never shown affection to each other, and certainly not to her. She let a sigh pass her lips as Bryce seated her.

He leaned over her shoulder and tucked a strand of hair behind her ear. "They've never hidden how they feel about each other. I was—I am lucky they chose to adopt me."

Yes, he was lucky. Perhaps that luck was rubbing of on her.

CHAPTER
SIXTEEN

After a meal filled with light conversation that told her much about Bryce's family, they took tall glasses of lemonade out to the deck and relaxed under the shade of the vine-covered pergola. "I see Bryce's handiwork here," she said, eyeing the thick mass of green.

Derrik leaned back and wrapped an arm around Tommy's shoulders. "Aye, our boy has a great many talents. 'Twas a blessin' when he came into our lives."

"I can certainly understand that." She did. Having the amazing man come into her life, only days ago, had drastically changed her outlook. Even if the memories had never happened, she was blessed by the man sitting next to her. And blessed by getting to know his family. She'd never really thought much about blessings, relegating that word to part of her parents unwanted vocabulary.

Pleasant silence fell over the group.

Until a blur of denim and pink tee shirt swirled across the yard and landed in her lap.

"Mommy!"

Trying to catch her breath, Carrie held the squirming child

reaped the reward of wet kisses on her cheeks and mouth. "I glad you're here. I miss-did you."

"Missed you," came Bryce's automatic correction.

Carrie smiled and stroked the white-blonde bangs back from Breanna's damp forehead. "I missed you, too. Where'd you come from?'

"Unka Jaye's house. Castin an' Belle was there. We played. Auntie Lara letted me—"

"Let me."

Breanna slid from Carrie's lap and stood before her father with her small hands pressed to her hips. "I know how to talk right, Daddy. Sometimes I like to talk like a baby. Sometimes I don't."

Bryce laughed and held his arms open. "Forgive me, darlin'? I'll let you talk however you want."

She crawled into his embrace and patted his cheek. "It's okay, Daddy. I know you want me to be the best."

"And you are. You're my bestest girl."

"Bestest isn't a word, Daddy, but that's okay. I'm gonna go sit with Mommy now."

"What? No loves for Granda and Pop Pop?" Tommy pouted his lower lip at his granddaughter.

"Oh, Pop Pop." Bree shook her finger at him. "I see you all the time. Not Mommy, I don't see her enough."

Bryce needed to nip his daughter's enthusiasm in the bud. As much as he wanted Carrie to be a part of their lives, to become Bree's mommy, he knew better than to push the situation. Especially after her revelations of the past night.

A heavy twitch of memory moved through his groin. Still amazed at her response to his lovemaking early that morning, he pushed at the remnants of guilt that had tainted his day. Had he taken advantage of her and her need for closeness and understanding?

He watched as Carrie and Bree shared whispers and giggles. They were beautiful together. His two beautiful girls. When Carrie glanced up and flashed him a grin, he had to shift position in his chair. Not that it helped, the movement only served to increase the awareness of his body's physical responses.

Damn. Not the time for this. Control. In his mind he whispered a few choice Faerie curses but the flowing syllables only reminded him of the words of seduction he'd used that morning. Double damn.

Tommy cleared his throat. Bryce looked up just as Tommy nudged Derrik's arm and indicated their son with a jerk of his head. Both smiled wickedly at him, eyebrows raised. Derrik gave a slow, exaggerated wink. Then both turned their attention from him and stared meaningfully toward Carrie.

Bryce took a deep breath. Da loved to tease, a fey trait long ago mastered. Knowing he was in for an intense round of teasing should his folks corner him alone, Bryce shifted again and rose to his feet. Better to diffuse the situation before he became any more of a target.

Breanna curled on Carrie's lap, her small thumb sneaking toward her slightly puckered lips. She'd be asleep in moments. "I think it's time to get Bree home for a nap. Looks like today's been busy for our little girl."

He reached for Bree but she shook her head fiercely. "Mommy take me, please?"

At Bryce's raised eyebrows, Carrie nodded. "I'll carry her."

"She gets heavy pretty fast," Tommy chuckled. "Here, let me help you up."

With his fathers pushing him out of the way and assisting Carrie to her feet, Bryce stood back and shook his head. He needn't have worried about his folks and Carrie. He should have trusted what he knew about her—and his folks. They were bound to love each other.

Tommy pressed a quick kiss to Carrie's cheek. "You come back anytime. Even without Bryce, you're always welcome."

"Aye. Dinna stay away. Yer presence brightens this house."

"Thank you. Don't worry, I love it here. You may regret giving me such an open invitation."

"Never." Derrik led the way around the side of the house to a tall, metal and wood gate. He bowed slightly to usher Carrie through the opening.

Bryce caught her arm and turned them to face his folks. "Hang on a minute. I have something to ask all of you."

He'd forgotten about his new job, and although Carrie knew, he thought keeping it a secret from his folks for a short time would give him some time to fully settle into the concept of permanent employment. Besides, it was fun trying to keep a secret from Pop's high curiosity levels. He grinned in anticipation.

"All that work I've done for Logan and Associates is paying off. The company is having a big dinner in a few weeks."

Tommy nodded. "I know. It's one of mine."

"Oh." A surge of disappointment centered in Bryce's chest. If Pop was in charge he wouldn't be able to join them at the table. "Is there any way you can get someone else to cover this one, Pop?"

"Why would I want to do that? This is one of the biggest events this quarter. Unfortunately, it's on the same night as a wedding reception, and a huge retirement party. All Zeroun's."

"So, that upstart caterer isn't stealing much of your business? What was his name?"

"Titus something—something Titus. Never heard anything but Titus. Nanceen was the only one of the family to actually see him. Nope, he's faded into the woodwork. Jaye and I talked about it—seemed like he just started up to cause trouble for Zeroun's then, when it didn't pan out for him, he was gone." Tommy grinned and shrugged. "No great loss."

"I've been invited to this dinner, Pop, and I really wanted you, Da, and Carrie to be my guests."

Derrik gave him a look so full of speculation, Bryce was afraid his Da already knew about the job offer. "An' why is this important to ye, me boyo?"

Carrie giggled at Derrik's choice of words. *Please don't say anything*, he sent silently to her. *I want this to be a surprise for them.*

She adjusted the child in her arms and shrugged. "She is getting heavy."

Bryce let relief color the smile he flashed at Carrie. "I'll make this quick then, unless you want me to take her?"

"Not just yet." She turned her attention to Tommy. "Please try and be there as a guest. I'd love the chance to get to know you better. Both of you."

Tommy pressed his hand against his heart. "How could I refuse such an eloquent plea? I'll impose on Jaysson. Have him take over the crew." Then he moved his hand to his forehead. "My gawd, to actually be served instead of being the server? I don't know how my old heart will take it."

O nce again, curled in the corner of Bryce's couch, Carrie sighed with full contentment. She was getting used to this room and the comfort of this piece of furniture. If she never had to leave this world, the world he created and surrounded her with, she thought she could be forever happy. Realistically, she knew what a pipe dream forever was, but still. She let those few romantic thoughts fill her as Bryce tucked his daughter in for a nap.

A warm presence at her side signaled Bryce's return to the cozy living room. He sat close, his leg brushing hers. "How long until you have to go... to work?" He tried hard to hide his discomfort with her job, and Carrie smiled her understanding. Now that she knew him, she didn't want to continue dancing either. Except, maybe for him. But that was a pipe dream as well and wouldn't last. However, she would be able to make him happy, at least for this one day.

"When I called Nightshade after going to the police station, he told me I didn't need to come to work tonight. Guess he thought the trauma of my remembering and having to report the attack would be too much. He's probably right. Besides, he wants me to be safe."

"Good. I want you safe as well. And here is the place to be safe."

"Bryce, I—"

"Please, no arguments. Won't you consider staying here? I've got that perfectly good guest room."

Heat filled Carrie's chest and crawled ever so slowly up to her face. The room was perfect. And good? Oh, yes. The heat intensified and she ducked her head to hide the red she knew had to be infusing her skin.

The touch of Bryce's hand as he lifted her face brought shivers of longing to chase the heat. She loved him, she knew she did. But, she didn't know how he really felt about her. The prohibitions and taunts, the degradation she had lived through as a child and young woman came to life in full, painful force. How could he like her—let alone maybe even love her—when she was nothing more than a product of her father's tirades?

"Carrie, my sweet one, what's the matter?"

She wasn't ready. "I don't think I can stay here. At least not tonight," she amended at Bryce's crestfallen expression. She touched his hand and waited as he twined his fingers through hers and tugged slightly to lay their joined hands against his thigh. Warm and comforting, the touch invited her to experience many things.

"If nothing else, I need to change clothes."

"After Bree wakes up, we could go pick up whatever you need from your place. I don't want you to be alone."

"I don't really want to be alone either, but I think, for tonight at least, I need to be. I don't know why, I have no explanation. I have to go with my feelings with this one."

"Your feelings? Where do I fit in your feelings?" His eyes widened briefly at his whispered plea, then narrowed. He turned his face from her and shook his head. "No, forget that."

"I can't, no, and I don't want to. Where you fit into my feelings is one of the things I need to think about tonight. When I'm with you, I can't think straight. My thoughts are all convoluted, like I don't know which way is up. Or down."

"But, Carrie—"

"I don't have to leave right now." She smiled gently at him and let the leaping of her heart at the sparkles in his eyes fill her.

She hated the thought of leaving. Hated the thought of being alone, even for one night.

"I'll stick around until this evening. I want to leave before it starts getting dark." She shivered against the thought of being out in the dark—alone. Even the heavy-duty locks on her door suddenly seemed flimsy and insubstantial. Maybe she should change her mind.

"I think I understand, sweetheart. And, against common sense, I'll go along with your wishes. This time. Just keep your phone close at all times, and call me if anything—do you understand—anything seems out of the ordinary."

"I understand. Thank you." Carrie leaned forward and kissed him. Bryce held himself still although his lips softened and moved sensuously under hers. She held the kiss a few moments before returning to her place.

"Tell me about Bree's mother."

Surprise widened his eyes. A strange swirl of something she couldn't decipher filled the pale green orbs before he turned his face away. What kind of nerve had she struck? She opened her mouth to take back the question but he squeezed her hand.

"I'm not proud of what I did. Although, probably not for the reasons you might think." Keeping a tight hold on her hand, Bryce angled to face her. He stared at their fingers. "You see, darlin', even though I always had a girlfriend, and never lacked a date for any event, none of the women sparked that special something within me. I wanted to experience the feelings, understand the strength of emotions that my folks have. All through my extended family, love ties are so strong they're almost physically visible." Bryce paused. Once he had seen the fiery blue sparks surrounding Jaye and Allyn and knew, that even without Faerie blood, there was a woman who would fulfill him the same way. He didn't need to see sparks; he would feel them in the depths of his soul. Carrie was that woman.

He sighed. "I knew it was stupid and that the sexual preferences of my folks had nothing to do with my own, but, I guess—no, I know—I had to prove it to myself. Bree's mother was a friend, one who willingly took me to her bed." He ducked his head and grinned. "She taught me a great deal."

A pink blush covered Carrie's cheeks before she waggled her eyebrows and winked at him. "If this morning was any indication —you must have been an A student."

Chuckling, Bryce lifted Carrie's hand, turned it over and kissed the palm. He trailed soft, open mouthed kisses to her wrist, up the smooth, soft skin of her inner arm, then touched his tongue to the inside of her elbow. When she shivered, he whispered a soft syllable against the dampness of her skin and looked up at her.

"Do you think so?"

"Oh, yeah. But... but what about her, what happened?"

"We were surprised when she became pregnant." This was the difficult part. He needed to tell Carrie what she wanted to know, but had to keep secret the Faerie heritage of his family. How quickly might Carrie run from him if she thought he was nuts and believed in an Otherworld? No matter that his Da was full Faerie, and others of his family carried differing measures of Fey blood. This was not a chance he was willing to take. Not just yet.

"Surprised? We're you using protection?"

"Not believing she could become pregnant, we didn't think it was necessary. Obviously, we were wrong."

"Where... oh, I remember. You said she died. I'm sorry."

"Shortly after Bree was born. She held our daughter a few moments, then handed Bree to me. She didn't say anything, but I could see in her eyes she knew she would die. She simply closed her eyes and the breath left her body."

"How sad for you. Would you have married her?"

"We didn't love each other, Carrie. I used her to prove myself a heterosexual man. She used me for pleasure. I'm not proud of what I did, what we did. But, I did get my darlin' daughter. I wouldn't change that for anything in this world—or any other."

A sad smile graced Carrie's face. "I understand. I can't tell you how often I've done, or thought of doing things to make some point. In fact, my dancing started out kind of like that. Maybe it wasn't trying to prove something, maybe it was more of a rebellion. In many cases, it's the same thing."

"Sure. I was rebelling against possibilities of what other people expected because I have gay parents. What were you rebelling against?"

"The expectations of my parents. Or rather, I think I was fulfilling those expectations, becoming what they'd always told me I was. Except, I'm a dancer only. I'm not a harlot."

"Harlot?" Startled by the word, he had to bite back a chuckle that would hurt Carrie.

"Their word. Straight from the lips of their religious leader."

"You're nothing like that."

"I know." She hung her head. "But there are times it's very hard to believe that I'm not. Consequently, I haven't seen my parents for a long time."

"That must be difficult for you." Devastated. That's how he'd feel if something happened and he couldn't see his folks. Despite his occasional rebellions, he loved Pop and Da with a fierceness rivaled only by his love for Breanna. And now, his love for Carrie.

Lost in his thoughts, he was startled when Carrie answered the question he'd forgotten he'd asked. "Nope, not really. I've grown accustomed to being without a loving family. I guess that now Nightshade is the closest thing I have to a family."

Swallowing heavily, Bryce took a chance. "What about me? And Breanna?"

"You'd want to be my family?"

More than anything in the combined worlds. Why did she have such a hard time believing it? "If you want us."

The golden brown of her eyes deepened to nearly black, drawing him closer. It was time he kissed her again. Past time. Too many moments had passed. Her lips parted, her expression softened. Their lips touched.

If Faerie blood ran through his veins, he would be covered by the luminescent sparks of a soulfire. Not even a molecule of doubt hovered near him as waves of pure pleasure rolled through him at just the simple press of her lips against his. That's all it took.

Bryce backed from the kiss and lifted one hand to caress Carrie's cheek. She leaned into the touch, then eased away. With gentle pressure he curved one finger under her chin and tilted her face for another kiss.

"Ooh, Daddy's kissin' Mommy."

Jerked apart by Breanna's happy chortle, Bryce reluctantly tore his gaze from the startled panic in Carrie's eyes but kept his palm against her cheek. He turned his face to his daughter.

Her bright blue-green eyes sparkled, and a smile blossomed around the finger stuffed into her mouth. He waggled a finger of his free hand, calling her to him. Bree skipped across the room and stood before him expectantly. Shaking his head, he pulled the finger from her mouth with a small suction that made a soft pop and Bree giggled. "Sorry, Daddy. I know I'm not supposed to." At his silent invitation, she crawled onto his lap.

Hoping that having the warm body of his daughter snuggled against him would diffuse his raging emotions, Bryce let his hand fall from Carrie's face. He ruffled Bree's hair, then kissed the top of her head. She turned her face to look up at him. "How much do you love this Mommy?"

Caught unaware by the question, Bryce fought the knot in his throat, making a choked, gagging sound.

"That's okay, Bryce. I don't think Bree really wants an answer to that." Although her heart had soared with the question, following her raging hormones, Carrie feared the answer. He couldn't possibly feel love for her. It was impossible.

"Yes I do, Mommy." Bree took Bryce's hand, played with one of his fingers, then pressed the hand over Carrie's. Breanna giggled. "That's better. I do want to know, Daddy. I wanna know if you love her as much as I do."

"Do you really love me, Breanna?" The question slipped unbidden from Carrie's lips. She bit her bottom lip and ducked her head. Why did she keep digging this deep, horrendous hole for herself? She'd never be able to deny her love for the darling girl—or her father. But, it was too soon. There was no way...

"I do, Breanna. I love her very much."

Bryce's words were so soft Carrie wasn't sure she'd heard them—and if she had heard them, she must not have heard correctly. She stared at Bryce.

He nodded solemnly. "Leave it to a child. Aren't they supposed to lead the way? I do love you, Carrie. No, don't say anything," he added quickly when she drew a shaky breath to speak." Let me get this out."

Breanna slipped to the couch between them and covered their joined hands with hers. She turned her smile from one to the other, then sighed the deep sigh of a child who has received her greatest wish.

"Carrie, I never thought popular songs could have it right. I remember a song, one that said something about loving you before meeting you. That's how I feel. It's more than feeling I know you, have known you forever. And maybe longer. When I saw you dance that night at the N B Tween—even though I couldn't see your face because of the mask—I knew it then."

"That was just a reaction to the dance." Glancing at Bree, she lowered her voice. "To my stripping." Time to diffuse the intensity, make him see his feelings for what they must really be. He couldn't really, truly love her. Not that way. It must be lust.

"Carrie. This has nothing to do with—physical attraction." He grinned and his gaze slid to Bree, who continued to smile up at them. "What I feel goes deeper. Far deeper than any feelings I've had before."

"I'm attracted to you as well, but..."

Bryce slipped his hand from under Bree's and used one palm to cup Carrie's cheek, the other to mimic the caress with his daughter. "But, now is not the time to discuss this adult talk."

"Oh, Daddy. You're silly."

"Maybe so, darlin', maybe so. Carrie, do you think I'm silly, too?"

She shook her head. Unable to form words, she just looked at Bryce.

Until Bree squirmed and climbed down to the floor. "I'm hungry."

After tugging his watch from his pocket Bryce popped open the lid and glanced at the face. "Oh, it's later than I thought. Where did this day go?"

"Same place it always goes, silly Daddy."

"You're right of course, darlin' And, you're hungry. How about you, Carrie?"

She didn't think she could eat anything, but nodded, and the hopeful expression on the little girl's face sparkled. Sparkles, that's how she felt when Bryce kissed her—all sparkly. The thought stretched her lips to a smile.

"That's what we like to see, isn't it Bree? So, how about going out for pizza? Your daddy got a new job today, I think pizza's gonna be a great way to celebrate."

Curious, Bryce leaned close to his daughter's ear. "Why did you ask me if I love this mommy? You shouldn't ask questions like that, darlin'. Sometimes adults have a hard time answering things like that."

Shuffling one foot over the thick carpet, Breanna dipped her head. "I sorry. Dinna mean to upset ye."

Bryce shook his head as he canted his gaze toward Carrie. "She's a little mimic," he explained. "One who tries to play on my sympathies by sounding like Da. It doesn't work."

By his grin Carrie understood that his daughter's ploys did work; he just didn't want the child to know. Then Breanna grinned up at her as well. The set of her small lips, nearly identical to her father's, told Carrie the child knew her mimicry worked. Very well. No surprise, the girl was an adorable bundle of energy and contradictions.

She stroked Bree's soft, blonde hair. "You should give your father an honest answer."

"I know, Mommy."

"And, you really shouldn't call me Mommy." Carrie hated saying the words. She loved being called Mommy.

'Why not? You will be. I think so." Bree nodded sagely and sucked her finger into her mouth.

Bryce hooked his index finger around Bree's fist and tugged the finger from her mouth. "Stop that. Now answer me, why did you ask that?"

"I have a new friend."

"What does your friend have to do with answering me, Breanna?" A hard edge tinged Bryce's question, one that demanded an answer. Yet, it was a tone so filled with love and respect. A wave of longing for what might have been crashed over Carrie. How different would her life be if just a little of this kind of love had been shown to her by her parents?

"Well," Breanna drew the word out then rushed on at Bryce's frown. "She talks to me. She said to ask."

"Does your friend play in the park? Does she go to daycare with you?"

"No, Daddy." Bree giggled. "She's like you, she's growed up."

Worry infused Bryce's face and Carrie experienced a corresponding sense of helpless dismay. Was someone stalking the beautiful girl—or was she just seeing specters since her own attack?

"Bree, look at me." Bryce held the child's attention for a few moments before he asked, "What does your new friend look like?"

A huge shrug lifted Breanna's small shoulders. "Don't know. I never see her. I only hear her."

Bryce's eyebrows lifted and he glanced at Carrie in confusion. This might be something she understood, a situation where she actually had some experience. She leaned closer to the small girl. "Have you had this friend very long?"

"Nope. Just before I finded you at the bookstore."

"Found, darlin', not finded."

Bree rolled her eyes in an expression worthy of a disgruntled teenager. "Daddy."

"Breanna." Bryce matched her tone and inflections. Then father and daughter laughed together.

Carrie leaned back and sighed. This was family, a marvelous time of sharing, with love and learning of each other. But, there was one other thing she needed to learn. If Bree's friend were a creation of her imagination, what reason could the small girl have for such a friend? Lottie was her protector, but with such a loving family, why would Bree need protection? Maybe it was just a type of wish fulfillment. Bree obviously wanted a mother.

"Hey, sweetie..."

Both Bree and Bryce turned to face her. "Yes, Mommy."

"Does your new friend have a name?"

"Course. Everybody does."

"Well?"

"My friend's name is Lottie. Can we get pizza now?"

CHAPTER

SEVENTEEN

Bryce followed Carrie to her apartment building and parked his sedan next to her vehicle in the narrow parking lot. Carrie rushed to his car door and leaned in the open window. "This is fine. I'll be okay now. You don't need to get out."

Fighting the shoulder restraint, Bryce angled to face her. "Are you sure?"

The soft stubble of a day's beard growth tickled her skin when she rested her palm against his cheek. Carrie nodded. "It's still light, and you can watch until I get inside the building. See the third window from the left on the third floor? When I get in my apartment, I'll wave from there." She glanced into the back seat where Breanna, ensconced in her car seat, played with the toy from her kid's meal. "Besides, you don't need to go through the hassle of getting her in and out of the car seat."

"It's no hassle."

"Yes, it is." She leaned further into the car and kissed him. Bryce's low groan vibrated through their kiss and Carrie understood how he felt. She wanted to be with him, tonight and forever. But, there were personal demons she had to fight, fears she needed to deal with. And to do that, she needed some time alone.

Reluctant to end the contact, she eased away from the heat of his lips. "It won't be long. I'll see you tomorrow."

"I'll be at my magic gig at five." Bryce smoothed one hand behind her ear, then held up a small coin sparkling in the early evening sun.

Laughing, Carrie curled his fingers around the coin and held his hand. Their gazes locked over their hands.

"Daddy?"

Bryce shook his head slowly as if clearing cobwebs from his brain and turned in his seat to face to his daughter. "Yes, darlin'?"

"Your new job means more money?"

"Quick grasp of the situation," Carrie whispered.

"I suppose so."

"We can buy more things."

"Within reason. Why?'

Breanna's eyes were bright, happy and sparkling and she clasped her hands tightly around her toy. "Daddy, can I have a pony?"

"A pony?"

Carrie choked back a chuckle at the surprise lighting Bryce's face. Bree must never have shown any previous interest in a pony. When Bryce glanced at back her, helplessness tinged his expression. She let the chuckle loose.

"So, Bree," Carrie said. "You want a pony?"

Bree nodded vigorously.

"Why do you want a pony?"

"Unka Iain's getting ponies for Belle and Castin. I want one, too." She paused in thought. "Please?"

A pony? Bryce looked like he was ready to strangle this Unka Iain.

"An' we could keep my pony at Unka Iain's house. Auntie Lara said so."

Bryce faced forward and rested his forehead against the steering wheel. His shoulders shook silently. When he lifted his head, he was chewing on his lower lip as if to keep a smile under wraps. He spoke without turning back to his daughter. "I don't know, darlin'. A pony is a big responsibility, even if Iain and Lara are willing to keep it."

"Unka Iain says everyone should know how to ride. So I can go to the Faerie hunt when I'm bigger."

Bryce's eyes widened and he glanced sideways at Carrie. She couldn't read his expression, but that touch of fear returned to swirl a dark green through his eyes. What did he fear? That Breanna's imagination would chase her away? He must have forgotten that she had an imaginary friend just like his daughter did now. One that shared the same name.

Carrie moved to the rear door, reached in through the window and ran her fingers over Bree's head. "I think your daddy needs some time to think about a pony. And maybe, he'll need to talk to your uncle to find out more about keeping such a big animal. Shall we let him do that? Give him that time he needs?"

Bree grinned at her and winked. "Okay, Mommy. We can do that." She lifted the toy and bounced it before Carrie's face, then lowered the molded plastic and frowned. "I wish you were coming home."

"I am home, honey."

"No, not here. Our house. You, me, an' Daddy."

Carrie touched her index finger to the tip of Bree's nose making her giggle. "Maybe another day. I have things to do here at my house."

"Okay." Bree's lower lip pouted making her small mouth even more like a perfect rosebud. "Kiss?"

Leaning as far as she could through the window, Carrie kissed Bree's cheek and received a loud, smacking kiss in return. "See you soon, Mommy."

After stroking Bree's soft cheek, Carrie returned to Bryce's window. His eyebrows curved high above his eyes and he blinked innocently. "Kiss?"

When she leaned closer, he captured her face between his palms, held her gently, and just as gently treated her lips to a sweetly sensual kiss that left her supporting herself against the warm metal of the car.

Breathless, she backed away, knowing that if she didn't beat a hasty retreat, there would be no retreat. "Give me a couple of minutes and watch the window."

"Sweetheart?"

"Y—yes?"

"Be careful."

His tender smile melted what was left of her muscles, and she struggled not to stagger drunkenly up the walk to the building. He did make her drunk, his kisses potent weapons on her senses. Pausing with the door open, she turned back and waved. Two arms, one long and masculine, the other pudgy and sweet gestured broadly from the car windows.

Carrie dug her key from a pocket in her purse and took the steps two at a time. She had the key ready by the time she reached the third floor and stood before her door.

A folded sheet of stark white paper was taped to the doorknob. She rolled her eyes as she fit the key into the deadbolt lock. The property managers were always leaving notes on everyone's door about some infraction. Idly wondering what it was this time, Carrie grabbed the note just before the door closed behind her.

She dashed to the window, took a deep breath, drew back the curtain, and stood before the clear glass. She waved and received the double wave in return. She remained in the window until Bryce drove away with one hand continuing to wave over the top of the car.

The curtains dropped back into place and she backed from the window. The early evening light barely found a way into her apartment, so she wandered through the rooms and turned on lights. If she was to chase the shadows from her soul, there could be no shadows or darkness in her environment.

The crisp crackle of the paper crushed in her hand caught her attention as she returned to the small living room. Might as well see what the managers wanted this time.

She plopped into a wide, overstuffed chair and curled her legs to one side. The page was folded twice, unusual for the managers who were usually in such a hurry to get through the building, it was amazing they took time to fold their messages at all.

Carrie frowned and opened the paper. Not the usual computer-generated missive, handwriting covered the page. A ball of unease settled low in her chest, then rose to wrap around her heart. The tiny, cramped, and shaking script could only belong to her mother. She dropped her gaze to the bottom of the page and the signature confirmed her fear.

Not only did her parents know where she lived; now they had left a note. Guessing what the note contained, Carrie crumpled it into a tight ball and threw it across the room. There was no place in her life now for tirades about her misconduct. No time for threats couched in supposed words of love. No desire in her to discover why now, after all this time, her parents tried to contact her.

Carrie bit back a sigh and stared unseeing at the furniture crammed into the tiny apartment. Now she'd have to move again. The sigh escaped. She knew where she would love to move, the loving home she would find. How long could she wait before she had to leave what used to be a safe haven?

Long enough to discover if Bryce truly loved her as he said he did. Now, along with putting memories into proper perspective, she had to deal with new, unwelcome interferences. Time to start a pot of coffee.

It would be a long night.

His bed was cold, empty—lonely. Bryce stroked the smooth cotton sheet next to him. Carrie should be there. Now and every night. He closed his eyes and imagined the feel of her skin.

Warm, smooth, and inviting. So responsive to his touch. He gathered the sheet in his fist, tugging against the tight fit over the thick mattress. Unable to raise his fist very high without releasing the crumpled material, Bryce pounded the bed repeatedly.

Damn and double damn. There had to be a way to ease his aloneness.

There was, but she was safe in her apartment halfway across town. Opening his eyes and knowing sleep would be impossible, Bryce stared at the ceiling. Patterns of light, barely indistinguishable from the darkness, danced across the smooth plaster. There, he could see his daughter's laughing eyes. And there, a favorite flower that grew only in the Faerie Otherworld. And there— Carrie looked down upon him.

Groaning his frustration, Bryce turned over and pressed his face into his pillow. Finally needing to breathe, he rolled to his side and stared at how the dim light from his alarm clock highlighted the outline of the phone.

Before he thought of the consequences, he lifted the receiver and dialed Carrie's number.

What was he doing? It was well past the middle of the night and she would be asleep. His brain told him to hang up before the second ring sounded, but he couldn't make his hand obey the command. It would hardly be a point in his favor if he woke—

"Hello?"

She didn't sound like she had been sleeping. Bryce scooted up in the bed and propped a pillow so he could lean against the headboard. "Did I wake you?"

"Who? Oh, Bryce. No, no you didn't. I haven't been to sleep yet."

"I miss you."

The sigh whispering through the phone line settled low in his body. "And I miss you. I've been lying here—awake— wondering what you were doing."

"Ah, Carrie, not that different than what you're doing. I couldn't sleep because I want you beside me."

"Even though this morning—oh, yesterday morning—was wonderful, I don't think I'm ready for sex again. Not yet, anyway."

"Um, sex is good, but that's not the only reason I want you. I need to feel your presence, to know that all I have to do is reach out my hand, and you'd be there."

Carrie released a choked bark of laughter. "You sound like a romance novel."

"If speaking the truth of how I feel means I'm a part of that particular genre, then so be it."

He heard rustling over the phone and imagined Carrie shifting position. He tugged another pillow to his side. But then, instead of imagining Carrie pressed against him, a scene from an old movie flashed across his inner vision. "So, do you like old romantic comedy movies?

"What? Bryce, what are you talking about?"

Laughter rumbled in his chest. "Don't you remember those old movies where the couple would be in their separate beds talking on the phone? They always did it with a split screen."

"Oh." Carrie giggled. "I know what you mean. But, wasn't there often a third party on the line, too?"

"We don't have to worry about that, Bree's sound asleep. Probably dreaming about ponies."

"I wouldn't be surprised. Did you call for any particular reason?"

"To hear your voice." Bryce paused. "So I could imagine you here with me. Why aren't you asleep?"

"Too many things on my mind. One thought merged into another until I couldn't shut my mind off."

"Was everything really okay when you got home?"

"Yes—no. There was a note on the door from my parents."

"I thought you hadn't heard from them in a long time."

"I haven't. This is really strange."

"What did the note say?" There was a long pause while he waited for Carrie to answer. "

I don't know. I threw it away."

"Don't you think—"

"No. I don't. Don't push me in this, Bryce."

He'd stepped over a boundary and immediately withdrew, but

couldn't keep the bite from his voice. "Sorry. I won't ask anything about them again."

"No," Carrie said on the exhale of a sigh. "It's my fault. I shouldn't be so sensitive, not when I don't care anyway. Bryce, I've got to go. I'll see you tomorrow. No, I mean later today."

There was another pause and Bryce sensed she wanted to say more. When the silence had dragged on to his breaking point, he whispered, "I love you."

"I know," came Carrie's whispered reply. "I think... I think I love you, too."

Before he could say good night, the irritating sound of a disconnected call assaulted his ear.

Carrie kept her hand on the phone receiver trying to gather her thoughts and calm her fiercely beating heart. She'd told Bryce she loved him. Something must have possessed her, otherwise she'd never have said those words out loud. But now, now she felt so good to have said it.

She huffed out a breath. As much as she dreaded admitting it, he was right, of course. She should read the note from her parents. Their treatment of her when she was a child had more to do with the woman she had become than she wanted to admit. Although, and she felt a smile draw her lips from their frown, quite probably not for the reasons they would suspect. Proud of the way she had made a life on her own after leaving home right after her high school graduation, Carrie had little to regret about her choices.

So, she rose and left the semidarkness of her bedroom and moved into the brightly lit living room. Leaving the lights on did nothing but increase her power bill, and she shook her head at her folly. If there were forces out to harm her, leaving lights on wouldn't stop them.

It took her a few moments to find the crumpled note. After digging the wadded paper from under a side chair, she sat on the floor and leaned her back against the chair. Flattening the page and smoothing the wrinkles captured all of her concentration for long moments. She could delay the inevitable no longer.

She rose to her knees to hold the note close to the table lamp. Not only did her mother write with a tiny, cramped script, but she had written in pencil. Lightly. With a frustrated groan, Carrie gave up and sat in the chair.

Daughter,

Daughter? They couldn't even use the name they'd given her. Although she hated Caroline, that salutation would have been better than daughter. Maybe she should just be glad they recognized a familial connection at all.

The amount of willpower Carrie needed to turn her attention back to her mother's note made her hands shake. She read silently for a few lines, then snorted and slapped the page onto her lap. What in the world was her mother talking about?

Shaking her head, Carrie reread the first paragraph. Okay, she understood how her parents thought, she'd been hearing their moral tirades her entire life. But then, her mother started going on about inappropriate relationships. Inappropriate? Her parents had no clue about relationships, any relationships—including one with a child. They had no right to make any comment on how any relationship she might have would be inappropriate.

Quickly scanning the rest of the short note, Carrie struggled to find some meaning in the odd assortment of disconnected thoughts. It was as if her mother were falling into some form of dementia. There was no cohesiveness to the note, except for the not so subtle criticism.

Only the simple signature *your parents* scrawled across one corner of the page ended the strange missive. No love or even an affectionately. Carrie folded the sheet and set it on the side table. What did she expect? There was nothing there. Not in a family relationship or in the note. She'd show the note to Bryce and ask his opinion. He would have no background on her parents, so he could give her an unbiased opinion.

Another cup of coffee would do her a world of good, the jolt of caffeine would help keep her awake. Another night of disturbed sleep might make her so exhausted she'd finally be able to sleep without dreams or fears.

With a mug of coffee warming her hands, she opened the curtains and sat so she could wait and watch the lightening of the sky signify the rising sun.

"You left the note as I instructed?"

The drab woman nodded slowly. "Yes, Mr. Avery. And I wrote the words the best I could remember."

Foolish woman, she should have transcribed his words while he spoke. No matter. It really didn't even matter if the note had been written or not, he'd only told the couple to write the communication to keep them occupied while he finalized his plans.

Titus nodded to himself and mentally ran through the list of preparations. When his choices were either to rely on fools such as these or do everything himself, he needed to keep his thoughts on track. This would be a minutely timed operation. One slip, and his plan would come to ruination. That could never happen. For this was only the first step in his revenge. He would receive satisfaction for the pain Zeroun caused him.

Muscles along his jaw tensed. He would break Jaye Zeroun, and destroy his family. Mentally, emotionally, physically—any way he could. The tempting thoughts of a physical retribution brought the heaviness of desire to his body.

Titus closed his eyes to block the sight of the couple hovering across the room from him.

"Mr. Avery, is anything wrong? Are you alright?"

The woman's whiny voice brought Titus back to the moment at hand. "Of course, Mrs. Newcomb. Just going over our next step. I have a short list of things that must be done at the compound before the acquisition is made. Would you and your fine husband be able to take care of them?"

The woman nodded. "Anything we can do to assist in your blessed work, Mr. Avery. I don't presume to understand your plans, but if you say they will save our daughter from an eternity of damnation, then we will do all we can." She glanced at her husband as if for confirmation. The man frowned and gave one sharp nod.

"Good." Titus glanced at a small sheet of notepaper he pulled from his pocket, then held it out to the woman. "Take care of these before noon tomorrow, then meet me as we discussed."

The woman glanced at the paper then back at her husband. Titus could read her thoughts by the expressions flitting across her plain, lined face. It was late and she wanted to be home, wrapped in the haven and forgetfulness of her bed. He wondered absently if she and her husband slept in the same bed, or even in the same room. They obviously didn't share much other than a blind obedience to their religious leader. And now, to him as well.

He graced them with a tolerant, benevolent smile. "I know it's late. Go home and rest. The duties I require of you can be done in the morning. Good night, Mr. Newcomb. Mrs. Newcomb."

The couple nodded in unison. The man took the paper from his wife, glanced at the short list, and stuffed the paper into his jacket pocket. Without another word, he preceded her from the room.

Titus grinned as the door closed behind them. He had forgotten what a pleasure it was to work with mindless, controllable fools.

CHAPTER
NINETEEN

The day dawned bright, the sun rising as a golden-red ball over the city horizon. Carrie still sat in her chair, still held the often refilled coffee mug, and still unable to order her thoughts. Confused over her parents' sudden attempts at contact, fearful of the strength of her feelings for Bryce, and just plain exhausted, Carrie closed the curtains, dumped her mug in the kitchen sink, and returned to bed. Tired as she was, she still wasn't sure she'd be able to sleep.

She had scheduled an appointment with a peer counselor at the rape crisis center late that afternoon. Throughout the night the one thing she had accomplished was putting her memories of that night into a place in her mind where she believed she could deal with them. Of the girls she'd been in contact with as a dancer, far too many had experienced similar assaults. Whether by a boyfriend or a stranger, it didn't matter. Carrie had often found herself a confidant; her ability to listen quietly must have made it comfortable for the girls to confide in her. In talking through the incidents, some of them had healed without further counseling.

Not that Carrie had much to offer. No sage advice, no personal experience. Until now. Unfortunately, in always being the listener and the recipient of secrets, she hadn't learned how to speak her own feelings. If she didn't feel at ease with the counselor they gave her, she didn't know if she'd be able to relive the rape yet again.

Carrie curled on her side and hugged a small pillow to her chest. No matter how difficult, this was something that she had to do. As soon as possible.

By accepting her and giving her a new, glorious memory to replace the trauma, Bryce had helped her find her way to healing. She understood that much. If he did truly love her as he said, he would always be there to help her. Wishing she was with him, holding him, loving him, learning from him, she hugged the pillow tighter.

In just that one time—their first time—her first time... Carrie took a deep breath and let it out slowly. He'd shown her so much. The echoes of his strange words returned to her mind. What language had he whispered to her? She hadn't recognized any of the words, although the cadence and sounds reminded her of a thick brogue. Amazingly, those words, whispered against her skin, released her from her fear and allowed her to physically love the man her heart chose.

Carrie closed her eyes. These thoughts were no less confusing than those consuming her during the night, but much more pleasant.

With the glow of her thoughts keeping the questions and fears at bay, Carrie relaxed. Close to sleep, she wanted to block out the calm, soft voice that called to her. However, Lottie was not to be ignored.

::Ye've done well, child.::

"Really? I'm not always sure," she whispered.

::Ye shall be fine. Ye've found the love meant fer ye, and ye shall soon understand the happiness ye deserve.::

"You always have said so, Lottie. But it's never happened."

::Until Bryce. A guid man, from a guid family.:: Deep sadness

tinged Lottie's voice, sadness so profound hot tears rose to
Carrie's eyes.

"Lottie, why are you so sad?"

::I am nae sad, child.:: Reverberations of pain and loss colored
the denial.

"Why can't I see you tonight?" Carrie squeezed her eyes tight,
crinkling her nose in concentration as she had when she was
young and needed Lottie's presence.

*::I am nae so far from ye, Carrie, but I have nae the energy to part
the veil.::*

"What's wrong, has something happened?"

::Oh, aye. Yet, 'tis no yer concern.::

"Lottie?"

::Aye?::

"Have you appeared to Bryce's daughter, Breanna? Why does
she need you? There isn't anything…"

::Nay, there is no!:: Lottie's emphatic words brought a whirl of
relief to Carrie. She hadn't realized how concerned she was over
the sudden appearance of Bree's invisible friend.

*::She is a truly happy child, who only wishes ye as her mathair. An'
ye needed—a bit o' proddin'.::* There was now laughter in Lottie's
voice. Relaxing into the sound, Carrie smiled; she'd long ago
become accustomed to the sudden changes in her friend's moods.
Soft, gentle laughter surrounded her. *::Dinna ye feel better havin'
told Bryce how ye feel about him?::*

"Yes. No. I'm not sure."

Easing awake from a dreamless sleep, Carrie lay still for a
few moments to gather her thoughts. She was ready to go
to the Rape Crisis Center and talk to the counselor. Able
to deal with the attack in a matter of fact manner in her mind, she
realized it probably wouldn't be so once she actually sat across
from someone and had to speak the words—again. Emotions
would definitely rule the day and the best she could hope for
would be to survive the onslaught. Being with Bryce afterward

would go a long way toward making her feel better. Maybe, just maybe, if things went well, she'd spend the night.

Stretching luxuriously and feeling the slide of the sheets against her skin brought thoughts of skin against skin, body against body. Of Bryce. Maybe it wasn't such a bad thing that she'd said those three words to him. She could call him now and say the words again. Practice makes perfect.

She and rolled to her side to stare at the clock.

Damn.

No telltale light indicated she'd set the alarm and she'd slept the day away. Her appointment was in less than half an hour. Surprised to discover the Crisis Center was in the neighborhood, now she was glad. It'd only take a few minutes to get there.

Carrie lunged from the bed, grabbed an easy outfit of jeans and a Henley from the closet, and bolted into the bathroom. There were few things she hated more than being late. Forgoing a shower, she washed just enough with a washrag to feel presentable, tugged her hair into a short ponytail with a wooden barrette, and huffed at the mirror.

Luckily, she wasn't out to make an impression, and would probably cry away any makeup she applied anyway. Tears still hovered at the back of her throat, the tightness constricting and almost painful. Leaving her haunted visage in the mirror, Carrie trotted through the apartment, slipped on a pair of sandals at the door, grabbed her purse and keys, and flew down the steps.

She made it to her appointment only five minutes late, and sat waiting on an old, overstuffed couch for another five before her counselor was free.

"Remember what we talked about last night, Daddy." Breanna gave Bryce a noisy kiss and skipped off to join the other children at the daycare. Before she climbed onto the slide, she turned and gave him a broad wave and called, "'Member my pony. Talk to Unka Iain."

Bryce returned her wave and shook his head. She wasn't going to let this pony thing go. Not that it was necessarily a bad idea, perhaps sharing the care of an animal with Iain's kids would help her learn responsibility. He shrugged and climbed back into the car. How responsible could one expect a four-year-old to be?

Before starting the car, he watched her play and an old worry resurfaced. Bree was half-Faerie, and he was concerned that she may have inherited some magical talent from her mother. The Faerie healers hadn't been able to tell, or even venture a guess at what age any talent might appear. How much longer could she spend two days a week at a normal daycare and not say or do something to raise suspicions? This was the kind of responsibility he needed to make sure she learned—control of any possible special abilities.

He stretched his fingers and stroked one hand against the other. A tiny coin appeared between his index and middle fingers. Grinning, he tucked the coin back in his pocket. He often wished he had real magic—Faerie magic. He'd felt inadequate as a young boy because, other than Pop, everyone in the family had some magic. Bree's cousins Belle and Castin had begun to show magical abilities. And they were only a few months older than his darlin' girl.

So many concerns. Although his family was always willing to listen and help out, he didn't have anyone to help share his deepest worries.

But would change soon. Carrie said she loved him. Loved him! And she already had a good, loving relationship with Breanna. If wishes were truly magic, the three of them would be a family soon. Very soon.

Bryce patted the manila folder on the seat beside him. A family man with a permanent job. The shopping trip would be much more fun with Carrie, and he knew she'd have some great ideas for his office, but Garr expected him to start furnishing the space right away. The vouchers in the folder were extremely generous, and would allow him to build his workspace with quality furnishings and equipment. Instead of working on his first project, he'd spent the sleepless night making lists of everything from desks and drawing tables to notepads and a variety of drawing pencils. Making the decision to pick out the basics and have them delivered before bringing Carrie to the office to help arrange things, Bryce gave Bree a final glance and headed for the office supply store.

TWENTY

"There is the house we will watch." Titus pointed across the street. Partially hidden by an overgrown bush at the edge of the park, but able to see the front of the indicated home clearly, Titus and Mr. and Mrs. Newcomb waited. Mrs. Newcomb wrung her hands together, shredding a tissue. Her husband remained stony faced, one hand wrapped tightly around a small, leather bound book.

Titus hummed a spritely dance tune and drummed his fingers on the van's steering wheel. Restraining his delight at the couple's uneasy reactions, Titus cleared his throat. "I have told you the background of the men who live in that house." A portion of the truth at least. "Now, the child they discovered and adopted is a man himself. And interested in your daughter. I don't wish for your daughter, or yourselves, to be contaminated by the sin-filled lives of those so-called parents. While I wish to save both men..." Titus paused to control the tremors of excitement in his voice. Saving the men was far from his plan. Destroying was a much better word. A much more satisfactory word.

Twin, harsh gazes turned from the windshield to him. "I fear we shall not be able to take both at this time. Once one has been saved, and renounces the evil of his ways, he shall assist us in returning the other to his proper place."

"Praises be," whispered Mrs. Newcomb.

"Certainly, my dear. Now, patience. It shouldn't be too long a wait."

One by one, the circle of tall, ornate stone jars slid toward a single plain jar standing alone in a spot of Faerie sunlight. With the rumble of stone grating against stone, the jars circled the jar restraining the magick of one banished. Slowly, each jar tottered, then lowered with the magically tightened stoppers pointed toward the sunlight.

"'Tis as if they pay homage to that one," the Faerie Queen whispered to the man next to her.

"I don't understand it, my lady aunt." Jaye scrubbed his hands through his hair and shook his head. "Has anything like this happened before?"

"I do not believe it to be so. I shall ask the historians. I have never seen movement of the jars where those who choose to leave Faerie store their magicks. Oh, at times, at times of great emotion I am able to feel the magicks. 'Tis as if they join us in our joys and sorrows. But never—this."

"It concerns me the jars move toward that particular container. Are there any other banished magicks besides Fiedhlim's?"

"Nay. His only. Would there be residual magick that might cause such an occurrence?"

Jaye glanced sideways at his aunt. "My lady, you ask me?"

She chuckled. "You hold much knowledge, Jayezer. Morem than one would expect considering your history and heritage. 'Tis why you are my Chosen and the heir to the realm."

"Yeah, I know. But this—I can't figure out. And that in itself, causes me a great deal of concern. Do you sense any magick user nearby? Someone who could be controlling the jars?"

The Queen stared sightless into the distance. "Nay, I do not. There are…" She shook her head. "Nay, 'tis nothing."

"Has Derrik been notified?"

"I called for you first."

Jaye gave a brief nod, closed his eyes and concentrated. The response from the leader of the Alastriona was swift and decisive. Jaye turned his gaze to the Queen. "He'll be here in a few minutes."

The scrape of movement silenced before the Queen could respond. Each jar lay on its side paying silent homage to the captured magick of the single banished evil-doer. A cloud drifted overhead and the spot of sunlight vanished.

A dark, lingering chill traveled the length of Jaye's spine as he and the Queen silently backed from the cold, unusual magick.

T itus straightened with a jerk and leaned eagerly over the steering wheel. "There. This is it. Once that one is gone, we shall rescue the other from evil and take him to the place of safety."

The trio in the van watched in silence as a tall man, long hair pulled back with a strange silver clasp, leaned toward his companion. The shorter, dark haired man rested his hands on the other's shoulders and their cheeks pressed together in a loving gesture.

Next to Titus, the woman looked away and shuddered. He grinned, then chided himself for the complacency. As easily as the plan was coming to fruition, just as easily could the day end in failure. He would tolerate no failure. Settling his face into a blank mask he returned his attention across the street.

The blond stroked the back of his hand over the other's cheek, then turned and jogged into the neighboring backyard. When he disappeared through a gap in the thick bushes, Titus started the van.

"We shall let the other return to the house and confront him there. Are you ready, Mr. Newcomb?" Titus glanced in the mirror at the man.

"I am." He pulled a small bottle and a bandana from a sack at his feet. After setting them on the seat beside him, he added a roll of thick gray tape and smiled a cold, satisfied smile.

Titus nodded in satisfaction. While biddable, this man still had some initiative. A shame he wasn't—

"He's inside," the woman whispered.

Titus revved the van's engine, eased them from the parking lot and into an alley behind a row of small, colorful Victorian houses. Silent, he held up one hand to forestall his companions while he peered into the neighboring yard. When his expression was composed to a concerned half-smile calculated to inspire confidence, he nodded. "Let's go."

Leading the couple through the backyard to the house, Titus let the satisfaction of the moment flow through him. It had been long and long again since he'd felt his plans coming together so well.

Single file, they stepped onto the deck and paused under a wide, vine-covered pergola. Titus twisted the doorknob and turned a triumphant grin toward Mr. Newcomb. The door opened soundlessly, and they stepped inside without hesitation.

Mrs. Newcomb clung to her husband's arm, hampering his movements as he twisted the cap from the small bottle and tipped the liquid onto the folded bandana. Titus leaned close to her head and wrinkled his nose at the mixture of fear and cheap cologne rising from her. "Wait here and watch the van. We will return momentarily."

"I... yes, of course." She released her husband with agonizing slowness. Titus restrained an impatient growl and the urge to rip her hands from their intense claw-like clutch. Now was not the time for her to have doubts.

Before he could hiss at her to move, she turned away and positioned herself to one side of the open door, angling her head to stare out toward the van. After a moment Titus touched the man on the arm and led him forward.

Music, low and pulsing, sounded from one of the front rooms. Papers rustled, the rhythmic tapping of a keyboard sounding a counterpoint to the music. The office door stood ajar. Their target sat at a computer facing a window. Titus nearly laughed. This was too easy.

He carefully pushed the door open and the two men eased into the room. Their quarry continued working, oblivious to the movement and intent behind him.

Closer.

Their prey paused, stretched, and lifted his arms above his head. Leaping the last few feet, Titus grinned down at the startled man, grabbed his wrists, and forced his arms down behind his back. Mr. Newcomb pressed the bandana over his nose and mouth.

The short struggle disappointed Titus. The glorious excitement faded too soon. He ached for a lingering enjoyment, a time to savor the thrill of his success.

Instead of being able to glory in the minor success, Titus gave a sharp nod and grabbed the unconscious man under the arms. Mr. Newcomb took his feet and they carried their captive through the house, out the back door now held open by the woman and tossed him unceremoniously into the back of the van.

Mr. Newcomb climbed in after him and reached for his roll of gray tape as Titus slammed the heavy doors. The mousy woman scurried to the passenger side of the van, her rapid breathing betraying her fear. The powerful scent brought a rise of sexual desire in Titus. Not for the dried up old woman, but for a lush, feminine body. One with violet eyes. One that would fear him and, in that fear, bring him momentary satisfaction. A lithe dancer's body, one he had watched for some time now at a club on the outskirts of town. Once his prize was delivered to the compound, he'd find her.

The woman beside him remained silent during the drive to the compound. Her husband grunted and struggled to bind their captive with the tape, yet not unduly injure the man. Titus rolled his eyes. The drug was enough to keep the prize subdued, the binding was unneeded. But, if the man derived pleasure from the act, Titus would not say him nay. Pleasure could be found in many ways, and he doubted the man received much in the angular body of his wife.

At the end of a long, overgrown road, Titus slowed the van and pushed a button on a small control unit. A large, metal gate opened with a series of jerks and clanks. The van eased over deep ruts and rain-washed gullies toward a squat, flat-roofed building. Two men waited by a steel door and stepped forward when the van stopped.

They dragged the captive from the van by his tightly bound arms, letting his feet trail in the dust. Titus watched with his arms crossed over his chest. At a short comment from Mr. Newcomb he nodded and the couple entered the building, following the captive.

Reverend Templeton stepped from the dark interior into the sunlight and blinked. "Ah, Mr. Avery. Your success pleases me. With our treatment, this man shall no longer be tempted by base, evil desires. He shall become pure in his love. It may take time, but my personal success rate is excellent. He shall become a true believer."

"I would wish nothing else, sir." Titus narrowed his eyes to stare at Reverend Templeton. Competition. That was the essence, the scent rising from the man. After a second of internal struggle, Titus relaxed and held out his hand. This one was no competition. Like the others, the man thought he served his own purpose while in reality, he now served Titus.

"If you will excuse me, Reverend. I have business to attend."

TWENTY-ONE

D rained and exhausted beyond the strain of her sleepless night, Carrie dragged her feet when she left the Crisis Center. She leaned against the side of her Kia and stared back at the huge old farmhouse that had been converted into offices and living quarters for abused women and children. An amazing place, filled with amazing women.

Never believing just talking about what happened could be so intense, and ultimately cleansing, Carrie made a silent vow. When she had completely put the rape behind her, she'd volunteer at the center. Helping others was bound to continue her healing process as well.

A deep sigh pushed her away from the vehicle and she tugged her keys from her pocket. Healing. She'd hoped this time with the counselor would be all she needed, but now she wasn't sure. It frightened her that, although the sex she'd had with Bryce was wonderful and she ached for more, memories of the assault could resurface at any time. Even during intimate moments with Bryce. He didn't deserve the pain her memories, her own pain, would cause him, didn't need to deal with a woman who was frightened of the very things she desired.

The counselor had told it was just as possible such incidents would never happen to her. Each person dealt with abuse situations in their own unique way. Since she'd felt so comfortable with Bryce, and wasn't afraid during sex, maybe she'd never have to worry about those recurrent memories.

It was a chance she was willing to take. Even if her fright somehow chased Bryce away or made him turn from her and believe she wasn't worth the effort.

He told her he loved her, surely an impossibility after so short a time. But, why not? She loved him with a love deeper than she'd ever thought to feel. Her love for Bryce was far beyond any dreams. And her love was strong enough she could leave him if that would be the best for him.

But how could she leave Breanna, the darling girl she loved from the first moment, from the first time Bree had called her mommy?

Mommy? The word brought a rise of panic as Carrie pulled from the parking lot. She nearly turned the vehicle back into the empty stall. How could she even think of being a parent? She had no proper role model. Her parents had been so cold and distant, only paying attention to her when she committed some wrong. The only emotion she'd experienced from the couple that bore her was the heat of religious fervor. She didn't know how to be a good parent. All she knew was what she experienced, and she wouldn't subject any child to that.

If she didn't know how, she did know how *not* to parent a child. Bryce had great teachers in his fathers, and was himself a wonderful parent. He'd help her. She could learn so much from him.

A tingling heat burned her face. She already had. The echoes of the strange words he'd whispered against her skin filled her with concentrated sensual delight, making her gasp at the sensation. How did he do that to her when he wasn't even there?

Catching a glimpse of her expression in the rear view mirror, Carrie rolled her eyes. How dreamy could one woman look? She looked like an infatuated fool. She grinned at her reflection. An infatuated fool was exactly what she was.

. . .

While Breanna chattered happily in her car seat, Bryce repeated the conversation he'd had with her daycare provider to himself. A boy had climbed to the top of the swing set and fallen to the pavement. Horror stricken, and all the way across the play area, the teacher had called to keep the other children away from the injured boy. She had been sure he was badly hurt, for he had fallen headfirst.

But, by the time she ran to the child, Bree had the boy's head in her lap while she sang to him. The teacher didn't recognize the song, so Bryce supposed it was a Faerie tune. He'd ask Bree when they got home.

Before the teacher could kneel to check the boy, he'd grinned at Bree and sat up. The teacher took him to the emergency room, but the doctors found nothing except for a few minor scratches, no signs of concussion or other trauma. The woman had been confused and concerned, telling Bryce of the incident so he wouldn't worry about the boy in case Bree mentioned the fall.

Was there was more to the situation than appeared on the surface? He watched Bree and was constantly on the lookout for any sign of Faerie magick. Could she have a talent for healing? He sighed. Maybe he was looking for magick where there was none. With the resiliency of childhood, perhaps the boy had merely knocked the wind from himself.

Running late, he drove directly to his folks' house to drop off Bree for the evening. Tempted to ask if she could spend the night, he shook his head. He'd imposed on his fathers too often in the past few days. Although they loved caring for Bree, and seldom told him no, Bryce was determined not to take advantage of their kindness to make his life easier.

Bree hugged his neck tightly when he lifted her from her seat. "You need to help Pop Pop."

Bryce kissed her sweet chubby cheek. "What do you mean, darlin'?"

"You can do it, Daddy. Lottie says so."

Ah, so this was another instance of her imaginary friend speaking for her. It probably had something to do with the pony. The idea seemed appropriate because Lara waited on the porch. But as he neared his cousin, the worry tightening her expression quickened his pace.

Lara held out her arms for Bree. "I'm taking Bree home with me. You need to go inside. Something's happened."

Bryce shifted Bree on his hip and grabbed Lara's shoulder. "What? Tell me."

"I'm going to keep Breanna safe with me, Bryce. Go to your da."

"Did something happen to Pop? Oh, my God, Lara. What happened?"

She indicated the door with a jerk of her head. "Don't worry about us, Bryce. They'll tell you..."

A single, huge tear trailed from the corner of Lara's eye. Leaden fear plummeted to the pit that was once his stomach. Indecision held him motionless for a moment before he leapt toward the door and slammed inside.

Derrik paced the width of the living room, his face a tight mask of anger and fear. That fear reflected in the expressions of the others gathered about the room. Fear Bryce knew had found its way into his eyes and the tight muscles of his jaw. All eyes turned to him.

Before he could ask what happened, Derrik strode to him, rested his hands heavily on Bryce's shoulders and leaned forward to press his forehead against Bryce's. "Yer Pop has been taken."

"Taken? Da? What do you mean?"

Derrik whirled and slammed his fist against an antique vase. The shattered porcelain sailed across the room. Fire blazed in his eyes when he turned back to Bryce. "Taken. Someone took him."

Jaye moved beside him and rested a hand on Bryce's arm. "We believe he was kidnapped, Bryce."

Confused, he drew his eyebrows low over his eyes and the

room blurred. "Why would anyone want to kidnap Pop? He has no enemies."

Jaye glanced at Derrik. A world of meaning passed through their silent communication. Derrik nodded once. Jaye drew a long breath. "It may not be a personal attack against Tommy. It may be whoever perpetrated this—obscenity—means to attack Derrik. Or me."

"Who would want to do that?" Anger chased the fear and he understood Da's attack on the vase. Who would dare? Another caterer? There were no others large enough to compete with Zeroun's and the company rarely offered bids on small occasions. Only that upstart Titus, who had disappeared almost as soon as he opened business. "That Titus fellow?"

"Uh, Bryce," Jaye looked even more uncomfortable and he turned away.

Two of the younger men left their conversation and Jaye's brother-in-law, Korin, closed the distance between them. The slender man shook his head. "Iain and I believe this may not have anything to do with family business."

"Then what?" Everyone sidestepped the issue. "Who took Pop?"

Derrik slumped into a chair and stabbed his fingers through his hair. The length hung over his face when he leaned forward. "Mayhaps 'tis because he is my Tommy. Because of our love fer each other." His voice broke. "My Tommy."

Bryce knelt before his da and took his hands. "You think this is a hate crime? My God, Da, after all this time?"

"Hate has no bounds, ye ken?"

"Aye, Da. I do." Bryce sat back on his heels and gave each of the others a long, hard stare. "So what do we do? Call the cops?"

"No!" Derrik lurched to his feet. "I shall find my Tommy." His fists clenched tight and the lines of despair etched deeper into his handsome face. "An' destroy the one who took him."

"Derrik." Jaye's voice was soft, low, yet commanding. "Derrik, you will not take the law into your own hands. We don't even know if this was of human instigation or of Otherworld origin."

"The Alastriona—"

"Will assist, and will discover if there is Faerie involvement. Once we know that, then, if appropriate, we'll take human measures."

Derrik collapsed back to the chair. Bryce took his Da's hands and tried to encourage him to loosen his tight fists. Derrik looked at him, but Bryce didn't think he saw him, being focused only on finding whoever had taken Tommy. Helplessness flowed through the rage and fear, forming complicated knots in Bryce's belly. How would they deal with this?

Jaye clasped one of Derrik's shoulders. "Until this is over and we find Tommy, you are relieved of leadership of the Alastriona." He paused and bent to peer into Derrik's startled eyes. "You're in no condition to command. Your second will lead until you return. Macaire."

A young Faerie stepped forward and gave a small bow with one palm resting flat against his chest. "Aye, m'lord?"

"You'll lead the Alastriona in Derrik's absence. Search the Otherworld and report to me. Any little difference, any overheard conversation, anything. Do you understand?"

Nodding, Macaire bit his lower lip and glanced repeatedly at Derrik. It wasn't until Derrik lifted his head and gave a sharp nod that Macaire gave his full attention to Jaye. "Aye, it shall be as ye say, m'lord." To Derrik he said, "We shall find Tommy, and return him to ye. Fear not, the Defenders of Mankind do not fail."

Bryce let a grim, flat smile touch his lips. The Alastriona would search Faerie for clues. He would do the same in this world. "Has anyone searched the house? How do we know this was a kidnapping?"

Iain moved into the close family circle, held out a dark blue bandana, and dropped the cloth into Bryce's open palm. Bryce stared at the material, then lifted it to his nose. A strange, heady scent rose from the fibers and he arched his eyebrows in question.

"They used a drug, I dinna ken what kind. A drug to subdue my Tommy."

"Da, I'm sure he's fine. We'll find him soon."

The single tear tracing its way over Derrik's high cheekbone and down his square jaw broke Bryce's wounded heart into a million, shattered pieces.

T he dry taste of cotton filled Tommy's mouth. Sucking on the insides of his cheeks, he tried to draw moisture to his mouth then groaned with failure. Total darkness met his eyes when he lifted his lids. Where was he? What happened?

A slow recollection of an evilly grinning face and the inability to breathe made him groan again. Where *was* he?

A hand touched his arm. Tommy jerked to sitting and grabbed his head to hold in the excruciating pain. Biting his lip kept back the moan vibrating his throat. "Who's there?" he croaked.

"I'm sorry. I didn't mean to make you jump."

The child's voice was soft and pitched low as if he feared to speak louder. "They used drugs to bring you here."

"I figured that out." Tommy ran his tongue around the inside of his mouth, but nothing worked to ease the sticky, cottony dryness. Straining to focus, Tommy searched the darkness trying to find any glimmer of illumination, something to use to orient himself. He sensed movement, then a small body eased onto the squeaky cot. "Where's here?"

"This is Reverend Templeton's compound."

"Templeton?" The name seemed vaguely familiar. Tommy rubbed his temples and winced. The drug left a powerful hangover.

"This is where the Reverend converts others to his church."

"Who are you?" The strange presence of a child outweighed Tommy's concern for himself.

"I... I help him." The boy's voice was tiny, quiet, and ashamed. "I don't want to, but he makes me."

Templeton. Now he remembered—rumors of the cult-like devotion of a growing religious movement within the city. There had been talk of how the cult created believers, but he had scoffed at the whispers. Maybe he should have paid more attention.

"Why?"

"Why do I help?"

It was a good question, but not one for which Tommy needed an answer. "Why am I here?"

"I tried to find out, but they would have seen me. The offices don't have many hiding places. I'm David." The touch of the small hand returned and Tommy rested his palm over the bit of warmth.

David wiggled his fingers and, expecting the boy to retreat from the contact, Tommy lifted his hand. Instead David patted his arm. "You're different than the others."

"Am I?"

"They said you're queer. I don't understand."

Tommy winced. Queer wasn't one of his favorite words, and although he had friends who identified themselves that way, he didn't. So, those whispers around the community were probably correct. Templeton was claiming to be able to cure homosexuality.

And he was to be the latest victim.

"I know queer means different or weird. But I don't think that's what they meant. It sounded... bad when they said it."

"It is, David." Tommy's head throbbed and nausea gathered in his belly. He groaned.

"You're gonna barf."

If it weren't so eminently true, Tommy would have laughed at David's matter-of-fact statement. Bile burned the back of his throat, hot saliva filled his mouth. He swallowed but the action did little good.

David scooted from his side, felt for his hand and tugged. "Come on, toilet's over here."

Thankful, Tommy let David lead him a few steps through the darkness and press his hand against cool porcelain.

When the contents of his stomach were flushed away, Tommy lifted his head and David's hand left his shoulder. The trickle of running water sounded loud in the darkness. Soon a paper cup was pressed carefully into his hand. The tepid water rinsed the bile from his mouth and he spat, hoping he hit the toilet. David took the cup and refilled it. This time the water was a bit cooler and Tommy drank gratefully.

"Thank you, David."

He felt the boy's shrug. "You'd never have found the toilet. And they don't clean any messes. Come on, I'll lead you back to the bed if you're okay."

"I think I'm fine. Just really thirsty now."

"I'll get you more water. They won't let you have anything else for a while. Not until you beg for it."

Beg? He wouldn't beg for anything from these idiots. Derrik would be on the trail and soon find him. *Ah, Derrik, I'm fine. I'll be okay. Don't worry. Just find me.*

The narrow cot was a welcome relief. His legs wobbled and the pounding in his head increased when he moved. David encouraged him to lay back, then patted his chest. "I gotta go. If they miss me at room check, they'll up the security and I won't be able to come back."

"David?"

"Yeah?"

"How did you get in here anyway?"

The boy chuckled. "I know ways around the compound. Go to sleep and you'll feel better. I don't think you'll barf again."

"I hope not."

The boy chuckled again but the sound sobered to a sigh. "They won't turn the lights on in here for at least a day. Something about depri... deprivation. I'll come back when I can."

The rustle of David's movements sounded precise and sure. Odd that the child could find his way so easily when Tommy couldn't even see his hand in front of his face. "David?"

"I gotta go."

"I know. How do you find your way so well in the dark?"

The short pause filled the room. "I'm always in the dark. I'm blind."

TWENTY-TWO

After checking her appearance in the thin strip of her rear view mirror, Carrie practically skipped into the fast food Mexican restaurant and eased past a group of children toward the back of the dining area. The magician's table, draped in black, encouraged her and she stepped forward eagerly.

A gangly, dark haired teenager sat behind the table, concentrating as he shuffled. He held the deck in one hand and cut the cards into three moving stacks with deft movements of his fingers. When he sensed her presence, he looked up and grinned. "And what trick can I do for you?"

Not in the mood to see anyone but Bryce, Carrie frowned. "Where's Bryce?"

The teen's grin faded and he set the cards to one side. "He's not here."

"I can see that."

"Hey, lady, I wish he was here, too, I've got a huge test tomorrow. He called. Some family emergency." The boy shrugged. "Don't know any more than that. Sorry."

Carrie turned on her heels and rushed from the restaurant. He hadn't called her. She slid into her vehicle, jammed the key in the ignition, then rested her forehead on the steering wheel. Why should he call her? Even though he had professed to love her, she was still an unknown to him. Besides, she wouldn't know what to do in a family emergency?

Maybe something happened to Breanna. Panic rose like bile in her throat and she jerked upright. She could be there for him, no matter what. Wasn't that part of what loving someone was all about—to be there in the bad times? Bryce had supported her when the memories of her assault ran roughshod over her. In return she'd be there for him, no matter what happened.

The trip halfway across town seemed endless, the rush hour traffic slow and congested. Carrie ached to scream at the other drivers and force them out of her way. The squeal of tires grated through her worry and with a start she realized the awful sound came from her car.

Slow down. If she had an accident she'd be delayed longer. Carrie leaned back in the seat and tried to take slow, calming breaths. The exercise did little good to slow the rapid, hard beat of her heart. Adrenaline surged through her when she finally neared the park and turned off onto a side street. Another corner and she was at Bryce's house.

The building was dark with no signs of occupation. Where was he? Frantic, she stared up and down the street. A silvery-blond haired man emerged from Bryce's folks' house and jogged past her. A familiar, god-awful green car screeched to a halt next to the curb.

Carrie left her car in Bryce's drive and ran to meet Nightshade as he rushed up the sidewalk. She clutched at his silk-clad arm. "What happened?"

The distracted, intense expression left his face and softened to a sad worry when he glanced down at her. "Come on, we'll find out together." He gave her a small smile. "I'm glad you're here, honey. Bryce will need your support. And love."

Oh, god. "Bree?" she croaked out on a choked whisper.

"She's okay."

Carrie froze and shook her head slowly back and forth. If Bree was okay, then it had to be one of his—

"Carrie, Carrie listen to me." Nightshade bent so he was eye level and shook her shoulder gently. "Carouselle, snap out of it. Bryce needs you to be strong. I know it's gonna be hard with all you've been through today, but try. For him? Honey? Carrie, can you do that?"

She could. Carrie bit back a dry sob and nodded.

"Good girl. Come on now, let's see what's happening and what we can do to make it better."

Nightshade knocked once on the door and opened it without waiting. He guided Carrie into the living room and they paused a moment before Nightshade angled her toward Bryce, then crossed to a group of four men. Carrie's heart dropped even further.

Hunched over with his head in his hands, Bryce sat alone on the couch. The low murmur of intense voices seemed to have no effect on his apparent grief. Carrie took one step and paused. A soft hiss from the men caught her attention. When she glanced toward them, Nightshade motioned sharply with one hand and a jerk of his head. She nodded and crossed the room to sit beside Bryce.

He didn't move as she slid closer, but when she rested her arm around his shoulders, he turned to her. Tears streaked his cheeks and pain dulled his eyes to a gray, moss green. Carrie opened her arms to him and he collapsed into her embrace. His lips moved against her neck. "Someone kidnapped Pop."

Kidnapped? She couldn't imagine that happening to someone she knew; it was fodder for forensic shows, not real life. "Oh, Bryce, is there a ransom?" Oh, what a stupid, thoughtless question.

Bryce drew back and scrubbed his palms over his face. "No. No note. Nothing. All we've found is a bandana with some chemical on it that was probably used to make him unconscious."

"Where are the cops?"

"Cops?" The tone of Bryce's voice rose sharply. "What can they do? We don't even know why anyone would want to hurt

Pop." He glanced quickly at the group of men and spoke softly. "Or anyone in the family."

"Bryce, you've got to call them. You can't expect to take care of this kind of thing yourself. What about your Da?" Carrie tore her gaze from Bryce's pain and searched for Derrik. He stood to one side, face infused with fierce anger as he argued with Nightshade.

A wry chuckle barked from Bryce. "He and Nightshade are probably arguing about calling the police as well."

"Well, you should. Call Detective Corley. I trust him."

"The family will handle this." The no nonsense tone made Carrie sit back. They should call the police. The authorities had the means and technology to ensure Tommy's safety and recovery. She lowered her gaze to her hands.

Bryce's fingers covered hers and slowly, she looked up at him. His eyes were soft and apologetic. "I'm sorry, sweetheart. But it has to be this way. There are things about my family..."

"Tell me so I understand."

"I can't." He looked away. "Not yet."

What other secrets did his family have? He'd been reluctant for her to meet his parents, understandable in a world where too many hated gay couples. Now, one of that loving couple had been taken away.

A niggle of suspicion found focus in her mind. Her mother had written about inappropriate relationships. A couple of the girls at the club had mentioned some group claiming to reform... her parents couldn't be involved with that—with this—could they? Their beliefs wouldn't take them that far afield. Would they? Oh, Lord.

"No."Derrik's exclamation rose over the other conversations. "I willna allow ye to do that." All eyes turned to where he stood toe to toe with Nightshade.

Carrie frowned. Nightshade's posture was subtly different as he calmly stood under Derrik's emotional tirade. His only reaction was the lift of one eyebrow. Then he turned, cocked his head toward her and Bryce and silently left the house.

"What was that about?" Carrie wondered out loud.

"I have no idea. Maybe you should go, too."

"Do you really want me to leave?"

Bryce grabbed her hand and pressed her palm against his chest. "No, I don't." He took a long, deep breath. "Time to do something. Korin and Macaire are checking their... neighborhoods. Jaye will stay with Da. Iain's going to look around outside then go home to stay with Lara and the kids. Bree's there with them. I don't know where Jaysson or Allyn are." He took a deep breath and fell silent.

She'd figure out who all these people were later. The main thing was that Bree was somewhere safe and she was here with Bryce. "Have you searched the house thoroughly?"

"I think Da and Jaye did. But, we can look again. Maybe we'll find something they missed." The color of his eyes lightened, as though a beacon of hope shone through them.

"Good." Carrie leaned forward and kissed his cheek. "Let's get started. The sooner we discover the clues, the sooner we'll find Tommy and bring your Pop back home."

She rose and tried to pull Bryce to his feet as well. He held back and when he looked up at her, she nearly cried from the renewed agony in his expression. Bending, she whispered, "I'll do anything I can to help. We'll find Tommy. I promise."

"You can't promise that. You have no control over what happens." The waver in his voice vibrated through her.

"I can promise this. It may not be much, but maybe it will help. Bryce, I love you.

F eeling as though days had passed, Tommy remained in total darkness. But in truth, he knew the passage of time had probably been only a few hours. When he wasn't sleeping, he gained a new appreciation for his hearing. And for other senses sharpening in the absence of light.

A nearly silent sound, like a well-oiled sliding door opening, woke him from a fitful doze. He held his breath and heard soft, short footsteps.

"David?" he whispered.

"Yeah. You heard me?"

Tommy sat and patted the cot at his side. "Amazing how much better my hearing is when I can't see."

"That's true. You know, I used to be able to see."

"What happened?"

The cot dipped slightly and David crawled next to Tommy. "My dad abandoned me, left me with Reverend Templeton. Then I couldn't see. No big deal. I saved you part of my breakfast." David stroked his small hand down Tommy's arm until he found Tommy's hand then pressed something soft against his palm. "It's only peanut butter, but it's better than nothing."

"Thank you. You said breakfast? How long have I been here?"

"Since yesterday morning. I can't stay. I've got to be a part of the service this morning. They might bring you, too."

"Why me?"

"Part of your in... indoctri... doctri—"

"Indoctrination?"

"Yeah. Oh, and make sure you drink a lot and rinse out your mouth before they come."

"Why?"

David giggled and slid from the bed. "So you don't smell like peanut butter, of course."

Bryce stretched carefully so he wouldn't disturb Carrie. She curled on her side on the couch with her head resting against his thigh. She'd refused to go home after they searched the house, even after the rest of the family had gone. Together, they kept Da company, sitting mostly without talking late into the night, taking comfort in each other's presence.

Bryce stroked his fingers over the tangles of her sleep mussed hair. He didn't deserve a woman as loving as Carrie. Her mere presence comforted him, while her gentle words had calmed Da when he raged his agony. How long would she stay if she learned the family's secret? Not many people truly believed in the Gentry, in Faerie folk. Bryce tried to imagine what her reaction might be when he took her through a portal into the Otherworld. She'd accepted so much already, both in his life and her own past. Maybe, just maybe, she could accept his heritage as well. He continued to stroke her hair, staring down into the relaxed lines of her face.

"Ye have to tell her soon, my son."

Bryce glanced up at Derrik's soft words. "I know, Da."

"Tell me what?" Carrie pushed against Bryce's thigh to sit and brushed hair back from her face. She wrinkled her nose and rotated her shoulders.

"You should have gone home and gotten a good night's sleep."

"I wasn't going to leave you." She glanced from Bryce to Derrik. "Either of you. So, what should you tell me?"

At any other time, Bryce would have admired her tenacity. But not now, not when he didn't have any idea how to broach the subject of Faerie.

A knock on the front door saved him from answering. The echoes of footsteps preceded the arrival of a red-haired young man. Derrik rose and gave a slight shake of his head at the man before taking him aside.

"Who's that? He wasn't here last night."

"Macaire. He's Da's, um, assistant. He's helping search for Pop."

"I still think we should talk to the police. Let me call Detective Corley."

"No. This is family business."

Hurt filled Carrie's eyes and she turned her face from him. "I'm only trying to help."

"Sweetheart?" He could think of no words to ease the pain for either of them, except to tell her the truth. Yet, this couldn't be the right time. Bryce held back the release of a deep breath. There wasn't any right time for this type of revelation. He rested his fingers against her arm and stroked gently. "Carrie?"

She turned back to him with a jerk. "Okay, don't tell me. But, when we find Tommy, we're having a long talk. And telling each other everything. Do you hear me? Everything."

Her perseverance made him smile despite the worry filling his soul. Nodding, he lifted his hand to her cheek. "Everything."

Derrik's low groan pulled Bryce immediately to his feet. He was across the room in long strides to where Derrik sank onto a chair. He knelt at one side of Derrik, Macaire crouched at the other, and both focused their concern on the man who bent double, holding his head in his hands. With a sharp gasp, Derrik sat upright and stared at Bryce. "'Tis my Tommy. Contactin' me. I dinna ken, but I can hear him in my head. Ah, my Tommy, where are ye?"

Derrik's wild-eyed appearance gave Bryce a moment of fright. Just as quickly the look was gone and Derrik sighed.

"'Tis gone now. My Tommy is safe, fer now. So he says. He dinna sound so well. Bryce, my son, we must find yer pop."

"We will, Da." He glanced back at Carrie who watched intently. "Maybe you should go see the, uh, Jaye's aunt. She may be able to help focus those thoughts and locate Pop."

"Aye. A guid idea. Macaire, ye are with me. Bryce ye must stay here—in case."

"I will."

"We will," Carrie amended. "You go do what you have to and together we'll find Tommy." She rose as Derrik shrugged off Bryce's hands and stood. Carrie hesitated, then moved forward to hug Derrik.

"Go on now. Don't worry. I'll take care of Bryce."

"Aye, I believe ye shall." Derrik turned to Macaire with a curt nod and the two strode from the house.

Bryce stretched to relax the tight muscles in his back and shoulders, then leaned back into Carrie's strong hands when she kneaded the muscles. He felt her take a breath and he tensed, waiting for her to speak.

"Anything you'd like to tell me now?"

TWENTY-THREE

Tommy had explored and memorized the tiny, closet-sized chamber in the dark, so when the sound of a key scraping the lock came, he stood, angled toward the sound, ready to face his captors. He wasn't ready for the flash of intense light burning into his eyes. Wincing from the spotlight, he covered his eyes with his forearm. Rough hands grabbed his arms and held them to his side. Without the protection, he couldn't lift his eyelids. Tears did nothing to cool the burning, only poured down his cheeks.

His captors shoved him forward and he stumbled. Unwilling to show any weakness before them, he remained stoically silent, as silent as his jailers.

By the time they pressed him onto a hard-backed chair, he could open his eyes enough to peer through the tiny slits. Not that he was able to see much through the blur of his tears.

The sounds of movement to one side, the whispers and shuffling of a group of people made him cock his head to listen. Further away, a low voice spoke urgently, the tones interspersed by a younger voice. David?

Tommy blinked rapidly. He had to see. Maybe he would be able to tell Derrik something to help the family locate him. Trying to send psychic messages to his partner was a foolish, desperate act of a foolish, desperate man and he gave a silent, self-derisive snort. While there were some humans who claimed to have similar connections, and it was a common enough means of communication for those of Faerie, he and Derrik had never experienced anything remotely similar.

Still, it didn't hurt to try. There was no doubt Derrik and the entire family were looking for him. Had the kidnappers left a note of any kind? Any clues? Tommy leaned back and rubbed his eyes. The tears were slowing and the spotty remnants of the flash of light faded.

When he was able to focus, he found himself in another small room. Instead of being totally enclosed, one entire wall was made of a thick wood lattice. Black window screening backed the lattice, enabling him to see shapes and shadows on the other side, but little detail of his surroundings.

The crash of a large drum reverberated through him. Tommy covered his ears and squinted toward the ceiling. Speakers, tiny yet obviously powerful, hung in each corner. The drum rolled again and the speakers vibrated. Closing his eyes, Tommy leaned back and clenched his teeth. They had taken him from total, silent darkness to a place of sensory overload. *Derrik, don't take too long. I'm okay for now. But, hurry.*

The lights dimmed, both in his tiny room and beyond the lattice screen. All movement and whispering ceased. With a third tremendous crash of drums a single spotlight focused directly in front of him. By angling his seat, he found a place in the lattice where the slats were further apart, the screen a wider mesh. The seemingly accidental configuration had to have been planned.

A man, tall, sandy-haired, imposing, dressed in a white shirt with rolled up sleeves and dark slacks, stepped into the spotlight. A sigh rose from the gathered people and a single voice, filled with ecstasy, rang out. "Reverend Templeton."

So, this was the man. Tommy steeled his will and turned his chair from the lattice. This show must be evidence of the man's attempt at programming and he'd have no part of it. In order to block the rise and fall of the man's voice and the joyous acclamations of the congregation, Tommy closed his eyes and silently recited a favorite poem; a Faerie love song Derrik often whispered to him late at night.

A woman's soft voice joined his own, speaking the words, in his mind. A woman's voice, but achingly similar in accent to Derrik's. He stopped the flow of the words, immediately losing the comfort of the familiar rhythm. The woman's voice continued for a few lines then paused.

::'Twill no be long, Tommy, an' ye'll be rescued.::

Okay, so now his imagination talked to him. Was the programming working and he didn't realize it?

Fey laughter, filled his head. ::Nay, I am no part of this ridiculous travesty. Yet, I have witnessed such afore. Ye are doin' as ye should. Dinna listen. Dinna let him find a weakness. Dinna worry, 'twill no be so long.::

"Who are you?" he whispered, afraid to open his eyes and chance losing the comforting presence.

::I am just one who watches o'er ye and yers.::

"I don't understand." Tommy rubbed his temples. The ranting of the man on the other side of the lattice was powerful, compelling part of his mind to listen. He forced himself to ignore the dynamic man and focused his thoughts on the woman.

"Tell me who you are."

::Lottie.::

The presence in his mind slowly faded. Lottie? Like Lottie, Bree's imaginary friend?

::Aye.::

Before he could digest that information, silence from beyond the lattice stole his attention. He turned and leaned close to the screen to peer into the other room. Templeton stood with both arms upraised as a small figure moved next to him.

The Reverend lowered one hand to the child's head. "Who seeks answers, healing from the blessed child, David?"

David? Tommy squinted to see the boy who had visited him during his dark captivity. Small and thin, the boy held his head high, facing forward, a grim expression tightening the young lips. His dark brown hair was chopped in ragged hanks, and he was dressed in a similar fashion to the Reverend Templeton.

A woman hobbled forward, leaning heavily on a cane. With labored steps, she climbed the short stairs to the dais and prostrated herself before the man and the boy. Tommy rolled his eyes to the ceiling and shook his head.

At a discreet shove from the Reverend, David stepped forward, one hand outstretched, until he touched the woman's head. The boy's lips moved, but Tommy heard nothing.

Evidently, the woman did, for she rose to her knees. After David touched her forehead, ran his small hand down the side of her face and rested his fingers on her shoulders, she gave a loud, astonished gasp.

The Reverend joined them, one hand cupping the back of her head, the other pressed to her forehead. He rocked her back and forth. Eyes were tightly closed and his face lifted to the ceiling, he spoke strange words.

The woman cried out. Templeton released her and she fell back with an undulating scream. David knelt beside her and felt for her hand. When he finally held her hand between his, she sat, stood, and walked a few steps without assistance or evidence of pain.

The assembly broke into chants of praise and hallelujahs.

Reverend Templeton smiled broadly as he broke the woman's cane over the edge of the dais. After she left the stage he raised his hands and received immediate silence.

Tommy slouched against the chair back. The chicanery and mass hypnotism used by Reverend Templeton was extremely effective. The man was more dangerous than the rumors indicated. When he was free, he'd make sure...

"... within the Blessings Chamber is a man. A sinner. A lover of men."

Tommy slid his chair back against the wall. A dangerous chill filled the Reverend's voice, and the responding rumble from his congregation filled Tommy with fear. The chill chased its way down his spine and he shook uncontrollably.

"We send David to heal this man, this poor soul who seeks redemption. David, who does not see as you or I, but sees the evil within us, and he who takes that evil and heals us, David, go to him."

But the boy held back, his blank eyes wide, his expression frightened. He shook his head. Templeton turned so that the congregation was unable to see his face, but Tommy saw him clearly. His eyes narrowed dangerously and he bent to whisper in David's ear.

The boy shook his head and took a step back, one hand held before him in denial. Templeton took a step toward him with a tight fist hidden from the assembly. Tommy rose and wrapped his fingers around the splintered wood lattice. He'd break through if the man touched a single hair on the boy's head.

Slowly, Templeton straightened, his shoulders tense. He grimaced before composing his features and turned back to the congregation.

"Witness the evilness of a homosexual. Even the pure heart of our beloved David fears to go near the one safely contained in the Blessings Chamber. We must pray for this one, and for others of his kind. Pray, my friends, pray with me."

As he lowered his head, he gave David a rough shove. The boy stumbled backward, then turned and, feeling his way along a side railing, fled the dais. Tommy sank back in the chair. What would Templeton do to David? The man's face had shown no evidence of tenderness or concern. If David had gone against his wishes... Tommy shuddered.

Derrik, hurry.

TWENTY-FOUR

The flagstone steps of Derrik's front porch were cold and hard against her bottom. Three days had passed since Tommy's disappearance, and although Derrik continued to receive the strange, mental messages, they were no closer to finding his partner than they had been immediately after the kidnapping. Feeling helpless and hopeless, Carrie leaned against a newel post and stared across the street at City Park. Life went on, people came and went, children played, dogs barked, lovers strolled hand in hand along the pathways.

But her life was on hold. All her energy, and all the energies of those around her, were directed to finding Bryce's father.

A lone man, dressed in black slacks and an open collared black shirt, incongruent next to the joggers and casual blue jeans, paced along the edge of the path. A tingle of recognition touched her. But, she couldn't place the slender, brown haired man. He walked to the corner, then returned, passing the parking lot and disappearing behind a stand of thick, flowering bushes. Carrie shook away the shred of dread. With all that was happening, it was no wonder she saw evil and horror everywhere.

Over the past days she'd come to know the men of Bryce's extended family and learned a little about each. She'd liked them all and looked forward to being with them under better circumstances.

But even with all the resources they seemed to have between them, they hadn't found Tommy. Nightshade had disappeared after that first day's argument with Derrik. Bryce was distracted.

Oh, she couldn't blame him for that, she was as well. Their relationship was just beginning and now there was no time for them to be together. Not until they found Tommy.

She had to do something. Despite the wishes of Bryce's family, she took a deep breath and made a quick decision. She tugged her cell phone from one pocket and a plain white business card from another. Hesitating, she stared at the phone, then back across the street into the park. The black clad man was still there. She acknowledged her decision and the possible consequences and flipped open the tiny phone.

B ryce stood in the doorway watching Carrie. She'd made a quick phone call, then sat staring at the phone for a long moment before tucking it back in her pocket. He was curious, but really didn't care. It seemed he didn't care about much— except finding Pop.

Bryce rubbed his thumbs over his tired, gritty eyes and yawned. He should sleep, but whenever he closed his eyes, possible scenarios blasted across his inner vision. Too many possibilities. He had to hold on to the hope that the mental calls Da received were really from Tommy, and not merely wishful thinking.

Fate must have it in for him. After the first time he'd seen her, it had taken so long to find Carrie, and now they had no chance to really get to know each other. When this was over, when Pop was home safely, he'd make it up to her. He didn't know how, but he would.

"Don't hover there, Bryce. Come sit with me."

The waver in her voice frightened him. After he sat, he

wrapped his arm about her shoulder and tilted his head to peer into her face. Tears wet her lower lashes.

"Sweetheart, what's wrong?"

"I just talked to Detective Corley."

She hadn't—had she?

Carrie turned to face him and reached up to clasp his hand to keep his arm in place. "Yes, I called him about Tommy. It's time for help, Bryce. You can't do this all yourself."

He sighed. "I know. I was going to talk to Da today about calling in the police. I'm out of ideas. What did the detective say?"

"He's coming over to talk to us. He also said that he wasn't surprised it took us so long to call. Seems that with all the media attention on police screw-ups, people are often reluctant to call in the authorities. I hope I did the right thing." Her voice and expression were forlorn and sad.

To console her, Bryce hugged her close. "You did. It was time. Maybe a fresh set of eyes will find something we missed."

Carrie snuggled against his side and rested her head on his shoulder. She fit perfectly there, her soft body pressed against his. He tightened his arm about her and rested his cheek against the top of her head. If only fate would give them a chance.

"Bryce, that's not all Detective Corley told me."

His heart plummeted to the pit of his stomach. "What else, sweetheart? You can tell me."

"Two nights ago there was another assault. A rape... like mine. Only this time he beat the girl badly. She was still able to give a description of sorts. Enough that they think it's the same guy."

"Carrie, are you okay?" She'd taken too many unending nightmares on her shoulders. It had to stop.

"Just scared. We've got to find Tommy and we've got to get this... this animal. Before any more women are attacked. So far, he's only assaulted dancers, but, who knows when that might change."

"We must have hope, Carrie. We have to have hope." Was he trying to convince her, or himself? Hope seemed in short supply.

The need to see his daughter and make sure she was safe grew

to a strong compulsion. Iain had passed loving messages back
and forth, but he needed the comfort his darlin' little girl could
unconsciously bring him. He couldn't risk bringing her back from
Faerie until Tommy was found and the kidnappers caught. He
wasn't sure he could survive if anything happened to his child. So
Bree had to stay safe.

However, he could take a few moments and cross through the
portal in Jaye's backyard to visit her. But that would mean leaving
Carrie alone. He was ultimately torn, and Bryce wished he had the
ability to be two places at once.

Soft, feminine laughter soothed through his mind. ::*Ye could
take her with ye. She misses yer daughter as well.*::

Bryce shook his head fiercely. He didn't need to start hearing
strange voices now.

"Bryce, what's wrong?"

"Just trying to make a decision."

"You're not angry with me, are you? Since we're not getting
anywhere, I thought it was time to call in the police."

"What? Oh, no, Carrie. I'm far from angry with you This is...
something else. I really miss Breanna."

"I know. Me, too. But, she needs to be somewhere that's safe,
just in case the kidnappers have more plans for your family. As
trusting as she is, she'd be an easy target."

Bryce sighed deeply. "I know. But, I hate to dampen her
enthusiasm, her joy. It's a fine line for a parent to walk, to keep a
child safe yet not frighten them with tales of boogey men."

"You do a good job."

"Do I?" Insecurity reared an ugly head. He felt hardly capable
to raise any child, let alone one who might be heir to Faerie
magick. "Sometimes I'm not so sure."

Carrie took his hand and held tightly to his fingers. He didn't
need words to know how she supported him and cared for his
feelings.

"This will work out, Bryce. We'll find Tommy and you'll be a
family again."

"No. We'll be a family." He drew her even closer and carefully kissed her. Her lips softened and she cupped the side of his face with her palm. The problems of the world faded as her mouth moved against his. There was nothing but Carrie.

Until hot, moist breath, followed by the swipe of a large, wet tongue jerked him from the pleasant sensations. He glared at the offending canine. "Noid! Stop that."

"We beg pardon, Bryce." The deep voice was filled with laughter, but when Bryce looked up, deep lines of worry filled the man's face.

Bryce rose and clasped the man's hand. "Stephen. I'm surprised to see you here." The man seldom left Faerie, so to see him in the human world brought Bryce to a new level of worry.

Stephen shrugged his wide shoulders. "Noid insisted. An' he is difficult to detour when something consumes his interest."

Bryce gave a tight chuckle and the huge, furry black dog sat and cocked his head to one side, the wide, dark brown eyes filled with intelligence. However, the lolling, wet tongue spoiled the image.

"Who might this beautiful young woman be?"

"Sorry, Stephen." Bryce held out his hand and tugged Carrie to her feet. "Stephen, this is Carrie Newcomb. Carrie, this is Stephen. Jaye's father."

Carrie squinted at the tall, dark haired man after he took Bryce slightly to one side to speak softly. Jaye's father? He looked barely older than Jaye. Granted, it seemed the members of this extended family didn't show their ages, but this man would have to be at least—seventy? The strong resemblance between the two men precluded the possibility Stephen was a stepfather. She should be so lucky as to have genes like those.

"Tell her, and soon. Can't you see the confusion?" Stephen's words were not meant for her to hear. Everyone had been counseling Bryce to tell her something. What could it be? She could think of nothing terrible enough to chase her away. Nope, she had a strong suspicion that Bryce was stuck with her. For the long run.

Making that admission to herself brought a wave of relief and a wash of delight through her. When they found Tommy, she'd tell Bryce the extent of her love and devotion to both him and Breanna.

Insistent, the dog nudged her hand so Carrie sat again and rubbed her hands over the large head, scratching behind the small ears. He gave a goofy doggy smile and drenched her hand with a soggy lick. "You're quite the fellow."

"That he is," Stephen said as the men returned to her side. "I believe he wishes to search the house."

"We've been over every inch time and time again." Carrie spread her hands to indicate that they'd found nothing.

"Aye, but not with Noid's keen senses. At least let him try." Bryce took her hand and grimaced at the remains of doggy affection, then wiped both of their hands against his denim covered thigh. "We sure don't have anything to lose if he tries. Come on, Noid, let's go inside."

Once inside the house, Noid trotted toward the office and pawed at the door until Bryce opened it for him. Carrie lifted her eyebrows at Stephen. "Smart fellow."

"Aye. Verra much so. At times 'tis best to let him have his way. He can be verra persuasive."

The humans stood in the doorway and watched as the large animal daintily sniffed his way around the room. He gave his shaggy head a shake and crowded out the doorway, lifted his head to sniff twice at the living room, then paced toward the back of the house. He spent little time in the dining area, concentrating instead on the kitchen and the back door.

Noid scratched at the door. When Stephen unlatched the screen, the dog nosed about the frame. Rising heavily on his hind legs, Noid pawed high on the frame and whined. He dropped to the floor with a loud thump then lunged upward again, whining. Bryce pushed the animal away and reached for something stuck between the doorframe and the wall.

"A business card?" Bryce stared down at the tan rectangle and turned it so he could read the printing. "It's from Miracle Hills."

Stephen held out his hand for the card. "What is this Miracle Hills?"

Carrie made a choking sound in the back of her throat. "It's a so-called church." Then her eyes opened wide. "My parents' church. Oh Lord, they couldn't have done this? Why?"

A loud knock at the front door turned the three humans toward the front of the house. Carrie giggled nervously. "That might be Detective Corley."

Carrie moved to answer the door and Bryce bent to rub the now calm and silent dog. "You're the best, Noid. We never would have found this clue without your help."

A heavy, shaggy tail thumped slowly against his ankle.

Detective Corley turned the card over and over in his hand. Bryce watched the movement from a detached distance. The man had good hands; he'd make a fine magician. Bryce shook his head. What the hell was he thinking?

"There's an ongoing investigation of the Miracle Hills ministry. Some strong allegations have been made against Templeton. Charges we've never been able to substantiate. This card is a definite link to his activities. You have no idea how or why it would be in your parents' home?"

"None."

"Unfortunately, we have been unable to locate Reverend Templeton's compound—a place where he conducts services and holds those he seeks to convert. Miracle Hills may have been created as a worthwhile ministry, but now it's a front for a cult that's suspected in a number of disappearances. Now, your father's included in that number."

"A cult?" Carrie leaned back. How could her parents have gotten involved in something like that? She stared at her tightly clasped her hands. Easily enough. From the first moment she could remember, her father had shoutedg tenants of right-eousness at her, seeking to wipe supposed sin from her soul. His zeal would make him an easy target for a charismatic leader. And her mother... was little more than a silent shadow, doing as her father commanded.

But why would they target Bryce's family?

She gave a small cry. Because of her, because of her involvement with Bryce. "I... I'm sorry."

Bryce covered her hand with his and gave a slight squeeze. "Sorry for what, sweetheart?"

"This is my fault, my parents—"

"Are being used like so many others, both now and in the past," Detective Corley stated in a tone that brooked no nonsense. "There is no fault to be laid, unless it's on Templeton." He tucked his small notebook away and tapped the tabletop twice. "Contact me if you discover anything else."

"Detective?" Carrie fought the old, inner voices of her parents as she struggled to make sense of this new twist in the horrific situation.

"Call me Rog." She supposed the first name basis and his easy smile were meant to calm her and inspire confidence. Carrie wrinkled her brow. Strangely, it did. "I can give you my parents' address. Maybe you can find something there."

"Thank you." He retrieved his notebook, turned a blank page toward her, and offered his pen.

T wice more his captors took him to the tiny, screened room, and twice more he sat through Reverend Templeton's tirades. Tommy suffered the bright lights, the noise and prayers, and the return to the silent darkness. David was not brought forward to perform healing, nor had he found his way to Tommy's prison. He feared for the boy, deathly afraid some harm had come to him because he had refused Templeton's orders.

Ensconced in darkness, Tommy sat on the cot trying to gauge the passage of time. But he couldn't stop the questions. How long had he been there? How long would it be before Derrik found him? Where was David?

The boy, the life and safety of the boy, meant more to him than he thought possible. Not since he first held Bryce, a tiny, deathly-ill baby, had he felt such protectiveness or discovered the

need to take care of another being. David said he had been abandoned as well. No longer. When Derrik came, David would leave
with them. "David, I promise you."

As if in answer to Tommy's softly spoken affirmation, the
silent slide of the wall panel alerted Tommy to David's presence.
The warmth of the small body that crawled next to him on the
cot, then curled close to his side erased a tiny fraction of his
worry. Then the sound of muffled sobbing and David's violent
shudders flared that worry to a high, bright peak.

"David, what's happened?"

"I... I couldn't get away to see you. I was scared they... beat
you... like me." He sniffed, wrapped his small arms around
Tommy's neck, and cried against his shoulder.

Tommy held the boy for long moments, softly stroking his
back and whispering meaningless words of comfort. Finally,
David pulled away and sat back, drawing long shaking breaths
between his sniffles. Pulling up one corner of the single sheet on
the cot, Tommy blindly searched for David's face.

A startled gasp of pain stopped him mid-wipe. Gently,
Tommy returned his fingers to David's face. He dried the damp
skin with his fingertips, pausing at the boy's groan when his hand
touched the side of his jaw. He let his hands rest gently on David's
thin shoulders. "I'm sorry, David. What happened?"

The boy's shrug lifted his hands. "Nothing new. He had one of
the guards punish me for disobeying orders. But... but I couldn't
pretend like he wanted me to."

"Pretend?" Tommy already had a good idea how Templeton
used David, but wanted the boy's confirmation.

"Yeah. He gets people to pretend to be sick or hurt. I touch
them and see the sin that makes them sick. He's taught me lots of
tricks that I use to heal the people."

"How long has he been making you do this?"

Another shrug. "Don't know. Maybe a couple years."

"Does he always have you punished if you don't obey?"
Tommy cupped his palm against David's damp cheek.

David nodded. "And sometimes even when I don't do it good enough."

"Oh, David. I'm so sorry."

"Ain't nothing you can do about it."

"Where else are you hurt?"

"I'm not hurt so bad."

"Uh huh. Show me."

David took Tommy's hand and lightly pressed it to his jaw, then moved the hand to his opposite temple, his upper arm, his side, one thigh, then turned slightly to draw Tommy's hand to his back.

"Oh, my God."

"They don't usually hurt my face, only places that don't show during the services. But I talked back. I told the guards I didn't like the words they called you."

Tommy didn't have to guess what kinds of names the guards used. He'd heard them his entire life and had learned to ignore the ignorant. Now, a young boy, a child, had borne the brunt of intolerance in his name. Tears burned his eyes. "Do you understand those words... what they mean?"

"Kinda. Will you tell me so I know for sure?" David lay his cheek against Tommy's upper arm.

"Those people hate me because instead of being in love with a woman, I'm in love with a man." Waiting for David to pull away from him, Tommy paused. Instead, the child snuggled closer to his side.

"That's what I thought. So? Why does that make people hate you?"

"I wish I knew the answer to that. The man I love, Derrik, he and I have been together longer than a lot of couples. We're a real family. We have a son."

"How'd you do that?"

Tommy chuckled. "We adopted him. He was abandoned when only a few days old. Once I held him in my arms, I knew Bryce was meant to be our child. He's a man now, and has a daughter of his own. I'm a grandpa."

"He's lucky. I wish I was like him. I wish... I wish you'd found me, instead of Reverend Templeton. I wish you were my dad."

Tommy's arms tightened convulsively around David to hold him and he cried out his pain and sorrow.

Tears drenched Tommy's face as well.

TWENTY-FIVE

With a gentle, persuasive shove in the center of his back from Stephen, Bryce approached Carrie. "Uh, Stephen will stay here until Da gets back and let him know what's going on. Would you like to visit Bree with me?"

A true smile brightened her face and dimmed some of the stress in her eyes. "I'd love that."

He took her hand. "I need to tell you something first. Let's go out to the deck. Then, if you still want to go..."

"Why wouldn't I? What's so terrible that you're afraid to tell me?"

Although he hated to admit it, he was afraid. Afraid she'd run from his craziness. Afraid she'd never look back. Afraid he'd never see her again. "Not terrible, but maybe difficult to believe."

After encouraging her to sit in a padded lounge chair, Bryce sat sideways in the lounger next to her and held her hand, playing with her fingers, trying to form the words he needed to say.

Carrie sighed. "I know how hard it can be to trust someone with a secret. You can't imagine how difficult it was tell you about the return of those memories, to tell you about the assault. I didn't need to be so scared. You accepted what happened and helped me. That's how I want it to be for you. I can't imagine anything to make me turn from you. I love you, Bryce. I do."

While numerous variations of what he had to say raced through his mind, Bryce decided the direct approach would be best. He captured Carrie's gaze and held it with his own. He expelled a long, slow breath. "I am human."

"Okay...?"

Bryce swallowed heavily. "Da is Faerie."

Carrie snatched her hand back, cradled her palm against her stomach, and glared at him. "I know your folks are gay, there's no reason to use such a demeaning word."

He held up both hands in denial. "No, no. That's not what I mean. Let me try again." At Carrie's dubious nod, he swallowed again. "Let me start this way. On this planet there are parallel worlds."

Heavy doubt filled her expression. Carrie cocked her head to one side and squinted at him. "Go on."

"One of these worlds is the Faerie Otherworld. The people there are like us, only magical. There is also a Fairy world that encompasses the tiny winged beings we usually think of in children's stories. Korin is from that world."

He paused to let her assimilate the extensive amount of information carried in so few sentences. When the wrinkle in her forehead eased and she nodded, he continued. "I really was found in a chemical toilet by Lara when she was four years old. She has the ability to form portals, not only between the worlds, but between times. Da could never discover what time or place I came from. Lara and Iain live in Faerie, in the Otherworld, and that's where Breanna is now. I... I would like to take you there."

There was a long, unbearably long pause as she studied him. "Are you magic?"

The question surprised him. He shook his head. "No, much to my constant dismay. That's why I studied human magic, to have some talent. Pop is human, too, by the way. As is Stephen."

"How old is Stephen? He doesn't look old enough to be Jaye's dad."

This might be even harder for her to comprehend and accept. "Stephen, and Noid, found a way to cross into Faerie where he met Kelene. They fell in love and he stayed. If... how do I explain this? He comes from northern Scotland in the eight hundreds. Living in Faerie slows the aging process."

Carrie glanced back at the house. "Obviously." Her lower lip was red from the deep imprint of her teeth. "How... how old are you really?"

A grin stretched his lips. "I really am twenty-six. I haven't yet spent enough time in Faerie for the process to really affect me. Pop spends a great deal of time there with Jaye, they're both in their fifties."

"That's hard to believe. And here I thought it was just good genes."

He had to know. "Carrie, do you believe me? Can you believe what I'm telling you?"

The moments of silence were deafening and Bryce had to force himself to breathe. Carrie stared into the air over one of his shoulders, her hands folded in her lap. He ached to touch her, to enfold her in his arms and never, ever let her go. But, he understood it had to be her decision whether to believe him or not. *Please, Carrie. Please believe me.*

::*Dinna worry.*:: The unusual feminine voice flowed through his head. ::*Visit yer daughter. Show Carrie the Faerie world through yer eyes. She believes, even is she dinna believe she does.*::

Bryce blinked and shook his head. Where was this voice coming from?

Carrie touched his knee. "Did you hear that? Did you hear Lottie?"

"I... I heard a voice." It was difficult to say aloud, but the reward of her smile was worth the admission.

"Lottie told me she would talk to you. She said she knows Faerie, and I have nothing to be afraid of there. That, in my heart, I really do believe. But, in my head, I'm not so sure."

"Come with me. Now. Let me show you the Otherworld, some of my favorite places. Please."

"How do... do we get there?"

"There's a permanent portal to Faerie in Jaye's backyard." He rose and held out his hand to her. Whether she took the offered hand or not would tell him much.

Carrie took his hand without hesitation and when she rose, she pressed close and kissed him. "Show me."

T he passage through the portal surprised Carrie. She'd thought there would be some flash of magic, some strange electric feelings. When Bryce first showed her the portal, all she saw was a wooden arbor covered with climbing roses. Yet, as she stared through the arch, the inner scene changed. First, as though she were looking through water, then clear. There was another world there, a forest of cool greens dappled with spots of sparkling sunlight. She clasped her hands before her breasts and sighed.

"I've dreamed of this place."

Bryce wrapped his arm about her shoulders. "Still willing to take these steps into Faerie? Sweetheart, are you sure?"

"I'm sure." She turned a smile to him. "Let's go see Breanna."

Returning the smile, Bryce led her forward. There was no odd tingling, no strangeness, nothing but the new, bright landscape to tell her she'd moved from one world into another. She filled her lungs with a deep breath of clean, unpolluted air. The colors were more vibrant and sweet smells rose from the profusion of flowers at her feet.

"Oh, Bryce, this is wonderful. Even better than my dreams."

"Lara's cabin is this way." Bryce pointed to a clear, well used path then bent to snap a light purple flower from its stem. He twirled the blossom in his fingers and the flower disappeared. Carrie gasped when he smoothed the hair behind her ear and tucked the flower there. "This is one of my favorite blossoms. I've never been able to get the plant to grow in the human world."

Gently touching the flower released a fragrance to wash over her, calming the churning of her stomach. "It's beautiful."

"More so when the bloom is part of you."

Slapping his arm playfully, Carrie glanced up at Bryce from under her lashes. "Such things you say. Let's visit Bree first, then you can show me around. I don't suppose we should spend too much time here." The joy left her heart for a moment. "Just in case."

"Time isn't an issue, sweetheart. Not now, not here."

She twirled in a slow circle, trying to capture each scene in her memory. If this were a dream, she hoped it would never end. Something about this place called to a hidden spot, deep inside her. A place filled by the peace she'd searched for all her life. A place she never wanted to be without again. Lottie's soft laughter whispered through her mind. The silent thank you she sent to her imaginary friend and protector received a wave of love in return. This was where she belonged. The joy was so great, she had to tell him.

"I believe in all this, Bryce. This isn't a dream or some strange conjuring of my imagination. Lottie was right, I think I've believed and been looking for a place like this all my life. A place like this—with you."

Bryce gathered her in his arms but before he kissed her, he stared into her face. She held his gaze, trying to put all her love and acceptance into her expression. She must have succeeded, for he lowered his lips to hers with a low groan.

His kiss was gentle and so sensuous she thought her legs would no longer hold her upright. He whispered another of those strange words near her ear and heat flowed through her. Reluctantly, she inched away from his body. "Is that a Faerie word?"

A ruddy blush covered the fair skin of Bryce's face. "Yes. One I learned from Breanna's mother."

"She was Faerie?" Bryce nodded.

"So Bree is half? Does she have any magic?"

"Although I suspect she has, we don't know for sure. I'm not sure what I'll do when she does exhibit a talent. Lara was her age when she started forming the portals through time."

"Well, we'll just have to keep an eye on her, won't we?"

"We? Carrie, sweetheart, what are you saying?"

"I... I'm not sure." But, she was. She wanted the whole shebang with Bryce. Love, marriage, family. And a strange Faerie Otherworld to explore. "I love you."

"You're not sure you love me?" He smiled tenderly as if he understood her confusion.

"Oh, no. I'm sure of that. I love you. Let's go see Bree."

Bryce chuckled, kissed the tip of her nose, and slid his hands up and down her arms. "And I'm sure of my love for you, Carrie. There is nothing more sure in my life." Taking her hand he stepped toward the path.

Bree saw them coming and ran screeching with joy from the small, sturdy cabin in a large clearing. Two other children followed her, a dark haired girl and a blond boy, neither much older than Bree. While Bree slammed into Bryce's open arms, the others stood back and stared at Carrie. The girl's expression was frank and openly assessing, the boy's solemn and studious. "Carrie, these are Belle and Castin, Lara and Iain's twins." Holding Bree tight in his arms, Bryce rose. "Kids, this is Carrie."

"My new mommy like I told you," Bree chimed in.

Belle smiled and stepped forward to take Carrie's hand. "Then you're Auntie Carrie. Come on, Castin," she said to her brother. "Take Auntie Carrie's hand. We'll show Momma an' Da who we found."

Led away by the twins' insistent tugging on her hands Carrie glanced back over her shoulder, but Bryce only shrugged and grinned broadly. Breanna waved, then turned her attention to kissing her father.

The children continued to pull on her hands until she stepped onto the long porch and paused before a bright red door. The door opened and a woman with curls as golden as Bryce's spilling wildly over her shoulder gave her a wide smile. "You must be Carrie."

"How did you know?"

"I'm Lara. Iain's spoken of you. And, I was at the N B Tween the night you danced and Bryce fell in love with you."

"Oh, but he didn't—"

"Oh, but he did." Lara's contagious laugh filled the clearing. "Why else would he have looked in every club, haunted every bar all those weeks looking for you. Come on in, let's chat."

"Not this time, Lara." Bryce moved beside her and Bree held out her arms to be held. The twins loosed her hands so Carrie took Bree and willingly suffered the onslaught of little girl kisses.

Bryce continued, "I don't want to be away long, but I've just told Carrie about the Otherworld and want to show her some of my favorite spots. Um, when we get back, could you form a portal that will return us not too long after we left? Just in case some-thing happens."

"Of course I will." Lara glanced at Carrie. "You know, Bryce is like a brother to me and Jaysson. Tommy's our uncle. I wish..."

"Me, too." Carrie sighed. Here she was enjoying time with Bryce, time away from the horror of Tommy's disappearance. The rise of guilt drew a line of tension across her back and she stiffened.

"Don't feel guilty." Lara touched Carrie's arm. "I know it's natural to feel that way, but try to enjoy your time here." At Carrie's surprise, she chuckled. "I'm usually pretty good at reading people. No magic in that, Carrie. Now, you two run along and have fun. Breanna's fine here with Belle and Castin, so there's nothing for you to worry about in that respect."

She took Bree from Carrie's arms and set the child on the floor. "Your Da and Carrie will be back in a little bit, okay?"

"Da and Mommy, you mean, Auntie Lara."

"As you say, sweetie." Lara faced Bryce and lifted her eyebrows. "Don't worry about a thing here, or in the mortal world. Enjoy yourselves. Your time is past due and you deserve these moments. Both of you."

Bryce whispered in Carrie's ear. "Let me show you your dreams, sweetheart."

"So, does Faerie live up to your dreams?"

They had ambled slowly along a myriad of pathways as Bryce showed her the Otherworld. While part of the Otherworld was mostly forests and rocky crags, he explained that other clans lived in environments as varied as those in the mortal world. Carrie was determined to see it all.

The rocky structure of the Queen's home held her awe for many minutes. Stones sparkled with crystals and the striation of many types of rocks made up the true fairy tale castle. Bryce promised her the inside was even more spectacular, and that he would take her there her another day. She would be introduced to the Queen.

"Sweetheart? I asked if Faerie measured up to your dreams." Bryce stopped and stood before her, a crooked grin on his face. "But I see you're mesmerized by everything."

"Oh, no, not so mesmerized as much as—oh, I don't know. It's like I know this place. When I said dreams, maybe they weren't real dreams. Lottie used to show me places. Places like this. Especially when I was terribly put upon by my parents. I always thought she made up the places. Now, I think she knows this Faerie Otherworld as well as you do."

"I'm glad you feel comfortable. Bree and I often visit here with friends and relatives."

"I wish... that I could, too."

Bryce's smile faltered for a moment then returned. "Carrie, I have one more spot to show you before we go back to real life. This is my favorite spot, my place in Faerie. I've never brought anyone here before. I've been waiting for the right person to share my glen with."

"And you want to share it with me?"

He pulled her tight against him and cupped the back of her head in his palm. "Don't you realize yet I want to share everything with you? All my life, my joys and sorrows, my love."

Carrie's eyes drifted closed and she waited for his kiss. Although he was close and the warmth of his breath brushed over her cheek, there was no meeting of their mouths. Carrie bit her lower lip and opened her eyes.

The love—and desire—shining in his eyes curled a responding need through her body. She pressed closer, but he stepped back. She moved toward him. He stepped back.

"Bryce."

"Follow me." He waggled his index finger at her and continued walking backwards.

This playful side of him was new, and she liked it. A lot. Fate hadn't given them much chance to be playful, not with her memories and Tommy's disappearance. But here, where the air itself was light, friendly and playful, here she could behave the way she'd long wanted to be, act the way that felt good to her. She could love Bryce with no limitations.

"Okay, sir. I'm gonna get you." Stretching out her hands, she quickened her pace. He matched her speed, even going backwards, and stayed just out of reach.

Joy surrounded them and they laughed together. Happiness caressed her and lightened the load of worry from her heart and soul. This was a magical place and she could imagine nothing better.

Or so she thought until they stepped from under the overhang of heavy tree branches into a narrow glade.

Bryce sidestepped to let her see the full panorama of his special place and Carrie gave a cry of delight. He turned to face the glade and grinned with satisfaction. With life's recent pitfalls, it had been some time since he'd visited and part of him had forgotten the peace and comfort to be found amongst the trees and flowers.

Carrie inched beside him and took his hand. "Got ya," she whispered. "Oh my, Bryce. This is amazing. You did this?"

"Yep, just me and Faerie nature. Many of these plants don't thrive at home, so I've gathered them here to enjoy. Come with me to the bower."

"Bower? Sounds..."

"It is. Very special." He hoped that it would become even more special for him. For them.

They walked hand in hand through ankle high grasses and patches of slightly taller, brightly colored flowers. Tiny dragon-flies danced around them, the hum of their rapidly beating wings a soft counterpart to the birdsong from the surrounding trees. Sunlight warmed their skin. Carrie stopped to examine many of the blooms, inhaling each fragrance and smiling at him. It was that smile, a smile only for him, one that, if he hadn't already been captivated by her, would capture him completely

From each plant Carrie touched, Bryce took a single bloom. As they crossed the glade, he wove them together. He stopped her before a natural arch made of branches bound together in a subtle Celtic weave. Carrie sighed and reached out to touch the branches.

He let her stroke the wood he'd spent years carefully bending and coaxing into the design. Each season had increased the complexity of his creation and now, with her next to it, the bower stood complete.

Joining his fingers to hers, he pulled her hand toward him. "For you," he said with a smile and slipped the bracelet of flowers over her hand.

In a smooth movement, he slipped her hand to the back of his neck and, as he had longed to do since entering the glade, he kissed her.

When Carrie's lips softened beneath his, he touched his tongue to the delectable fullness. With a soft sigh, she granted him entrance and danced her tongue along his. Her other hand wrapped around his waist and she crushed herself against him. The cushioned press of her breasts against his chest, the mindless shifting of her hips centered longing low in his body. He returned the movement and felt her response in the way her fingers tangled in his hair.

Breathless, he tore his lips from Carrie's and gazed into her eyes. Dark with desire and heavy lidded, her expression told him much. He only need ask. "Will you, sweetheart? Will you enter the bower with me?"

A bright sparkle touched her eyes. "I thought you'd never ask."

Barely allowing a breath of air to come between them, Bryce backed her into the cool shadows and helped her to sit on a thick cushion of fragrant grass. The sounds of the glen faded until Bryce was sure she could hear the fierce beating of his heart. Delighted, she glanced around, and brushed her hand over the natural carpet, giggling as the sprinkling of tiny flowers tickled her palm.

Bryce lifted her hand and kissed the palm, turning her giggles to soft kitten-like sounds of pleasure. He moved the caress to her inner wrist, nudging the flowers aside with his nose. A trail of kisses toward her elbow made her gasp and her skin quivered against his lips.

"I love you, Carrie. I will always love you." Bryce cupped her face between his palms. "Carrie, my sweet one, will you make my life complete by marrying me?"

"M... marry you?"

Carrie didn't believe—no, she couldn't believe—the words she'd heard. It was easier to believe in the Faerie Otherworld than it was to believe Bryce wanted to marry her. To tie himself to her —forever. No, she must have heard her own wishes in his words.

"In truth, sweetheart. I want you to be my wife, my partner, my lover, my friend. Bree already calls you mommy."

"You want me to be her mother?" That might make more sense if not for her background.

Bryce made her look into his eyes. He ran his thumbs over her lips and she ached to capture one in her mouth. No, that would be a poor substitute for his kisses and the strange words he mumbled against her skin.

"Yes. But, did you understand me, Carrie? Even more than that, I want you for me."

"Why?"

"Carrie, listen to me. I want you. I love you. I need you. Share my life, be my life."

"What if... I do it wrong?" She voiced her deepest fear then caught at her lower lip with her teeth and tried to turn her face from him.

Gentle pressure from his palms held her in place. Bryce shook his head slowly from side to side. "Oh, sweet darlin'. How could you think that? Never wrong, Carrie, never wrong. I'll ask once more. Will you marry me?"

The strange light in his eyes made her believe his words. This was her chance, and if she let the moment slip by, she was a fool. The biggest fool in any world. She lowered her gaze. "Yes."

"Yes?"

Carrie let Bryce angle her face until she gazed into a love so powerful she knew she had given the correct answer. The only answer. "Yes," she repeated.

Bryce's mouth was close to hers, the soft tickling of his lips as he spoke made her lips tingle. She tingled everywhere.

"I created this bower for this moment. I always knew I'd bring the woman I loved here. There's been no one else who means what you do to me. No other has seen this place."

Carrie tugged on a lock of white-blond hair behind one of Bryce's ears. "Stop talking romance and kiss me. No, make love to me."

With a groan that passed from his body into hers, Bryce eased her back on the fresh, dark green grass and lowered himself next to her. "Are you sure?"

"Didn't I just say no talking? I'm sure Bryce. As sure as my love for you has brought me here, here to you. Love me, please?"

Carrie didn't know what to expect, but this wasn't quite what she'd had in mind. Instead of kissing or touching her, Bryce turned her to face away from him and molded his body to her back. Spooned together, he wrapped one arm over her side and rested his palm just below her ribcage. Then he remained still, except for the restless movement of his thumb.

He wanted her, she could tell that from the hard presence of his groin against her bottom. But when she tried to wiggle against him, he moved his hand to her hip.

"Just let me hold you for a while."

The strange plea in his words intrigued her, so she nodded silently and pressed back, trying to get even closer. With a slow sweep of sensation, he moved his hand, this time to cover her stomach. The stroking of his thumb continued. His breath flowed evenly past her ear.

The soft insect sounds, the gentle breeze flowing through the bower, the heady scent of grasses and flowers, combined with her recent sleepless nights should have sent her quickly to sleep. While she couldn't deny the comfort and belonging of the moment, she felt strung as tightly as a violin string. The denied passion curled deep in her body threatened to explode within her. A tiny moan of frustration vibrated behind her clenched lips.

The rumble of Bryce's chuckle quivered against her and she shuddered in response. He lifted his head and touched the tip of his tongue to a sensitive spot just below her ear. He followed the damp caress with a whispered word.

"Bryce," she moaned.

He eased one leg over her hip and rose over her as he turned her to her back. Straddling her thighs, he braced his hands on the ground to lean forward. Nudging her cheek with his, he encouraged her to turn her face to one side. Then he licked a spot beneath her other ear and whispered again.

At her even louder moan he sat back and smiled. When he made to lean forward again, Carrie planted her hands in the center of his chest and shook her head. "I don't need those words, Bryce. I don't need anything but you. You seduce me, not the words."

A tiny frown marred his delightful mouth.

"No, Bryce. Not the words... this time. You're the only magic I need."

The confusion faded from his eyes, replaced by a deep, deep green, and he smiled. Carrie returned the smile, then stroked her palms down his chest and over the jerking muscles in his abdomen. He looked down, watching her hands move over his chest and linger at the row of buttons closing the front of his shirt. Silent, he held his breath. She fumbled with the tiny, white disks. When his shirt was open, she pressed her palms against his skin. The air burst from his lungs in a delighted gasp.

Carrie took her time exploring his chest and belly. Breaths short and heaving, he held himself still when she traced a line down the center of his chest, curled her touch around his navel, then rested her fingers at the waist of his jeans.

"My... turn," he gasped.

She had no buttons, but the hem of her tee shirt was loose, so Bryce slipped his hands under the soft material to find even softer skin. Inching his hands upward, he smoothed his palms over her belly, down her sides, and dipped his fingertips lightly into her navel. Her back arched and she clutched his waist in mute encouragement. Willing, he obliged and covered her breasts with his palms. Mute no longer, Carrie moaned.

"Carrie, sweetheart, lift your arms." Bryce's voice was ragged and harsh.

Smiling, she did as he asked and he pulled the shirt over her head, tossing it to one side. With her arms still lifted, her breasts were plump temptations he didn't try to resist. Planting wet, openmouthed kisses over the fullness, Bryce moved over her. She buried her fingers in his hair to hold him in place. The words of Faerie seduction hovered in his mind but her body responded without his speaking. He closed his lips around one nipple and tugged. Carrie whimpered. The sounds of her pleasure chased the flowing syllables from his mind. All there was... was Carrie.

Forcing the material off his shoulders, Carrie pushed at his shirt. Unwilling to leave his study of her breasts, Bryce angled and shifted, lifting his arms one at a time until the shirt was gone. She smoothed her hands across his back, around his sides, then to the front of his jeans where she pressed her palm over the bulge. Bryce jerked and bit back a groan.

"That's got to be painful." Carrie grinned wickedly. "Don't you think...?" She stroked her fingers over the worn denim and down the metal zipper. Shuddering, Bryce leaned back.

"I'm thinking..." he said as he batted her wandering hands away and reached for the button, "...perhaps you should join me."

"Join?" Carrie wiggled and Bryce rose to his knees. "Joining sounds like just what I had in mind." She unfastened her own jeans, slipped out of them and her underwear before Bryce had unzipped his. "What's taking you so long?"

Her breathless laughter spurred him to greater speed, although lowering his shorts over his insistent body slowed his impatient progress. By the time he tossed the jeans to the pile of clothing, Carrie had lain back on the grass, her arms lifted to him. Her smile of welcome tightened the intensity of desire and Bryce had to pause, taking deep breaths, before lowering himself beside her warm, responsive body. He didn't think he could wait much longer. Hell, he couldn't even think.

Carrie's breaths, heavy yet languid, matched Bryce's, and when he stretched beside her, she half turned to face him. His face was set in tense lines, the desire low and heavy in his body. She knew how he felt. She didn't want to wait and didn't need anything else to make her ready for his love and the feel of his body. Bold, and without preamble, she wrapped her fingers around his erection.

"I don't want to wait. I'm ready now." She stroked him and sighed.

His eyes closed and he swallowed heavily. "Carrie... I..."

"I love you, too. Bryce, don't say any more." Carrie lifted her shoulders and pressed her mouth to his. His lips moved with hers and he accepted the gift of her tongue, chasing it back into the heat of her mouth. Slowly, ever so slowly, Carrie eased to her back, drawing him with her. She continued to stroke him and Bryce matched her stokes, moving ever lower until he touched his fingers to her wetness.

Some dark part of her mind hinted that she was too bold, too wanton, too easy. She was a whore. Before the thoughts coalesced to an understandable form, a bright flash, like the slash of a sword cut through the darkness. The dark shattered to brilliant green sparkles as she cried out with pleasure. The words were gone, leaving only the deep green of Bryce's desire hooded eyes.

The tingle of sparkles washed over her as Bryce settled between her thighs. His mouth took bold possession of hers and he took her body, sharing the strength of his passion. Unable to hold back her cries of powerful delight, Carrie released her pleasure. Bryce groaned with her. Groaned again when she wrapped her legs around his hips.

Deeper, she drew him deeper. Trying to restrain the frantic need, Bryce withdrew slowly and entered her just as slowly. Carrie gasped at each thrust, her eyes closed, her face tight with pleasure's tension. He watched her, angled his body and thrust again. She hid nothing from him, showed him every emotion, and when her lids lifted heavily, her love for him burned like a bright shooting star.

The tight pressure of her legs and the way her nails dug into his shoulders increased his tempo, his desire, his mindless need for her. Capturing her cries with his kisses, cradling her head in his palms, Bryce found heaven.

Her inner muscles tightened around him, and she moved her legs to plant her feet against the ground. She pressed her hips up to his and tossed her head from side to side. Bryce inched one hand from her head, treasuring the feel of her damp skin, until he passed the palm over one of her distended nipples. She arched into his hand, so he lingered, tugging on the turgid peak as he thrust. Tighter. Her body clutched him. Hot, wet friction pulled him to the center of their joining.

Carrie's eyes shot open and she gave a wild cry. Her eyelids drifted closed and she shuddered. He chased the shudders across her skin with his hands and with the frenzied thrusting of his body.

She'd exploded and shattered. Little bits of her had to be scattered about the bower. But no, she was still whole, still writhing against Bryce, still accepting the gift of his body. She basked in the glow of her aftermath and grew more sensitized to every nuance of Bryce's movement and the feel of every inch of him against her, inside her. She met his increasing thrusts, gasped at the friction, moaned at the slide of skin against skin. Oh, Lord —again!

Shouting his release, Bryce joined her cry.

After a long moment, he leaned his sweaty forehead against hers and kissed her.

"I love you," they whispered in unison.

"We've been gone a long time, Bryce. I hope they didn't need us for anything."

"Don't worry, sweetheart." The endearment flowed through her, renewing the passion she thought sated. Ah, if he could do this with just one word—and not even a magical word—she'd be his willing captive forever.

"...at Lara's."

"What?"

With a knowing grin, Bryce repeated himself. "Remember how I asked Lara to create a portal for us when we returned? And that she is able to open portals in time? We'll be able to return home not that long after we left. So, if any new information has surfaced, we'll be there."

"Good. I'd hate to be..."

"Hate to be what?" Bryce stroked his hand down her arm, grinned wickedly, and cupped her breast. The stroking continued, this time his thumb stroked over her nipple, bringing the bit of flesh to delightful attention.

Heat filled her face. "Hate to enjoy myself so much, and not worry about what's happening to anyone else, when your father may be in danger."

His hand dropped away, the sharp inhalation and low groan from Bryce made her sorry she had spoiled the sensual aura still surrounding them. Although she would gladly linger longer in this new world, the problems waiting in her real world were far more important than the bliss she'd discovered with Bryce.

She was going to marry him. While it was true she hadn't known him that long, it was long enough to know. And whether that was some special kind of magic—Faerie or just Bryce himself —she didn't know. And didn't care. She was, for the first time in her life, truly and ultimately happy.

Once back at Lara's cabin, they spent a few precious moments with Bree, who excitedly showed them where Iain was going to keep the ponies. Bryce gave Carrie a look over Bree's head that melted her heart. A look of parental love, now a shared love between both parents. A love spilling over to surround the child.

It was that love that pulled them back through the time portal Lara created. Love for Tommy and Derrik.

A split second after they entered Jaye's backyard, the tiny phone in her pocket chimed. She had to let loose of Bryce's hand to retrieve the noisy rectangle and she frowned at it before she flipped open the mouthpiece and spoke.

"Yes?"

"About time. I've been calling both you and Bryce."

"Oh. Nightshade, has something happened?"

"I have some information for Bryce, honey. Is he there with you?"

"Yes. We just got back from visiting Breanna."

Nightshade gave a low chuckle "So, he finally told you."

"Told me?" Carrie lifted her eyebrows, looked askance at Bryce and held the phone away from her ear. "Does everybody know about Faerie except me?"

A faint red covered Bryce's cheeks and he shrugged. "Can I talk to him?"

Carrie kissed his cheek and pressed the phone into his hand. "It's okay—I know now. The best parts."

Bryce leaned toward her, wanting to forget the phone pressed between their palms, wanting to forget the problems, to remember only the feel of her in his arms, of her surrounding him. But Carrie lifted one hand to give him a gentle shove in the center of his chest. "Talk to Nightshade."

When he lifted the phone to his ear, the sounds of Nightshade ranting and shouting brought a fresh rise of worry. "Nightshade, whoa, what's going on?"

At the sound of Bryce's voice, the tirade stopped abruptly. "Bryce. I think I've found where Tommy's being held. But, I don't want to tell Derrik until I'm sure. The fool'd go rushing in without thought. God, I wish there was a man who loved me so powerfully."

Pop had been found? Bryce clutched the phone so hard he was afraid he would crack the plastic casing. His hand shook. A look of terrified worry on her face, Carrie held tightly to his arm. To comfort her, Bryce touched her cheek. "Nightshade thinks he's found Pop."

Carrie jerked back. "Oh. Where?"

Bryce shook his head and turned his attention back to the phone. "Where?"

"Honey, I can't tell you that."

"Nightshade," Bryce drew the name out with a low undercurrent of warning.

"Come with me tonight."

"But Da—"

"We'll let him know when we find Tommy. You know he'd run off half-cocked." A chuckle rumbled through the phone. "And your Pop wouldn't like that at all."

Bryce couldn't help it. He grinned. Nightshade was incorrigible. "I'll meet you. When and where?"

Nightshade paused and cleared his throat. "Ready for a covert operation, honey?"

"Nightshade." This time the warning was lighter, the man would pass on the information only when he was ready.

"I'll pick you up at dusk. We'll go in under full darkness. Wear black."

"Black?"

"Honey, haven't you ever watched those action adventure movies with those brawny men?" Bryce gave a wry snort as he pictured Nightshade's delicate shiver of delight. "Really, Bryce. We need to be as invisible as possible. There might be guards."

Guards? Where was Pop? "Okay, if you say so."

"Be at your house so the big D doesn't get wind of the operation. Oh, and honey?"

"Yeah."

"Congratulations."

"For...?"

"Carrie. At dusk, darling." The line went dead.

Bryce slowly lowered the phone and clicked the mouthpiece closed. Carrie's fingers trembled with rhythmic spasms around his arm. He handed her the phone and enfolded her in a tight embrace. She was his lifeline, a steady anchor in the drama unfolding around them.

"We need to check in with Stephen and Da. Then, unless they need something, I need to get to my house and get ready for tonight."

"What's tonight?"

Bryce took his time formulating an answer. Carrie deserved to know the truth, but he still hesitated. Something in Nightshade's tone gave him a bad feeling. Covert operation?

Bryce closed his eyes, he thought he could handle a dangerous situation to save Pop, but could Nightshade? The flamboyant man was far from the macho adventurers he always talked about.

"Nightshade's found Pop, and we're going there tonight to get him out. He doesn't want Da to know just in case he's wrong. Da would do something crazy and probably endanger Pop even more."

"Nightshade's doing something like that? Something possibly dangerous?" Carrie turned away and threw her hands into the air. "What's he thinking? What are you thinking? You can't do something like that—something so dangerous. We've got to call Detective Corley."

"No." Bryce took her shoulder in a firm grip. "Let me do this first, then if nothing pans out, we've lost nothing but a little time. I'll take Nightshade to Rog myself."

"I don't want you, or Nightshade, in any danger. It's bad enough we don't know what Tommy's going through, what's being done to him."

Bryce took a shaking breath. "I know, sweetheart. I know I'm not hero material, but I've got to do something." He shook his head and laughed, "Neither is Nightshade. But neither of us can simply sit and wait. I... I'm getting frantic, Carrie. This afternoon I was able to forget all this for a little while. A little, glorious while."

As he hoped, the lines of her face softened in sensual memory and she leaned closer. "A glorious while." Carrie's lips firmed to a flat, determined line. "Tell me what I need to do. Don't tell me to just sit and wait. I'll go crazy worrying."

"We'll talk while I get ready. First—"

The gentle touch of her lips against his gave him courage. He's never thought of himself as an action hero type, that was more Jaysson's personality. For himself, he'd need all the courage he could find. He moved his mouth over hers, neither taking possession of the kiss nor giving Carrie total control.

"I thought I heard someone out here." Laughter followed Stephen's bland statement. Although Carrie gave a momentary start and attempted to pull away, Bryce took his time ending the kiss. His family was openly affectionate—and she would have to grow accustomed to it.

She gave him a brief, loving smile when he finally arched back. She would.

"I see the trip to Faerie was... pleasurable."

Bruce tucked Carrie close to his side and tightened his arm about her waist.

"Aye, you don't need to say more. I'm happy for you. Derrik has returned, but there is no news."

"How did he take the news that we contacted the police?"

"He seems resigned to it. And he feels helpless, for Jaye willna let him resume leadership of the Alastriona. All we can do is wait."

Bryce cleared his throat. "Do you think he'll be okay? I've neglected things at home, and at work, and I should spend a little time—"

"Aye, your Da understands that. Jaye and Allyn will be with him this eve. Go talk to him, then be on your way. With the little phones, you'll be only moments away. He doesna expect you to put life on hold."

"But it is, Stephen. It is."

Stephen clasped Bryce's shoulder and held tightly for a moment. A long look passed between the two men. One of Stephen's eyebrows lifted. "Be careful. Dinna make your Da worry about you as well."

Then Stephen turned to Carrie and kissed her cheek. "I'm glad you liked my Faerie world. I shall expect to see you there oft now." Calling to the huge black dog investigating a flower garden, Stephen strode toward the portal in Jaye's backyard.

After he disappeared through the arbor, Bryce led Carrie into the house. Derrik slouched in his chair, Jaye and Allyn shared the couch.

"Da?"

"Ah, Bryce. I am glad ye have returned. Where have ye been?" Derrik looked up, glanced at Carrie's face, then focused his gaze on the bruised flowers encircling her wrist. "So, ye finally told her."

"Aye, Da."

"'Tis time, son. 'Tis time." He rose in a fluid motion, planted both hands on Carrie's shoulders, and kissed her cheek. "'Tis happy this makes me."

When he made to turn away Carrie touched his shoulder to hold his attention. Dark smudges under his eyes marred his fair skin. His blue eyes were dull and lifeless. "Thank you."

Solemn, he nodded and returned to his chair. Bryce shuffled his feet like a schoolboy having to confess to a small infraction. She knew he was concerned about leaving Derrik, worried about finding his father safe and unharmed, and lost about how to tell Derrik. She glanced at Allyn and the older woman gave her a gentle smile and a short nod. Didn't they always say behind every man...

Carrie knelt beside Derrik's chair and took his hand. "Derrik?" His head turned slowly to look at her but only the vaguest of recognition sparked his eyes. "Derrik, Bryce has been neglecting his work. He needs to spend an evening catching up. Is that okay? Will you be okay if he works at his house? We'll keep both our phone lines open, just in case."

Allyn rose and brushed at her skirt. "I think that's a fine idea. Jaye and I will be here, and I'm going to try and get Derrik to eat something."

He shook his head. "Nay, Allyn, I canna."

She fisted her hands at her hips and Carrie ducked her head to hide a smile. "Don't be saying nay to me, Derrik. You'll eat something. I don't want Tommy accusing me of not taking care of you while he's away. Don't make me have Jaye order you..."

A bitter chuckle rumbled from Derrik. "Nay, Allyn. Dinna get yerself in a snit. I shall try. For my Tommy if fer nothin' else." He glanced over his shoulder at Bryce who immediately moved closer. "Ye go an' do yer work. Yer new job is important. Take care of what ye need to do. Dinna worry. Ye'll know when we know anythin'."

"Aye, Da. I know." Bryce bent to hug Derrik as Carrie rose. Allyn touched her sleeve. "Take care of Bryce and we'll watch over Derrik." She lightly touched the flowers. "I'm so happy he finally told you. Remind me, when this is all over, to tell you how long it took Jaye to accept Faerie."

"Are you...?"

Allyn chuckled. "I'm as human as you and Bryce. We're the lucky ones, considered Friends of Faerie." She touched Carrie's hair in a loving gesture. "You've much yet to learn about our family."

TWENTY-EIGHT

"You understand what you need to do?"

Carrie took a deep breath to calm a flare of unreasonable anger. They'd been over this way too many times since returning to Bryce's house. He was nervous, so she tried to silently forgive the repetitions.

"I understand. Don't worry about us here. You just be careful."

Bryce tugged a black Polo shirt over his head and pulled the hem toward his lean hips. Carrie tried to force moisture to her dry mouth. How could she be so—inspired—by him putting his clothes on?

Who was she kidding? Everything about Bryce inspired her. She settled on her side, stroked the plain, dark purple comforter covering the bed, and watched him reach into a drawer for socks.

Everyday actions of a normal, everyday life. That's what she'd wanted all her life. A normal lover. A normal family. She caught herself before she snorted in disgust. There was nothing normal about her relationship with Bryce, unless a love so powerful all else faded in comparison was normal.

She had a feeling in his family, it was.

The mattress dipped as Bryce sat to put on socks and athletic shoes. He leaned forward to tie the shoes, giving her a fine view of the muscle movement under the knit shirt. Then, he glanced over his shoulder, grinned, and flopped to his back on the bed.

Reaching up, he captured her head in his palm and encouraged her to join him in a kiss. Keeping the contact simple was difficult when she wanted to deepen the kiss and keep him there with her. Finally admitting her fear, Carrie let tears fill her eyes and spill down her cheeks.

When the wetness touched Bryce's face he carefully twisted his lips from hers and stroked his fingertips over her face. "Don't cry, sweetheart. I don't mean to be a crazy, repetitive fool. I know you understand what to do. I'm just... really nervous about all this."

Carrie let the tears fall without attempting to stem the tide. "I know. That's... not it."

"I'm afraid, too." Bryce tugged her close and wrapped his arms tightly around her. "But, I have to do this. If there's any chance we can rescue Pop, I have to. I can't let Nightshade go by himself, and he would. He's not... well, made for this kind of stuff."

Carrie had to chuckle. "You don't think so? I've met some pretty tough drag queens in my day."

Bryce joined in the moment of levity some of the stress lines eased from the corners of his eyes and mouth. Too soon, the serious light returned to his eyes. "I don't think this is going to be solved by a bitch fight."

"He'll be okay. You'll watch out for each other."

"I'm surprised he doesn't want to wait for help from the Alastriona."

"You've never told me who they are. Derrik is their leader?"

Bryce scooted to the end of the bed and rose. He glanced at the clock and Carrie followed his gaze. Only about ten minutes before Nightshade was scheduled to arrive. He held out his hand and helped her from the bed. After a deep, lingering kiss, he led them from the bedroom.

"The Alastriona," he said as they descended the stairs, "are the Defenders of Mankind. They're part of an ancient clan of

Faerie who guard the portals between the worlds. There have always been humans who are considered Friends of Faerie—"

"Yes, Allyn mentioned that."

Bryce nodded and double-checked his pockets at the front door. "One of the duties of the Alastriona is to protect these people and guide them safely between the worlds. Until recently, there was little danger. Now... their jobs have become more difficult. And more important."

"So, they're the cops of the Otherworld? No wonder Derrik didn't want a human cop called in. I've heard there can be a lot of disagreement and charges of misuse of proprietary information between law enforcement agencies."

As she'd hoped, Bryce laughed. "Ah, Carrie. You know the right things to say. I love you. When Pop's home, we'll gather everyone together and tell them."

"Tell them?"

"That you've agreed to be my wife."

"Oh."

"Carrie?" Bryce bent slightly to look directly into her eyes. "You haven't changed your mind?"

Pain flowed through his eyes dulling the sparkling green; fear tightened his lips. The physical force of his uncertainty blasted against her and she took a tiny step back. At her retreat, Bryce's eyes closed and he turned away.

"No, Bryce." Carrie clutched his arm and he froze. "Don't turn away from me. I haven't changed my mind. I have no doubts. I love you more than I could have ever imagined possible. I would die without you. Look at me."

It took an eternity for Bryce to face her. She stroked her fingers over his eyebrows and the deep lines etched between them. She touched his face as if memorizing each line, the varied textures of his skin. "With so much worry over Tommy, our lives together aren't foremost in my mind. Find your Pop. Then I'll proudly stand beside you and make the announcement. Please, Bryce. Don't ever doubt me."

He shook his head, captured and kissed her fingertips.

A short, single blast of a car horn stole the gentle mood from them. "That's Nightshade. I've got to go." He didn't move.

"I know." Carrie gave him a gentle shove. "The sooner you go, the sooner Tommy will be home. And the sooner we can really be together—as a family."

After a deep breath, Bryce absently kissed her cheek and exited the house. He paused at the bottom step and turned. "You remember what—"

"Yes, yes. Now go."

He flashed her an endearing, teasing grin then trotted to the dark sedan waiting at the curb.

Bryce paused before opening the car door. First, he bent to make sure it was Nightshade; the dark, uninteresting sedan wasn't the man's normal style. He gave a mental shrug. Nightshade's lime green Volkswagen would be rather noticeable.

"Get in, man." Nightshade hissed when Bryce finally opened the door. "It would be just our luck for Derrik to take a peek outside about now."

Settling himself on the cloth seat, Bryce studied his friend.

Nightshade pulled away from the curb and drove silently for a few blocks before he turned a firm-lipped expression to Bryce. "Different look for me, isn't it, honey?"

Only able to nod, Bryce wondered where Nightshade had gotten the get up, and the car. Nightshade had pulled his hair back and braided the length at his nape. He wore a dark tee shirt and fatigue pants with bulging pockets. He glanced lower and Bryce arched his eyebrows in surprise. He'd never seen the man in anything but sandals, and now Nightshade wore black combat boots.

Nightshade patted the seat beside him, found what he was looking for, and tossed it sideways to Bryce, who stared down at the knit cap. "What's this for?"

"Your hair. I'm not so concerned about your skin, but, honey, that hair of yours will be like a beacon to the bad guys."

They reached the edge of town and headed out on a wide, gravel road. As he drove, Nightshade pulled additional items from a bag at his side. Soon Bryce had a thin flashlight with a powerful, focused beam that left spots before his eyes when he tested it, a leather wrapped packet of tools, and a length of thin rope clutched in his hands.

Nightshade refused to say much as he drove, concentrating instead on watching the road both before and behind them, continually checking the odometer. So Bryce sat back and fingered the rope. What the hell was he doing?

The car slowed to a crawl and Nightshade turned off the lights. The thin strip of moon peeking between swiftly passing clouds gave them little light, but Nightshade seemed to know where he was going. He turned the car down a dirt road, little more than a parallel set of tire tracks through a pasture, and leaned forward over the steering wheel.

"Almost there. Listen to me, Bryce. You have to follow my orders exactly."

Orders? Bryce stared at Nightshade. The set of his face was somehow different, the masculinity he normally disguised prevalent in the harsh lines around his mouth and the tense set of his jaw. This was a different man.

Nightshade sighed, stopped the car and, still gripping the steering wheel, leaned back. He stared straight ahead. "You deserve an explanation if you're going to follow me into this lions' den. A lifetime ago I was part of an agency, an, uh, type of special forces." He held up one hand when Bryce drew breath. "I can't tell you which one. Let it suffice to say I ended up on too many hit lists to continue. I had to go into hiding."

Subtly, as Nightshade turned to face him, his face changed, softened, became the flamboyant Nightshade Bryce knew. "And, honey, ain't I done a fine job?"

Bryce shook his head. "I don't understand."

"When we've gotten Tommy free, I'll tell you more. There's no time for explanations. Just do as I say and we'll be fine." He waited for Bryce to nod, then climbed from the car. "We walk from here. Follow me."

Numb, both from worry and Nightshade's strange revelations,

Bryce gathered his supplies and followed Nightshade's sure, silent steps to a wooded culvert. How much danger was Pop in that it warranted such caution? He forced himself not to gasp and turn back to the car when Nightshade pulled a gun from a pocket and tucked the weapon into the back of his waistband.

T wenty minutes before she was scheduled to return to Derrik's home, Carrie sauntered up the sidewalk as casually as she could. She couldn't sit alone in Bryce's house any longer. Her imagination shifted into overdrive, and none of the scenarios she'd come up with had a happy ending. Lottie, normally there to calm and redirect that imagination, was conspicuous in her silence. The only help was to join the waiting family.

Carrie chewed on her lip. She took a chance coming here now, knowing she'd have to slip away to call Detective Corley at the proper time? Questions layered on top of more questions. Unfortunately, the answers were as elusive as her happy endings.

She knocked once on the door, then walked in and paused at the arched entryway to the living room. Derrik still slouched in his chair, staring forward, looking into the distance at nothing. Allyn had her legs curled under her. She held a drawing pad in her lap, but the pencil hung loose from her fingers.

"Carrie. We didn't expect to see you back this evening. Where's Bryce?" Allyn set the pad on the end table and patted the couch at her side.

"He's still working. I thought I should leave him alone for a while. Maybe he'll get more done that way."

Allyn arched her eyebrows and Carrie felt heat filling her face. "Don't worry, child. We all know how it is to be in love." She glanced at Derrik. "Luckily, few of us have faced what he's going through now."

"I pray this will be over soon." *Please be over soon. Keep safe, Bryce.*

Derrik looked up at her thoughts, and she had a brief fear he'd been able to hear them. But he merely gave a one-sided smile. "I'm glad yer back. Where is my son?"

"Still working. He'll be over later."

"'Tis amazed I am he let ye from his side." The heat in Carrie's face flamed fiercely.

"I see ye still wear the flowers. He took ye to his special place. Aye?"

"He did. It was... is beautiful."

Derrik's smile briefly touched the other side of his mouth. "So, then somethin' guid has come of this tragedy." The smile faded, his shoulders hunched forward, and he was lost again in his private misery.

"Can't we do anything, Allyn? I can't stand seeing him so miserable."

Allyn sat back and cleared her throat. "In Faerie, when two souls are meant to be together, there is a thing called the soulfire. It's very rare, but..." she grinned, "... common enough in this family. Some experience the soulfire physically. With Jaye and I, blue sparks fly from our bodies. Derrik has never believed he could experience the soulfire, but I've seen it."

"Sparks?" Carrie's body experienced the memories of the strange tingling that was more than sexual desire. She'd definitely felt inner sparks.

"Uh hum. But, with Derrik and Tommy it's more like a fiery, red-orange aura surrounding them."

"That's amazing."

Allyn gave an elegant shrug. "Perhaps. And perhaps it's just something that we, as jaded humans, have learned not to see. Rather like... invisible friends."

Carrie couldn't speak, so only nodded. There was so much she had to learn about Bryce's extended family and the world of Faerie. It could take a lifetime.

Jaye returned to the living room, wiping his hands on a dishtowel. "Soup's on. Oh, Carrie, when did you get back? Will you and Bryce join us for supper?"

"Bryce isn't here, so it'll be just Carrie. This time." Allyn leaned forward and unclenched Derrik's fingers from their grip on the chair arm. "Time to eat, Derrik. Carrie's going to have supper with us."

"Carrie? Aye, 'tis guid." He shook his head and for a moment seemed the gentle man she had met only a few days before. Then his eyes became hooded as if he were looking inside himself.

Her heart lurched at the dull pain emanating from the once vibrant man. Bryce and Nightshade had to be successful. They had to be. She wasn't sure how much longer Derrik would be able to function in this defeated state.

Derrik turned toward the dining room and muttered, "Aye. We do as we must."

B ryce kept his eyes focused on the center of Nightshade's back. He wasn't allowed to use the tiny flashlight and the moon gave barely enough light to brighten the clouds, let alone send any illumination to highlight the uneven ground at his feet.

Totally out of his league, he forced himself to concentrate on the occasional whispered comment from Nightshade.

Not far from the car, Nightshade had pointed out the dark shadows of buildings. Now, as they skirted the squat structures, lights flickered on then disappeared as the inhabitants seemed to move from place to place. Nightshade led them toward the rear buildings, where there were no lights and no signs of habitation.

Bryce stumbled in a dip in the grassy pasture and fell heavily to his knees. Instantly, Nightshade was at his side, helping him to rise, silently assessing his condition. Bryce's opinion of Nightshade's abilities quickly evolved to frank, intense admiration. The man's lithe, easy movements told of intense training and incredible knowledge. Still, Bryce was sure, once this operation was over, the old Nightshade would return and vehemently deny any of the actions they took that night.

Lost again in his thoughts, he nearly ran into Nightshade, who turned, frowned, shook his head, then smiled broadly. His white teeth were bright in the dim light and Bryce shuddered. There was something—predatory—in the smile.

"We go in here," Nightshade hissed at him. Bryce nodded and looked for a doorway. There was none. Nightshade poked his shoulder and pointed to a window eight feet from the ground.

At his questioning look, Nightshade grinned again, took the rope Bryce had slung over his shoulder, and moved under the window. Bryce came up beside him, ready to give him a lift toward the window, but Nightshade released a slow breath and leaped upward. He caught the window ledge with his fingertips, hung motionless for a moment then hauled himself through the opening. Bryce held his breath until Nightshade popped his head out of the dark window, motioned Bryce closer and tossed down the rope.

Bryce eyed the rope with distaste. He hadn't climbed a rope since high school, and even then not well. Being physical was Jaysson's passion, not his. But Nightshade needed help and if Pop was in there, he'd do anything to help him. He grabbed the rope and wrapped it around one fist.

Before he even had a chance to think about rope climbing techniques, his feet left the ground. Tightening his grip on the thin rope, Bryce let himself be lifted to the window until he could hook one arm over the sill and scramble inside. Nightshade met him with a knowing smile and arched perfectly groomed eyebrows as he coiled the rope, slipped it back over Bryce's shoulder, and patted the coils in place.

With one finger pressed against his lips, Nightshade indicated with the other hand which direction to go. He slipped a small flashlight into his hand, flicked on the narrow beam, and moved away. Bryce turned on his own flashlight and followed.

They inched down a dark hall, the twin beams of the flashlights bouncing along the walls. Nightshade paused, took Bryce's hand and readjusted his hold on the flashlight. With the beam held at shoulder height, he was amazed to find he could see better.

He followed Nightshade closely, staying a pace behind the man's easy movements. He wasn't sure what might happen, but understood the enigmatic man could handle the situation better than he could.

They followed the straight hall, turned toward the inner part of the building, then turned again. His sense of direction failing him, Bryce became lost in the darkness. Finally, Nightshade paused before a door, ran the flashlight beam around the thin outline of the opening and nodded grimly. An electronic keypad replaced the doorknob. Indicating Bryce should hold his light trained on the keypad, Nightshade took the packet of tools from him. Moments later with the face panel removed, a jumble of wires, like an octopus of colored insulation hung from the open hole. With deft, sure movements, Nightshade snipped and rerouted the wires. He stepped back, angled each of them to opposite sides of the door and pressed a single button.

The door opened silently.

L eaving the others sitting in silence, Carrie excused herself from the table. Derrik had only picked at his food, moving pieces around the plate. Not that any of them had much appetite, and even though Jaye's meal was attractive and tasty, most was left on the plates and in the serving bowls.

The night sounds of the city greeted her when she stepped onto the deck. She thought of the musical birds and insects of Faerie and the contrasts between this world and the Otherworld. At this moment, she preferred the quiet innocence of

Faerie, but feared in the long run she might miss the action and noise of the human experience. Bryce had managed to live in both worlds, as had much of his extended family. She could do that as well, with Bryce to guide her and Breanna to show her the way.

Carrie leaned on the railing and stared into the night sky, wishing she could see the stars more clearly. Were there stars in Faerie? Of course there must be, but how much more brightly would they shine than here? She sighed, loving the sparkling twinkles above her.

Sparks. Allyn had told her a little about the Faerie soulfire. Carrie wanted to know more, and curiously, wanted to see the manifestation of souls meant to be together. Deep inside, she wanted to experience such a remarkable oneness with another.

A gentle smile eased the tenseness of her face. She could experience being one with another. She could—she did—with Bryce. She didn't need sparkling lights or flaming auras to tell her they belonged together. Nothing was needed to validate the song of her soul when she was with him. Loving him was so easy. The rest of life that was hard.

She couldn't imagine what her parents would say about her getting married. Maybe she wouldn't have to tell them anything. Her relationship with her new family would be hers alone.

Somehow, though, they must know something since her mother had alluded to it in the note taped to her door. The notion that Bryce would insist on telling, then inviting them to the wedding hovered uncomfortably in the back of her mind. Family was important to him, maybe because of his abandonment, or maybe just because he was lucky enough to have had a loving familial relationship. A loving, caring, large family.

Twisting her wrist to catch the light from the kitchen window, she glanced at her watch. It was time. She turned to face away from the house and took the cell phone from her pocket. She'd memorized the number she needed to call, but dug through her pocket for the slip of paper where she'd written specific directions during a whispered call from Nightshade.

"Detective Corley, please." She waited long moments before a rough voice answered.

"Corley went home at the end of his shift, ma'am. How can I help you?"

"I have to speak to Roger Corley. It's... it's about Reverend Templeton."

"I can take your information, ma'am."

Frustration blazed through Carrie. She didn't dare trust this to anyone else. And she needed to tell him now, or Nightshade—and Bryce—would be in even greater danger. "No, only Detective Corley."

"Ma'am, I—" The voice stopped abruptly and Carrie could hear an urgent conversation, muffled as though a hand covered the phone's mouthpiece.

"This is Roger Corley."

"Oh, thank God. This is Carrie Newcomb. I have information for you about Reverend Templeton."

"Let me get settled here, Carrie. Some little voice in my head told me I needed to return to the station. I thought I had forgotten some damned paperwork," he mumbled over the sounds of settling into a creaky chair. "Okay, I'm set, go ahead."

"I have directions to where Tommy MacAlister is being held. There's a rescue going on right now, and they need back up."

"What the hell? Who's in there? You should have let me handle this, Carrie."

"Who's not important. You have to get there as soon as you can." Carrie spread the scrap of paper on the rail and angled so the kitchen light highlighted her rapidly written directions. Hopefully, she could still decipher them.

"These are precise directions." Carrie took a deep breath and slowly repeated the route, mileages, and landmarks. Detective Corley responded with faint syllables of encouragement and surprise.

"This is close to where we've been searching. How did you come by this information?"

"Just go. Now. Please." She touched the button to disconnect the call before the detective uttered another word. A deep breath rushed from her lungs. She'd done her part, now if the police did theirs...

"I thought there was something going on."

Carrie whirled to face Jaye who leaned against the doorframe with his arms folded over his chest. Shadowed by the lights behind him, his face remained hidden and she couldn't determine his expression.

"Oh, I... uh..."

He took the steps forward to reach her and rested his hands on her shoulders. "Bryce?"

Tears filled her eyes. It was a relief for someone else to know, but also she felt a surge of failure for the secret operation. It couldn't be a premonition of... of...? She shook her head to clear the fuzz, then nodded. "And Nightshade."

THIRTY

A black cavern yawned before them. If it were possible, the room was even darker than the hallway. Flashlights trained on the floor, Bryce stepped into the room in front of Nightshade.

"Now what?" a tired voice said from the darkness. "Another attempt to convert me?"

Relief washed through Bryce at the sound of his father's voice. The sarcasm dripping from the words proved Tommy hadn't been broken by his captivity.

"Pop?" Bryce took another step forward and lifted his light beam toward the voice.

"Bryce? Dear God, please don't let this be my imagination." Creaking sounded to one side and Bryce swung the light toward it.

Surrounded by the thin beam, Tommy sat on a narrow cot, his back against the wall, one hand covering his eyes in a protective manner.

Bryce closed the distance between them and wrapped his arms around his father. Tears burned behind his eyes and he struggled to speak.

"Pop, oh, God, Pop."

"Bryce, I can't believe it. How'd you get in here? What about the guards?"

Nightshade cleared his throat. "Ah yes, the guards. They'll be making rounds before too long. We've got to get going."

Tommy loosened his hold on Bryce and peered blearily over his son's shoulder. "Nightshade? That you?"

"You'd best believe it, honey. Are you able to walk?"

Dim light reflecting off the wall showed Tommy's confusion. "Nightshade?"

Nightshade backed out the door and stood in the hall, head tilted to one side, listening. "Not much time." He shone his flashlight beam on his wrist. "And, if Carrie did her part, the authorities will be here soon. We need to leave. Now!"

Bryce rose and held one hand out to Tommy who stood unsteadily. Bryce wrapped his arm about Tommy's shoulder and winced. In these few days, he'd lost weight. But his steps were sure as they started across the room. Tommy froze in the doorway and clutched the side of the opening. "David."

"Come on, Pop." Nightshade's pacing made him nervous.

Tommy shook his head. "No. We can't leave without David." He faced Bryce and squinted at him through the darkness. "I won't leave without him."

Nightshade took Tommy's arm and tried to tug him into the hallway. Tommy shook off the hand, grabbed Bryce's flashlight and shone it upward toward his own face. Blinking rapidly and squinting through watering eyes, he said, "Look at my face. I'm not leaving without David."

Bryce glanced helplessly at Nightshade. He didn't know what to do. Who was David?

Nightshade leaned close and pressed on Tommy's hand so he lowered the flashlight. "Come with me, Tommy."

"No."

They had to get him out soon. Nightshade had made it abundantly clear they needed to be away from the compound before the police arrived. Bryce wasn't sure why that would be so important, but maybe, with Nightshade's past...

"Pop, you go with Nightshade. I'll find this David for you." Relief eased the tension from Tommy's body and he clasped Bryce's shoulders. "There's a secret panel on the wall opposite the cot. I'm not sure how to open it, but I think it goes into the room where they keep him. Tell him who you are, and he'll come with you. Hurry."

Tommy pulled Bryce into a fierce hug. "I love you, my son."

"Love you, too, Pop. Now, get going. We'll catch up with you."

Nightshade gave him a doubtful glance, then shrugged and motioned down the hall. "Door and stairs to exit on the left. Do *not* go to the right. Keep to the shadows. Don't waste time." He leaned closer and whispered, "If you can't find this person, leave."

Bryce glanced at Tommy who rubbed at his eyes before he gave a short nod of understanding. As much as Tommy insisted, his own rescue was of prime importance. Anyone else... could wait.

After he watched Nightshade lead Tommy toward the exit, Bryce turned back to the interior of the room. He quickly scanned the small space and cringed at the cot, the open toilet, and dirty sink. Wanting only to follow Nightshade from the horrors he imagined in the building, he searched the wall across from the cot, slowly drawing the flashlight beam back and forth over the scarred plaster. A nearly invisible line, one that would barely show if there was full light in the room, indicated the side of a small opening. Bryce ran his fingers along the seam until he detected a shallow depression. He pressed. The panel slid to one side, revealing a long, low tunnel. Thinking of old science fiction movies where the actors were always crawling through the tubes and tunnels of their ships, he bent and inched forward. He held the flashlight low, only a few inches in front of his feet, to lessen the chance of the light being seen through other possible cracks along the wall.

He hadn't gone far when he faced a dead end. Running his fingers along the wall, he found a depression similar to the first. He pushed.

A low panel slid open. "Tommy? Is that you?"

A child's voice? Bryce took a cautious step into the room.

"Who are you? You're not Tommy. Where's Tommy?" Panic rose along with the pitch of the young voice.

"Shh. I'm Bryce."

"Tommy's son?" Disbelief colored the child's question.

How did the boy know that? Bryce felt his own surge of disbelief. "Yes. We're getting Pop out of here—"

"Oh, good." Elation and sadness melded in the two words. "It'll be better when he's safe."

"He wants you to come, too."

There was a rustle, then the patter of bare feet across a hard floor. Bryce lifted the flashlight beam a fraction and a boy moved into the circle of light. A very thin boy, with bruises on his face and arms. Bryce bit back a gasp of dismay and crouched before him. "David?"

A cocky grin brightened the young face for only a brief moment then, he sobered. "Yes, sir. I'm David. Are you really gonna take me out of here?"

"It's what Pop wants." Bryce watched the boy's face. His expression was animated and his eyes cast about as he spoke, but Bryce wondered how much David saw. His eyes were points of lifelessness in the young face. He waved his hand before David's face.

"No, sir, I can't see. I'm blind." He caught his lip between his teeth and tears pooled on his lashes. "Now you won't take me, will you? 'Cause I'm damaged."

Unable to resist the forlorn expression, Bryce cautiously leaned forward and embraced the boy. David held himself stiff for a moment, but relaxed when Bryce gently stroked his thin back and ragged hair. "That doesn't matter a bit, David. If Pop wants you along, then you're definitely coming with us. Anything you want to take with you?"

"I don't have anything. Reverend Templeton says possessions are the wealth of the devil." Bryce didn't doubt that a bit, although Templeton was rumored to own vast tracts of land and properties. And if his treatment of others was any indication, he was a devil himself.

"Pop and Nightshade will be waiting. We'd better hurry." David nodded, confidently took Bryce's hand and pulled him toward the passageway. "I'll bet I can do better in the dark than you. They never turn any lights on over here."

"Do you know the stairs to an outside exit?"

"Yes. Hurry."

They passed through the tiny space that had been his pop's cell. Bryce shuddered again at the dismal place. It was probably better if Pop's captors never did illuminate the bleakness.

"Come on. Hurry up."

Bryce let a grin at the boy's exuberance relax his face. He understood why Tommy had been so insistent. The child was obviously abused, and Pop would never allow a child to languish in such a life. Neither would he, for that matter. Neither would he.

Bryce stumbled on the steep steps, but David caught his arm and held tightly until he was steady. Silent at Bryce's finger against his lips, David waited while Bryce eased the door open and peered out, scanning the yard surrounding the building. Compared to the near total darkness of the building's interior, the pale light from the sliver of moon made the distant trees stand out in sharp relief.

They needed to make it to those trees. When he squinted, Bryce thought he could see the vague outlines of Nightshade and Tommy crouched together.

"We have to cross a bit of open ground here, David."

"I... I don't know if I can. I don't have any shoes. They don't let me have any except at services." He sniffed softly. "I... I can... go back to my room. I know the way." He turned and reached for the handrail leading back up the stairs.

"Don't be silly." David paused at Bryce's light tone. "I'll carry you." The boy was so thin, Bryce doubted he weighed much more than Breanna. At the boy's shocked expression, Bryce amended his statement. "If that's okay with you."

"You'd do that... for me?"

A welling of sorrow burned again behind Bryce's eyes. What deprivations, what horrors had this child suffered? "Of course for you, David. And for Pop. I see him waiting for us. You don't want to disappoint him, do you?"

"Oh, no. Never, Bryce. You can carry me, if you think you can."

"Hey, I'm stronger than I look, kiddo." Bryce scooped David into his arms. At first the small arms wrapped around his neck were tentative, but as Bryce strode forward, they tightened and the stiff little body relaxed against him.

They reached the trees without incident and as Nightshade turned to lead them back through the culvert to the pasture where they'd left the car, the sounds of vehicles pulling into the front of the compound roared loud in the night.

THIRTY-ONE

He hated gravel roads. No matter how carefully he drove, pieces of rock flew up to tear tiny chips from his vehicle's new paint. Titus drove much slower than he liked—speed thrilled him almost as much as power over another—and cursed when his sporty car bounced over deep ruts. Unable to contemplate the success of his plans while concentrating on driving, Titus turned on the radio and searched for the classic, heavy metal rock station. The loud, throbbing, angry music soothed him.

Headlights sparkled in his rear view mirror. There were seldom others upon this stretch of road and a faint niggle of concern tickled his mind. What had that fool Templeton done now? Titus shook his head and pulled off the road into an abandoned farmstead. He drove his Pantera behind the crumbling barn and, shutting off the engine, waited.

He counted two minutes before a line of cars sped by, raising dust that hung low over the road in the dim moonlight. He was far enough from the road not to be seen in his dark blue car, but close enough to discern the identity of the passing vehicles. Police.

Titus exited his car and stomped around the weed-infested

ground, muttering fierce curses under his breath. There could be no doubt where the vehicles were going, and he spared few thoughts as to how the authorities would have discovered the location of Templeton's compound.

Growling in frustration, Titus jogged toward a low hill, hoping he could see the compound from there. He topped the rise and slipped to a stop on the tall grass. Swinging his arms to regain his balance, Titus bit his lip and tasted blood. The coppery taste served to increase his anger and he kicked at a low clump of weeds.

Distant sounds of the invasion at the compound carried though the quiet night to mix with his anger. The sound of a racing engine filtered through the other sounds and Titus froze, silently listening.

There, to the left. No headlights announced the closeness of the oncoming car. Titus crouched, then flattened himself against the ground when a dark sedan sped by at the base of the rise. He lifted his head high enough to see the profiles of the car's occupants.

He didn't hold back the explosion of vile curses.

THIRTY-TWO

B ryce glanced over his shoulder to the back seat. David curled against Tommy's side. Bryce gave his Pop a smile he hoped was full of encouragement and received a tired grin in return. David's blank eyes searched the interior of the car, cringing at tiny noises, acting as though he expected them to turn the car around at any moment and take him back. Tommy laid his hand over David's clenched fist and the boy stilled.

Nightshade remained silent until they entered the city. "I'll drop you off and see you tomorrow."

Tommy reached over the car seat to touch his shoulder. "No, you'll come inside so we can thank you properly. Never thought I'd say this, but, Nightshade, you're my hero."

Nightshade rolled his eyes. "Honey, the things you say. No. I can't come in. I can't let anyone see me in this get up. It would ruin my reputation. And I've worked so hard to get where I am."

Bryce chuckled but sobered quickly. There must be a way to make both Pop and Nightshade happy. Nightshade needed to keep this part of his life secret. Strange, so many men struggled to keep their gay personalities hidden, not a macho, secret agent background. Bryce felt a slightly hysterical laugh building at the base of his throat. This night had been... he couldn't' even think about it. All that mattered was that Pop was safe, and they'd saved a child as well.

"Bryce," Tommy pleaded, exhaustion heavy in his tone. "Convince him."

Nightshade cast a sideways glance with a minute shake of his head. There would be no convincing the man who sat tall and fierce behind the steering wheel. At that moment, Bryce had no doubt Nightshade could kill a man—had killed. He closed his eyes and when he opened them, his Nightshade had returned. The slightly pursed lips and limp wave of his hand comforted Bryce, bringing him back from the power of his imagination. A compromise, that's what they needed. "Would you be willing to drop us off, go home and... change and come back?"

"Oh, honey, what a plan. Yes, Nightshade could do that." He gave Bryce a grateful glance and turned the sedan down Tommy's street.

After confronting her, Jaye had left the house briefly, and Carrie supposed he was contacting that group Bryce had told her about—the Alastriona. But, with the human authorities on the way, she didn't see any use for Faerie peacekeepers.

Jaye returned and they sat together in the living room and, in an effort at normalcy, had even turned on the television, though she would never be able to say what program blared across the screen. Derrik, slouched in his chair, stared at his hands and gave only monosyllabic responses if asked a question.

Carrie's heart bled for the man, his pain was palpable. Beyond what she had done, there was nothing more she could do. *Hurry home, Bryce.*

::*They come.*::

Carrie sat up straight and inched forward to sit on the edge of her chair. Lottie's voice resounded in her head. ::*Go outside, child. They're here.*::

Excitement rushed through her and she rose, gave a single

dismissive wave to Allyn who made to rise with her, and forced herself to walk to the front door. She longed to run, to fling herself through the opening and fly into Bryce's arms. But she held back, stopped on the top step and clutched the pillar, watching a dark sedan pass under a streetlight and pull into the driveway. The post supported her as Bryce exited the front seat, helped Tommy and a child from the back, and moved slowly toward the house.

When Bryce lifted his gaze to her, she cried out softly and launched herself into his arms. The sound of the car pulling away barely registered. She rained kisses over his face. The strength of his arms about her held back her tears; the stroke of his hand over her back calmed the remnants of her fear.

A throat clearing separated them, but Bryce kept her hand in his. Tommy smiled at their clasped hands. "Dare I hope to receive so fond a welcome?"

Carrie gave another cry and reached out to hug him. This was one of Bryce's fathers, a man she already loved—more than she cared for her own parents. "I'm so happy you're safe."

"Carrie, will you watch over David for a few minutes? Much as I love your welcome, there's one I want even more."

"Oh, I'm sorry. I shouldn't be so—"

"No, dear girl, you should be." Tommy knelt next to the boy and ran his hand over the small shaggy head. "Will you let Carrie bring you inside in a few minutes? I'll go in with Bryce and... and see Derrik. Is that okay?"

"Yes. You go ahead." He reached out blindly, and after staring until Bryce nudged her, Carrie took the small, thin hand.

"We'll be fine. Derrik needs to see you."

"And I need him. Bryce, Give your old Pop an arm to lean on, I'm feeling the strain of the past few days."

Bryce and Tommy moved toward the porch and David tugged on her hand. "Bryce saved me from that place. From Reverend Templeton. Tommy wanted me to come home with him. I hope... hope that's okay." Huge, round tears dripped slowly down the boy's thin cheeks and his lower lip trembled.

Carrie understood his fear and knelt to gather him in her

arms. After a moment's hesitation, he wrapped his arms around her neck.

David sniffed then said, "She said you'd take care of me, too."

"She?"

"The angel who helped me find Tommy."

B ryce faced the room, one finger to his lips when Jaye and Allyn stared at him. He cleared his throat. "Da?"

Derrik didn't raise his head. The only movement of his tall, lithe body was a tiny shrug of one shoulder.

Tommy stepped around Bryce. "Is that any way to respond to your son? Haven't we raised him with more respect than that?"

The muscles across Derrik's back tensed and with infinite slowness, he lifted his gaze. "My Tommy?"

Tommy took another step forward and opened his arms. "I'm home."

Derrik shook his head as if clearing cobwebs from his brain. His blue eyes flashed and he rose to his feet. As if he didn't believe Tommy actually stood before him, he moved forward slowly, still shaking his head.

With a drawn out sigh, Tommy closed the short distance and reached up to catch a single tear hovering on Derrik's cheek. "Derrik, I really am home."

Jaye and Allyn each touched Tommy on the arm as they passed, but he gave little indication he saw anything but the man before him. Bryce smiled and followed his aunt and uncle into the kitchen. His fathers needed time for their reunion.

He turned back before entering the kitchen. Pop and Da were enfolded in a powerful embrace. A faint red-orange aura surrounded them, flaring more brightly when Derrik whispered in Tommy's ear.

Bryce backed into the kitchen and ran into Allyn. "Soulfire." His awed whisper was harsh and strained with longing.

Allyn hugged him. "You've never seen it?"

He shook his head. "Well, maybe. Once when I was little I thought... God, Allyn. That's amazing."

"Thank you for whatever you did to bring him home."

"Nothing any son wouldn't do."

Jaye gave a rueful chuckle. "Don't be so sure of that, Bryce. It's amazing what some people will—or won't—do for a loved one."

Allyn sat at the small kitchen table. "Where did Carrie go?"

"Oh, no, Carrie. She's out front. I'd better bring them around back to give the folks a little more time together before we all gang up on them." Bryce sprinted out the back door.

"Them?" Allyn's question followed him across the deck.

A fter sitting with David on the porch steps and talking quietly about Tommy, Carrie felt a deep empathy for the boy. She wondered where he had gotten the bruises on his face and arms, and strongly suspected there would be more covering his body. As emotionally abusive as her father had been, at least he had never hit her.

"Carrie?" David touched her leg. "You want to know about me, don't you?"

Perceptive child.

"You can ask me questions. It's okay."

The boy's voice wavered and he yawned. Then, his stomach growled. Carrie grinned, first things first. "It sounds like your tummy would answer anything I might ask you. How about if we get something to eat first? There'll be plenty of time for questions later."

"I suppose. I bet the police want to talk to me about Reverend Templeton, too. I've never talked to a policeman before. I... hope they're nice."

She knew one nice cop, and if she could arrange it, Rog Corley would be the only one to talk to David. Somehow, deep inside, she knew he would be gentle with the fragile child. "Do you want to talk to the police?"

"I think so. They did lots of bad things there. They wanted to make Tommy change. I tried to help him, and I made them mad. That's why Reverend Templeton had them punish me." He touched the bruise on the side of his face.

"Oh, David. That should never have happened to you."

"But, my dad didn't want me. He signed papers so Reverend Templeton could take me. I try to be good."

Carrie hugged David to her side. "I'm sure you're very good. Now, how about we go inside and find something to eat?"

"I am hungry. A little."

"Good, come around to the back door then."

Bryce's voice startled them both and David clung to her for a moment before he blew out a breath that stirred the hair hanging over his forehead. "Bryce, you scared me."

"Sorry, kiddo. If we go in the back door, we'll give Pop some extra time with Da."

They rose and David stumbled, so Bryce lifted him and carried him piggyback. He had to bend nearly double to get through the back door, but didn't release the boy until he sat him at the table. Carrie sat opposite David and leaned back in the chair. She loved watching Bryce with children. His ease, kindness, and concern were part of the many reasons she loved him so much.

Bryce turned to Jaye and Allyn. "This is David. He was also being held by Templeton. While Pop was there, they got to know each other and, of course, Pop insisted David come home with us. David, meet Jaye and Allyn."

The boy held out his hand and Jaye shook it. "Nice to meet you, sir. I know about you. You're Tommy's business partner." His blank eyes turned unerringly toward Allyn. "And his wife."

"I'll tell you more later," Bryce cautioned. "Right now, David's kinda hungry."

Allyn turned toward the refrigerator. "We have leftovers from supper. No one felt much like eating. How about a sandwich for now?"

"That would be fine, ma'am."

"No ma'ams here, David. Call me Allyn. I'll have a snack for you lickity split."

While she layered leftover beef on a thick slice of bread, Bryce pulled Jaye to one side and spoke urgently with him. Carrie watched her lover hungrily. She'd been more worried than she cared to admit, and now that he was home safely, she didn't want to let him out of her sight.

Swinging his legs and plucking at the placemat on the table, David sat silently. When she could tear her thoughts from Bryce, Carrie wondered about the boy's true story and how he came to be in Reverend Templeton's compound. Allyn placed the sandwich in front of David and adjusted the plate so he could find the sandwich easily. She cast Carrie a look of motherly concern then sat at the table.

David carefully felt the edge of the plate, then found the sandwich. He lifted it and took a big sniff. He quickly dropped the sandwich back onto the plate and sat back, his hands in his lap.

"This must belong to you. This isn't my sandwich."

"Of course it is."

"No, it's not peanut butter."

Allyn made to rise. "Would you rather have peanut butter?" David reached out his hand, dropped it back to his lap and whispered, "No. I don't really like peanut butter. But... that's all I'm allowed."

A lump, thick as a spoonful of peanut butter, lodged in Carrie's throat. "Only... only peanut butter?"

David nodded. "All three meals. Unless I've been bad. Then I get nothing."

The look of horror in Allyn's eyes surely must mirror her own. Carrie took David's hand and touched his fingers to the roast beef sandwich. "That changes now, David. If you don't want peanut butter, you don't have to eat it. Ever. This is roast beef left over from supper." She took her hand away and held her breath until the boy picked up the sandwich and took a tentative, tiny bite. He chewed slowly and smiled.

"Much better than peanut butter. Thank you."

"Eat up, young man," Allyn commanded in a tender voice. "And if there's anything else you want, you only need to ask."

A beguiling grin brightened David's face before the expression turned wistful. "When I did good, and Reverend Templeton was happy with me, sometimes... sometimes he'd let me have potato chips."

"And you like chips?" Allyn signaled for Jaye to join them at the table.

Bliss filled the young face. "Oh, yes."

Allyn tugged on Jaye's sleeve until he bent so she could whisper in his ear. "Don't we have some chips at home? Would you run and get them, please?"

David paid fierce attention to chewing his sandwich, eating rapidly, as though he feared the food would be taken from him. Carrie suspected that might have happened more than once. Anyone who would feed a child only peanut butter sandwiches could just as easily take them away. The more she heard about Reverend Templeton, the more she discovered unwelcome hate within her. Despite her upbringing and her father's attempts to teach her to hate those who were different, she'd always been able to tame those feelings. Now, she could think of two who would deserve her hatred.

Allyn sat a glass of milk before David, took his free hand, and wrapped his fingers around the plastic cylinder. "Milk."

"Thank you."

David placed the last of his sandwich on the plate and used both hands to lift the glass for a long drink. His eyes grew wide. "It's cold." Carrie chewed on her lower lip. Hadn't he had cold milk either?

David sat back with his hands in his lap. "Where's Nightshade?"

Bryce gave a low chuckle, but Carrie sensed the nervousness behind the sound. "Nightshade? He had to change." He glanced at Jaye who had returned to set a crinkly bag of chips on the table. "I'd like to keep this story until Da's here. That way I only have to tell it once."

"We're here, my son. Tell yer tale."

Derrik and Tommy entered the kitchen. Derrik held Tommy's

hand and stared regretfully when Tommy shook his hand free and knelt beside David's chair. "Are you okay, David?"

The boy turned in his chair, reached out, and hugged Tommy around the neck. "I had roast beef. Not peanut butter. And cold milk." He looked hopefully toward the table, "And maybe some chips."

Tommy ruffled his hair. "That's wonderful. Would you like to bring the chips into the other room so we can all sit and talk?"

"Sure. But you'll have to show me the way."

Doing better than showing, Tommy lifted David from the chair. Bryce grabbed the chips and followed his folks back to the living room. Derrik passed his chair, sat on the couch with Tommy close to him, legs touching. David settled on Tommy's other side. The rest took chairs; Bryce sat in Derrik's chair and pulled Carrie down to sit on his lap.

Eyes clear of the pain of the past days, Derrik cast a loving smile at Tommy, who helped David open the bag of chips. "Bryce, I dinna ken how this all happened, but ye have brought my Tommy home to me. To all of us."

"Da, I—"

"Nay, Bryce. Dinna say more about it. Tell us what part Night-shade played in all this. Someone brought ye home, I do remember hearin' the car. David mentioned Nightshade. What did he have to do with this?"

Bryce grinned. Da was returning to normal, his inquisitive, peacekeeping nature showed itself. He was about to reply when Carrie squeezed his thigh.

"I know," he mumbled. To the room, he said, "Nightshade somehow found out where the compound was. He drove me out there and showed me the building where Pop was being held."

"Why isna he here? He should share in this time of joy. He is part of yer family."

"Aye, Da, I know. But, he wanted to change first." This would be the tricky part. It was true Nightshade wanted to— needed to change. But not in the way those in the room would suspect. Even Carrie knew Nightshade didn't want the full extent of his participation known, but had no idea the reason why. It was a strange secret, one Bryce would keep as long as necessary. "Uh, while we were in the compound, Nightshade got some mud on his shoes. He wouldn't come in with messy shoes. You know how he is."

Derrik chuckled. The sound sent warmth deep through Bryce. Da was on the mend. "Aye, that we do."

Bryce squeezed Carrie's waist and she leaned on his shoulder to kiss his cheek and whisper, "Well done."

With a smile just for her, he returned the kiss, lingering a moment against the warmth and freshness of her skin. Pop was safe. Da back to normal with his Tommy at his side. Carrie was in his arms. These tribulations were nearly over, and he and Carrie would be free to start their lives together. Maybe he'd ask if Bree could stay just a little longer in Faerie to give them some needed time alone.

Carrie wiggled and his body responded with instant urgency. Oh yes, they needed time alone. Adult time. Sure that eventually the police would show up at the door, he reluctantly admitted he couldn't leave his folks to face them alone. He would need to continue the ruse of Nightshade's involvement. But, when he had the chance to get the man alone, there were some questions Nightshade would answer. Maybe. He'd known Nightshade almost his whole life, but the revelations and behaviors of the night had come as a complete, stunning surprise.

Carrie adjusted her position again. Bryce splayed his hand over her lower back. "Careful, sweetheart."

"I'm sorry." She turned to the others in the room. "I need a little air. I'm going to take a short walk and be back when Detective Corley gets here."

Derrik sighed. "Aye. Since ye called him, we shall have to talk wi' him. Perhaps they apprehended the ones who did this."

David paused in his single-minded enjoyment of the potato chips and lifted his sightless eyes to Derrik. "I hope so, too. I don't want to go back."

Tommy pulled David onto his lap and wrapped his arms tightly around the boy. The chip bag crinkled loudly. "You'll never go back there. Never." He glanced sideways at Derrik, who smiled gently, then turned to Bryce and rolled his eyes.

His folks were considering something, something that had to do with the boy. Caught up in his thoughts, he barely noticed when Carrie stood. But by the time she had crossed to the door he felt the loss of her body.

"I'll be back in a few minutes. This will give you some family time." Her lip quivered and she rushed from the house.

Family time? She was family now. Even if he hadn't already asked her to marry him, her help and acceptance by his family granted her a place with them. He pressed his hands against the chair arms.

Allyn stopped him with a shake of her head. "Give her a little bit, Bryce. She's not used to family and needs some time to adjust. We've sprung an awful lot on her in just a few days. You happened fast."

"No faster than I fell in love with you, darlin'." Jaye reached across the space between the two chairs and took his wife's hand.

Allyn gave a low chuckle. "Remember how long it took me to accept that love? Almost as long as it took you to accept your place in Faerie. She'll be fine, Bryce. She just needs that time."

Bryce settled back in the chair and fought his reluctance to acknowledge the right in Allyn's statement. He'd give Carrie the time she required, then ask her to join him in the time he needed.

.

THIRTY-THREE

A breeze cooled the night and the light clouds hiding the moon earlier had disappeared, leaving a pale light to slightly brighten the areas between the streetlight glows. She glanced toward Bryce's house, but there was another person walking a dog there, so she crossed the street to stroll along the edge of the park. A single, dark sports car roared down the street. The quiet, peaceful night soothed her nerves.

So much energy had been used trying to find Tommy and dealing with Derrik's depression. Bryce had been strong, a support to his fathers, and to her. How unfair that he had to deal with this so soon after her memory of the rape appeared. The wedge of pain still hovered between them and she hoped the experience wouldn't come back to haunt her time and again. She wouldn't have been able to deal with the sudden onslaught of emotions without Bryce. She shuddered, all at once concerned about walking alone so late at night?

Then she shrugged. Having never been the type to fear the night, or dark places, she had always discounted she would become a victim. That wasn't true now. But Carrie refused to give up the quiet joy she felt in a nightly walk when she wasn't at work.

She paused at the drive for the parking lot. Now that Tommy was home, she had no excuses not to go back to work. The job itself held no appeal. She loved dancing, and would never give that up, but now she wanted a one man audience. If... no, when they got married, would she still have to work? Of course she would. She couldn't expect anyone to support her.

While she struggled with her personal desires and the practicalities of real life, the sports car pulled into the drive. Before she could back away, a man sprang from the driver's seat, grabbed her around the waist, and pulled her toward the bushes. A scream rose in her throat, but died when the man raised his hand and covered her mouth and nose with a vile smelling cloth.

C arrie hadn't been gone that long, but Bryce still worried. It was late, dark, and she was walking alone. Although she hadn't shown any nervousness at going for a walk by herself, Bryce experienced an agonizing pain low in his belly. He loved her, so of course he worried. The past days probably served to increase the worry and Bryce fought to contain the need to rush from the house and find her.

Finally, despite the knowledge he couldn't always watch over her, like he couldn't always be there for his daughter, he excused himself and strolled to the front porch.

He paused on the step and scanned the street. A lone woman walked rapidly toward him, but the figure was too thin to be Carrie. He squinted through the patchy light from the streetlights into the darker shadows of the park. A lone, dark blue sports car sat in the parking area.

The concern deepened and he stepped onto the sidewalk meaning to search for Carrie. The thin woman called to him. He didn't want to give directions, he didn't want to have to deny a homeless person's request for money, he didn't want anything but to find Carrie.

The woman clutched his arm with surprising strength. "You know my daughter."

Bryce glanced into the lined face. Something sparked a memory, something remotely familiar about her eyes. "Do I?"

"You do. Carrie Newcomb. She needs help."

"You're Carrie's mother?" This mousy woman was the woman Carrie refused to acknowledge? She seemed more frightened than abusive.

Her fingers clawed into his arm. "There. Across the street. A man in the car took her... into the park... she... was unconscious."

Bryce stared at her. Someone took Carrie? He tensed. "What—"

"The same man who kidnapped the man who lives here." After pointing at the house she shook his arm. "I don't know what to do. Help her."

Adrenaline surged through Bryce and he uncurled her fingers from his arm. "Go to the house and tell them what happened. Call the police. I'm going after her."

He gave the woman a gentle shove toward his folks' house and watched for only a second before turning toward the park.

Just as he reached the curb, Nightshade pulled up in his bright, lime green car and waved gaily. This was the Nightshade he was accustomed to, but not the Nightshade he needed.

Bryce leaned into the open car window. "Someone's got Carrie in the park. Come with me."

The grin disappeared from Nightshade's face and he nodded once. Bryce heard his light footsteps behind him as he ran toward the sports car. Inspecting the vehicle as quickly as he could without spending precious moments, he passed by, then paused at the edge of the grassy expanse of City Park. Where...?

Nightshade pointed to a thicket of bushes surrounding the base of a stand of trees. "There. We start there."

Bryce ran toward the trees, Nightshade hot on his heels. An irreverent thought flashed through his mind. How did Nightshade run wearing sandals?

The sounds of struggle rustled loud in the night, louder even than the combined pounding of his heart and his feet on the hard ground. *Carrie.*

Nightshade grabbed his shoulder and yanked him back. "Let me. He might be armed."

Bryce shook his head and surged forward. Carrie was in danger, a danger he could have prevented by insisting she not go out walking alone. Now it was up to him to save her.

Nightshade wrapped both arms around Bryce's chest and held him back. "No," he hissed close to Bryce's ear. "Carrie might get hurt."

Struggling against his friend's hold Bryce growled a curse low in his throat.

A gasp and low moan sounded from the darkness. Freed from Nightshade's hold, Bryce leapt forward, Nightshade at his side. The force of their advance parted the bushes. Ignoring the intrusion, a brown haired, mustached man ripped Carrie's tee shirt from neck to hem. The sound echoed through the silent night. Shimmering tears filled Carrie's wide eyes; and she pulled her lower lip between her teeth.

"Stop," Bryce growled. He took a step forward, his fists clenched and rising.

The man glanced up. The desire glazing his eyes intensified the protective anger consuming Bryce. He flew at Carrie's attacker, knocking the man to his side. One fist connected with the man's shoulder, the other grazed his face. The moustache ripped half from his face and dangled over his mouth. Shocked to stillness, Bryce stared at the false facial hair waving back and forth. The man drew in a sharp breath, rose to his knees, then stood in a lithe, fluid movement.

Nightshade moved to the side and held out one hand, palm facing Bryce. "Take care of Carrie. I've got this bastard."

The wail of sirens rose in the distance, growing steadily closer. The man straightened, glaring defiantly as Nightshade moved closer. "You won't be attacking women again."

With a laugh that chilled Bryce to his core, the man turned on his heel and dashed away, the movement so fast and surprising neither Bryce nor Nightshade reacted in time to stop his escape.

Moments later the roar of a car engine, followed by the squeal of tires, drowned out the advancing sirens.

Clenched fists tight at his hips, Nightshade faced the departing vehicle and mumbled under his breath, "Damn. I'm out of practice."

"Carrie? Sweetheart?" Bryce knelt beside Carrie, lifted her shoulders, and crushed her in his embrace. She was silent for a moment then, after a long, shaky, breath, gave one sob and was silent again.

Bryce glanced up at Nightshade, who still faced the street. As if feeling eyes upon his back, he turned. "Got the license number as we entered the park. Hope those sirens are for us."

"Are you ready to go back to the house, Carrie?" Frightened by the flat, dull expression in her eyes, Bryce was concerned how much this assault would set back her recovery.

"It was the same man." Carrie clutched her torn shirt over her breasts.

"What, honey?" Nightshade knelt beside her as well.

"The same man who raped me. He was... going to do... to rape me again." She glanced at Nightshade and blinked, her eyes now clear. "You have the license? Good. Then it won't be hard for the police to get him. They will get him... won't they?"

"They will, honey. And if they don't, I will." Nightshade stood and held out both hands. "We need to go. I'm sure the cops will want to do their forensic thing here, so we'd best not mess up the area. And, you'll be more comfortable in the house. Come, my dears."

At that moment Bryce appreciated Nightshade more than ever. The calm voice, alternating between authority and the man's normally flippant and irreverent tones, helped ease the intense pain of Carrie's latest horrific experience. Keeping Carrie close, he rose and let Nightshade lead the way back across the green expanse of the park. Derrik, expression fierce as an ancient warrior, met them in the parking area. At Bryce's nod, he relaxed and joined the trio in crossing the street.

The rest of the family waited on the porch, expressions of

horror and concern filling each face. Carrie relaxed against Bryce's side until the thin woman who claimed to be her mother stepped forward with one hand outstretched.

The siren wailed to silence and a squad car that pulled into the drive, Carrie angled her upper body toward the woman. "What the hell are you doing here?"

A team of forensic experts followed Nightshade back to the park. Detective Corley sat with Bryce's immediate family around the large dining room table. Carrie rolled up the sleeves of one of Tommy's shirts and glared across the expanse of polished wood at her mother. How dare the woman intrude on her chance for happiness. The older woman sat with her head lowered, her hands clenched tightly in her lap. It gave Carrie a small satisfaction that she looked uncomfortable.

"I'm not sure where to start." Detective Corley positioned his notebook on the table and tapped the end of his pen against the page. He turned to Tommy. "I'm glad you're safely home, Mr. MacAlister. I really need to get some information from you."

Carrie only half-listened to Tommy's experience. The detective took occasional notes, asked a few questions and encouraged Tommy with gestures and wordless comments. David, sitting with his eyes closed on Derrik's lap, added occasional comments and clarifications to the dark, dismal picture being painted of Reverend Templeton's control and operation. Finally, the detective asked, "Why do you think you were targeted?"

Tommy shrugged. "Other than my choice of partner—"

"That's exactly why."

All eyes turned to Carrie's mother. "A man came to my husband claiming your relationship was harming our daughter. I wasn't sure, but Harold was convinced."

"By Reverend Templeton?"

"No." She shook her head. "By Mr. Avery. He said he was helping the Reverend. He said taking you to the compound would help save Carrie's soul."

"My soul doesn't need saving, Mother."

"I know. But your father—"

"He made you help, didn't he? Why haven't you left him? He's never let you be who you are—you've always kowtowed to what he expects. That's all he ever wanted of me, too. But I couldn't—I couldn't be how he expected. What you expected." Carrie covered her face with her hands and leaned her elbows on the table. Tears trailed between her fingers.

A hand came to rest gently on her shoulder. "Sweetheart?"

"I'll... I'll be okay." She forced herself to look across the table at the mousy woman who had given birth to her. "Why did you stay with him?" Carrie winced at the accusations in her tone.

"Where would I go?" Her mother spread her hands. "True, your father was... is controlling. I thought he loved me when he took me from my father's home. But, he wasn't any different than my Father. Both men were so controlling, but I thought that was how my life was supposed to be. It was my fault I wasn't happy. Until you were born. I was happy then. For a short while, Harold wasn't so... angry and demanding. But when you wouldn't listen to him either... Oh, Carrie. I'm so sorry."

"Mrs. Newcomb, what did you have to do with Mr. MacAlister's kidnapping?"

She dabbed a wadded handkerchief at her eyes, took a deep breath, and spoke with a confident voice Carrie had seldom heard coming from her mother. "We helped Mr. Avery watch the house. Then, when the tall man left, we came in the back door. While Mr. Avery and my husband... drugged him, I watched out the back door. I held the van door open while they put him inside. I rode in the van out to the compound. I... I know I shouldn't have, but I was afraid. I wanted to somehow let someone know because I didn't want them to hurt anyone. Mr. Avery had the desire to hurt someone in his eyes. I know the look." She dipped her head.

When she lifted her gaze again to the stunned silence in the room, her eyes were dry, "I had one of Reverend Templeton's cards. I stuck it between the doorframe and the screen door. I hoped someone would find it and look for Mr. MacAlister there."

Bryce gave Carrie's shoulder a squeeze. "We did find the card. That's when we called the police. Thank you, Mrs. Newcomb. We had no idea where to start looking before that."

"It... it really helped?"

"Yes, ma'am. It did."

Carrie glanced sideways at Bryce. He sounded truly grateful. To her mother?

"And thank you as well, Mrs. Newcomb, for being here tonight. If you hadn't directed me to the park, I might not have found Carrie before... before..." His words trailed away and a collective heavy sigh rose around the table.

"Carrie?" Her mother stretched her arm across the table. She held her hand flat, palm up in a reconciliatory gesture. "There is so much for you to forgive of me. I understand if you never want to see me again. If you want to..."

Carrie couldn't look at her mother. Deep in her heart the blame she had long laid at her mother's feet dissipated. She was as much a victim as Carrie had been. But she wasn't sure she was ready to let the anger go quite yet.

Her mother sighed and drew her hand back. "Detective, is there another officer I could talk to? I think it might be better for... all of us."

"Certainly, ma'am." Detective Corley rose with her and led the older woman toward the living room.

Carrie took a deep breath. She was so tired and feared the night would never be over.

Derrik leaned to whisper to Tommy who nodded. Then Derrik rose and carried a sleeping David upstairs. Entering the room, Detective Corley glanced at the retreating man then let out a whoosh of breath as he sat.

"Now, about the boy." The detective took a deep breath. "I'll have to call soc—"

"You will not." Tommy slammed his palm against the table-top. "You will not put that boy into the system. He'll stay here."

"But, sir—"

"Don't 'but, sir' me. If you take David away, we'll have to fight to get him back. I fully intend for him to join this family. Derrik and I will adopt him."

Carrie stared at the furor of the normally calm man. Surprised at his insistence, she sat back to see what would happen.

Jaye poked his head around the corner. "What's going on in here?"

Tommy pointed at the detective with a shaking finger and sputtered. "This... this man wants to put David in the social services system. He wants to take David away."

Patting Tommy's shoulder, Jaye sat in the chair Carrie's mother had vacated. "Calm down, Thomas. Detective Corley, I was raised in the system, and I don't wish any child to be placed in a similar position. With David's blindness, it might be even more difficult to place him in a suitable home. What could be more suitable than leaving him with people who already love him? Isn't there something we can do to prevent this?"

Before the detective answered, Tommy started muttering. "Bryce was never in the system. We didn't have any trouble adopting him. David needs me, needs us. Who'll know how to take care of him, understand what he's gone through?" He stared wide-eyed at the detective. "I saw how Templeton used him. I've touched the bruises left after the punishment when David refused to follow orders. I've heard how they never fed him anything but peanut butter sandwiches. He hates peanut butter."

Detective Corley sighed. "Until we find his parents—"

"He has none. David told me his mother was dead. His father abandoned him after signing some papers."

"A Relinquishment of Parental Rights?"

Tommy shrugged. "What it boils down to, Rog, is that I plan on adopting David. Until we can take care of the official procedures, he's not leaving this house. This is his home now. I won't let him be uprooted again."

A smile brightened the detective's tired expression. "I understand, and I'll do what I can. You'll still have to talk to a case worker, but I'll add my recommendations that David be fostered here."

Thankful Tommy wouldn't have to go through any more trauma that night, Carrie lay her head on the table, cushioned in her crossed arms.

"This has been a long day for all of you. I've got just a few questions I have to ask now concerning Carrie's assault, then that will be it for tonight. I'll have to speak with each of you again tomorrow, though."

"That's okay, Detective." Bryce scooted his chair closer to Carrie's. She sat up and reached for his hand. "We'll do whatever we can to help apprehend all of those trying to hurt our family."

"Good. And please. Call me Rog. I'm really not into titles and honorifics."

Comforted by the way Bryce stroked his thumb over the back of her hand, Carrie offered Rog a tiny smile. "That makes it easier to talk to you, too."

"Carrie, the man who attacked you tonight—"

"Was the same man as before."

"You're sure of that?"

"Oh yes. His hair was different—lighter, and he has a mustache now—but the laughter was the same. He used some drug on me, but I don't think I was unconscious very long. Just long enough for him to get me into those bushes."

"If I set you up with an artist, do you think you could describe him?"

"I'll never forget his face. Yes. I can do that."

"The mustache was fake."

Startled, Carrie stared at Bryce.

"It was fake. It came half off when... I punched him in the face." Bryce shrugged as he explained. Carrie nearly chuckled at the self-satisfied glint in his eyes.

"And your friend gave us the license number. We'll have him in no time."

Carrie appreciated the detective's confidence, but she wasn't so sure. There was something—illusive—about her attacker. She suspected he could hide very well in a crowd, blending in so he would be overlooked. She wouldn't voice her concerns now, and she'd work with the artist. She'd do everything she could to catch the bastard.

"Do you need me to come down to the station tomorrow?"

"Would you be more comfortable here? Lucidea Galvagin is the artist, and she uses computer composites to create the perp's face. She'll have you pick out samples of each feature, then put them together. It can be done here."

Relieved, Carrie released a breath. "That would be great."

She remained at the table while Bryce and Tommy walked the detective to the door. Picking at the edge of the table runner, she tried not to think. But her mind whirled with possibilities and implications and what ifs. She needed to get away from everything. At least for the night. Then maybe, tomorrow she could face describing her attacker. Maybe tomorrow she would be able to think about the things her mother had said. Maybe tomorrow... Carrie gave a bitter bark of laughter just as Bryce returned.

"What?"

"I'm thinking like Scarlett O'Hara."

"Huh?" Bryce's blank expression made her giggle. It was an honest, happy reaction in the midst of the pain.

"A twentieth century literary heroine. One who would always think about her troubles tomorrow. Like her, I don't want to have to deal with anything now. I'm not sure I'll want to do it tomorrow. But I will. I need some sleep, Bryce. I just need to sleep."

"Let's go home." He held out his hand and drew her up to him. He kissed the tip of her nose, holding her as if afraid she would break. She appreciated his concern, but really needed to be locked in his powerful embrace. She was numb, and she needed to feel.

"Please, hold me tighter. I can't feel you."

He complied with a low groan. There. Now she could feel his touch. He shook, the tremors transferring to her, and she angled her head to look at him.

"What's wrong?"

Closing his eyes, Bryce drew a shuddering breath. "After today, you can ask that?" Then he smiled, a sad smile, but a smile. "Let's go home."

He turned her and started toward the front of the house.

"No." Carrie held back.

His eyebrows arched high over the questions in his eyes.

"Not your house. Not my apartment. Can we...can we go back to Faerie? Too much is happening here—the police are in the park and patrolling the neighborhood. I'll feel safest in the bower. Can we go there?"

"Of course. Just let me tell Pop so they can contact us in case we're needed." He disappeared into the living room. Unsure she'd make it that far before collapsing Carrie clutched the back of a chair to hold herself upright.

Bryce returned, Derrik close on his heels. Before Derrik entered the dining room, he opened a narrow door and pulled out two blankets and a pair of pillows. He handed them to Bryce as he passed, stopped to kiss Carrie's cheek, then faced a broad expanse of wall. His fingers moved and he spoke a soft word.

The wall blurred and Carrie blinked. It wasn't just Faerie; it was Bryce's glade. She jerked when Bryce touched her arm.

"Da insisted on opening a portal right to the glade," he explained.

"Aye, ye are exhausted an' ye dinna need a trek through the forest before ye rest. Go now. I dinna believe anythin' will happen that ye will need to be here until late in the morn. Dinna fear, sweet girl, dinna fear. Bryce shall watch o'er ye."

Carrie moved forward and hugged Derrik. "Thank you. Now, you go watch over Tommy."

The smile that touched his firm lips filled with so much love it brought tears to her eyes. The same expression filled Bryce's face when he looked at her. And it shone down on her now when he stood next to her, wrapped his free arm about her waist and led her through the portal into Faerie.

T itus roared into the parking lot behind his apartment
building, the endless stream of his curses louder than
the squeal of his tires. The bitch would be able to recognize him, and others had seen him sans the irritating facial hair.
Foolishly, he'd left his car in plain sight. No doubt they had the
license number as well.

Not that it would do them much good since the license had
been stolen. But, the sleek form of the Pantera was unusual in the
city and recognizable.

He rushed to the apartment, grabbed the phone, and began
slamming a few belongings into a bag as he waited for the call to
go through.

"I've been discovered," he barked as soon as a voice answered.
"I'm leaving. You know what to do. I'll bypass the first and second
contingency. Contact me at the third location." He listened a
moment. "No, I don't know how long. There's a good chance
Zeroun will now know who I am. You will increase your efforts in
the other place... No. Continue no matter what... I *will* have what
belongs to me returned. Then Zeroun, and his entire clan, will
suffer. I'll contact you when I'm settled... No. I will contact you."

Titus slammed the phone against the wall, snapping the

receiver in two. He tossed the pieces aside, opened the safe bolted to the closet floor, and added the contents to the bag.

No regret hampered him when he paced through the luxury apartment. He didn't care that he was leaving this life. He did care he was forced to make this move long before he planned. Plans that went awry angered and frustrated him. And anything to do with the damned Zeroun and his kin fell short of his goals.

He sprinted to his car, zoomed through town and out onto the interstate. The first stop was not far. He didn't wish to give up the sleek power of his vehicle, and a place in a nearby small town would alter the color and provide him with a new, preferably out of state license. He offered himself a cold smile in the rear view mirror. A new identity awaited him. A new identity he would perfect, and when Zeroun had once again become complacent, he would be ready. He would return. Woe, and death, to any whom stood in his way.

B ryce jerked awake and leaned up on one elbow to look around the bower. The bright sunlight of midmorning shone in the glade but hadn't touched the deep shade of the bower. Bryce angled so he could look down on the woman sleeping next to him. Faint bird song rose to fill the glade with sweet sound.

Late the night before, under the light of the Faerie moon, he'd spread one blanket over the soft grass carpet in the bower, positioned the pillows, and lay beside Carrie. She'd fallen asleep even before he pulled the second, light blanket over them. So, he'd spooned against her back, wrapped his arm over her waist, and let the peacefulness of the Otherworld seep into him. He hadn't thought he would sleep, but even the wildness of his thoughts couldn't keep the healing serenity from him. He had a niggling suspicion some magick had been at work as well.

Letting Carrie sleep, he lay on his back and stared up through the woven branches above him. The sky was clear cerulean and cloudless. Occasional soft breezes blew over him, caressing his skin. He loved it here. Now, Carrie seemed to as well. He loved her, and he worried about that love. So many traumas filled her past. Struggling with those memories could prevent the survival of their love. He would do anything for Carrie, anything to insure their love would last and grow stronger.

There was a soft tug on the hair over his ear and a tiny giggle. He sat and looked around. Carrie still slept peacefully, one hand curled under her cheek, a calm smile on her face.

The tug came again and Bryce turned his face from Carrie. A pair of pale yellow wings lifted a tiny woman level with his eyes. She gave an odd, airborne curtsey then waited expectantly.

"Yes?" Since Korin had married Nanceen and accepted the rule of the fairy folk, the once mythological peoples were common visitors to the gentry of Faerie. This tiny creature seemed to want to tell him something.

"M'lord Korin sends greetings to his nephew, Bryce of the Bower."

Bryce rolled his eyes. As down to earth as Korin seemed, there were times his Goodfellow heritage and the temperament of the original Puck showed through.

"What is your message, little one?"

"It is requested you return to the world of humans. The woman, Carrie, is needed as agreed upon the night afore this day. One known as Rog awaits her."

"I'm coming." Carrie yawned, stretched then opened her eyes. Staring at the fairy, she sat slowly and lifted one hand to point. "Is that... that...?"

"I be of the true fairy folk, Miss." With that, the fairy turned with a proud cant to her head and fluttered away.

"Fairy folk? But..."

Bryce rose and began folding the blankets. "We'd better start back so we don't keep the detective waiting long. I'll explain as we go. You see, a long time ago, the beings who look like us, called the gentry, coexisted with the smaller fairy folk. The winged people, leprechauns, boggarts, the Bean Sidhe, all of them are a part of that Realm. Someday, we'll have Korin tell you the whole story, but because he is a descendent of the original Puck—"

"Puck. Like in Shakespeare?"

"Yep, that's him. Because Korin is his descendent, Korin is the ruler of those folk. I told you my family has a thing for Shakespeare." He grinned at her expression as she tried to work through what he had just told her. Then he chuckled. "And when I first met him, Korin had wings, too."

"I do have a lot to learn about your family." Carrie stood and brushed at her clothes. "I feel really wrinkled, but I don't suppose it will matter. Let's get this over with." She paced from the bower.

She tipped her face toward the sky and sunlight sparkled highlights through her hair. The breath caught in Bryce's throat. No fey woman was ever so beautiful to his eyes. No other woman would hold such a large piece of his heart. No, not a piece, but his entire heart. Hoping to need them again soon, he tossed the blankets deep into the bower and hurried to her side. He took her hand and they crossed the glen. When they reached the edge of the woods, a portal opened and Derrik appeared.

"Korin said ye would be along soon."

Detective Corley explained the raid on Reverend Templeton's compound while the artist set up her laptop and accessories on the dining room table.

"Did you find any other... prisoners?" Tommy asked.

"No, sir. But, we did apprehend the Reverend. Found him in bed with one of his female parishioners. And another man."

Tommy chuckled. "Ah, so, he doth protest too loudly."

Rog gave one snort of laughter, then sobered as he faced Carrie. "I'm sorry to tell you this, but the man..." Ruddy color formed a thin line over his high cheekbones.

Carrie frowned. What could this other man have to do with her? If it had been her attacker, why would Rog be embarrassed to tell her? "Who was it, Rog?"

"Carrie, I'm sorry. It was your father." He stared down at his hands.

The announcement didn't surprise her. It didn't make her sad, or angry, or—anything. The numbness returned in full force. How much more of a hypocrite would the man prove to be? A touch of concern forced her question. "Does my mother know?"

"I had to tell her this morning. She took the news... as well as could be expected. Actually, she seemed rather relieved."

Carrie gave a sarcastic snort of laughter. "I don't doubt."

Bryce cleared his throat. "You should talk to her."

Carrie turned her gaze to Bryce. She knew he'd say that eventually. Although part of her wanted to argue the fact, a greater part of her heart knew he was right. Her mother had hinted at her father's abuse. She gave Bryce a smile. "I know. I will."

The relief and pleasure in his expression filled her with a joyful determination. The load of baggage she carried with her, the past she brought to their relationship was large, but not any more than she could handle, with his help.

Maybe she should deal with all this before they got married.

"I'm ready whenever you are." The artist sat next to Carrie and angled the laptop so they could both see the screen. "Let me explain what we're going to do here."

"Okay, Ms. Galvagin."

"Sounds like everyone's on first name basis here, call me Lucidea. Now, we used to have to go through books of facial features and compile the individual features into a composite drawing. With this new equipment, the features are automatically put together when you pick them out. Then, we'll fine tune. Ready?"

Carrie nodded. Rog ushered the others from the kitchen to let the women work. Carrie missed Bryce's presence beside her, but realized he would also be a distraction. She didn't want to think about how the attacker looked. She didn't want to see his face—even if it was just a computer rendition. And Bryce would have tried to save her from any pain creating the composite drawing might cause her. He was a dear, wonderful man, but she couldn't let herself depend upon him for all her emotional support.

Using the computer under the direction of the artist was easier than Carrie thought, and before long they had a credible face. More than credible. After the fine tuning, the composite looked almost exactly like the man who attacked her. Both times.

Lucidea added just a slight almond shape to the eyes. "That's it. That's him." Carrie shuddered. It was remarkable. Then, she remembered. "Wait. Bryce said that the moustache was fake. Could you make the face without it?"

Chuckling, Lucidea complied. "How's that?"

"Good. Now, however he looks, he'll be found. Won't he?"

"The authorities will do their best. Unless he's an idiot, I doubt this perp's still in town. So it may take some time."

"Oh, I understand." Feeling stupid, Carrie shook her head. "I know that. Now what?"

"Now I'll print out a copy of each of these faces and let you take a look at the hard copy. Sometimes we notice things on the paper that are missed on the computer screen."

While the pages printed, Carrie studied the program icons. "How'd you get such a neat piece of equipment?"

A sad light entered Lucidea's eyes, but she quickly shook it away and smiled at Carrie. "I did a three dimensional reconstruction on a skull in Scotland recently. The department here received some expensive forensic equipment as payment." She grabbed the first page from the tiny, portable printer and handed it to Carrie.

After studying the face, Carrie nodded. "Yes. Almost as accurate as a photograph. This is the man."

As if sensing they were done, Bryce peeked into the kitchen. "Uh, Carrie. Your mother's here. Do you want to talk to her?"

Might as well get started unloading the baggage. She set the printout on the table and nodded. Bryce gave her a pleased grin and signaled to someone behind him. Mrs. Newcomb timidly entered the kitchen.

"Mom. I'm so sorry to hear about Father."

"I'm not. Maybe it was just the push I need to finally divorce him. Maybe. I'm so used to someone else making decisions for me, I didn't know how to make one myself." She squared her rounded shoulders and smiled at Carrie. "Now that choice is taken from me, and I have to decide. I won't stay long, I already have an appointment with an attorney. I just wanted to see how you are... handling all this."

"I'm going to be okay. Can we... can we talk again soon?"

A timid smile lightened her mother's dreary face. "I'd like that. I've got a lot to apologize for, many amends to make to you."

Carrie rose and took her mother's hand. "We both do."

T he police had gone. Carrie's mother had soon followed. Bryce held up a copy of the computer generated face. This man who attacked Carrie had also masterminded Pop's kidnapping. What reason did he have to prey upon the family?

Anger blossomed in Bryce's chest and flowed through his body, tensing his muscles and tightening his jaw. He should have beaten the man to a pulp. Bryce shook his head at himself. Better that the police find him and prosecute him to the fullest extent possible. There would be no way he'd let the creep escape again.

Jaye knocked on the back door and entered. "Just wanted to let you know Tommy took David to Faerie to visit Bree and Lara's kids. Derrik's going to meet them there a little later. First, I've got some things to discuss with him."

"Good. They both need to get away for a while." He held up the composite drawing. "Carrie's mom identified this picture as Mr. Avery. So there's no doubt that the rapist is also the kidnapper."

"Avery? Wonder if that could be the same Titus Avery, the guy who tried to ruin business by undercutting Zeroun's catering a couple months back. I've never seen him. Let me take a look."

Jaye took the page and stared at it. His eyes widened, his face paled, and he slumped into a chair. "Oh, god. Not him."

"Jaye, what's wrong?"

Jaye only continued to stare at the drawing and shake his head, so Bryce called for Derrik. When his Da rushed into the room, Jaye silently handed him the printout.

Derrik's reaction was much the same; his face paled, his eyes grew wide, he slumped into a chair. "Nay, it canna be him."

"I don't know how he did this, but it is him. That would explain why this family has been targeted."

Bryce leaned over Derrik's shoulder and pushed at the sheet of paper with his finger. "What are you talking about?"

"Sit, my son. Do ye remember who Lara discovered in the past?"

"Besides Iain? Sure, the Faerie who had been captured by his own portal when he tried to destroy Jaye and Allyn."

"Aye. An' ye remember his magick was taken from him an' he was banished to the mortal world, to another time, another place. Or so we believed."

"Are you telling me this is Feidhlim? You're kidding, right?"

Jaye rose to pace the width of the room. "No, Bryce. He's not. Somehow, Fiedhlim must have been able to control when and where he was sent. He still has supporters in Faerie, and they must be assisting him here. Damn, this complicates things." Jaye leaned over the table and drummed his fingers on the surface. "We've got to find him. He won't stop in his quest for revenge against me. I can't allow him to harm anyone—especially those I love."

"Ye must speak wi' the Queen, Jayezer. 'Tis a thing she must ken."

"First we'll gather the family. Let them know of the danger here. Then, we'll alert the Queen."

Bryce sat and scrubbed his hands over his face. They were living in a never ending nightmare. How could he bring Carrie into this mess and put her in the face of more possible danger? But then, how could he not—for his life would be worth nothing without her beside him.

He realized Jaye spoke to him, so he focused on the commanding voice. "... in one hour. Here."

.   .   .

Bryce was waiting when Carrie stepped out of the bathroom. Refreshed from a quick shower and a change of clothes, she cast him a smile that soon turned to a frown when she recognized the worry in his face.

He held out his arms and she walked into his embrace. "Now what's wrong?" she whispered to his chest.

"Looks like you'll get to meet the whole family—in full force in less than an hour."

"What happened?"

Sighing, he angled them toward the bed and sat on the edge. He half-faced her and gazed into her eyes. "The man who kidnapped Pop, and attacked you, is Faerie. A Faerie who had his magick taken from him because twice before he tried to destroy Jaye and this family. It was thought that he had been banished to another time and place in the mortal world, but somehow, he's here."

"So, what's going to happen now? We can't call Rog on this one."

Bryce chuckled as she'd hoped he would. "I doubt he'd believe any of it, anyway. No, this will be something for the Alastriona to handle. Jaye returned leadership of the Defenders to Da. They'll discover where Feidhlim is hiding. And take him back to Faerie for another judgment."

Carrie remained silent then took a deep breath. "Bryce, I know this is hard on your family. And I know I have a lot of my own problems right now. About getting married—"

"No, don't say it." Panic tightened the tiny lines around his eyes. He shook his head fiercely. "Don't deny me now. Please, Carrie."

Carrie cupped his cheek in her palm. He leaned into the caress and closed his eyes. "Look at me, Bryce." She waited until his lids slowly opened and exposed his heart and soul to her. "I wasn't going to deny our love, or deny you. I was only wondering if we could get married right away. No waiting. Today if we could—but I know we can't—but I would."

"I don't want to put you in any more danger, sweetheart."

"I know. Marry me and I'll feel safe. Marry me and you'll be there to protect me. Marry me and love me. It's all I want. Now and forever."

"We could, if you wanted, be joined in the Faerie way, then have a human wedding later. Because of their independent, fun seeking natures, there aren't many of this Faerie clan who choose to join with another for life. But there is a way."

"In your glade? Could we be married there?"

"It would be the fulfillment a dream, sweetheart. Carrie, are you sure?"

Her answer was to smooth her hand back to his ear and tug lightly on it to draw him closer. "Very sure," she said and guided his lips to hers.

Tain, Lara and Korin she knew, but not Lara's brother Jaysson or Korin's wife, Nanceen. Also present were Stephen and his wife Kelene and Nanceen's twin sister Kaelea. Nightshade sat quietly in one corner, while David was firmly ensconced between Tommy and Derrik. The tight knit support of the extended family group gave Carrie a sense of peace so strong she was afraid she'd burst from the new, wonderful strangeness. Now she was a part of the family. And, should she totally reconcile with her mother, the older woman would be welcomed as well. After experiencing the love of the extended family, she really did hope to add her mother to the group. Tommy didn't seem to hold a grudge against her mother, or even against the Reverend Templeton. Bryce's parents were fascinating and amazing men.

Jaye stood in the middle of the room and cleared his throat but before he could speak, Bryce rose and stood beside him.

"May I speak first, Jaye?"

Jaye's brows drew together but he nodded and sat on the arm of Allyn's chair. "Go ahead."

"We, as a family, are about to embark on yet another quest against Feidhlim. The past few days have been painful." Bryce glanced at David, then caught and held Carrie's gaze. "And joy filled. During this time Carrie discovered and accepted Faerie. And she accepted me. We wish to be joined in the Faerie way as soon as possible, then, when the danger to the family is contained, we'll do a human wedding."

A ripple of surprise rounded the room, then heartfelt congratulations filled the air. Carrie accepted the congratulations, relieved that she was accepted so readily.

"Tonight," she added. "Tonight in Bryce's glen. Will you all be there with us?"

While all agreed to join them, Bryce returned to Carrie's side, kissed her soundly, then grinned at his family.

"It's a good thing to temper the quest with such joy," Jaye said as he rose again. "Carrie, let me give you an official welcome to the family. The hugs will come later. Now, to deal with the problem of Fiedhlim."

Carrie let the family's discussion roll around her. Instead, she tried to imagine the ceremony involved in a Faerie joining. Then, she imagined what it would be like being married to Bryce, being Breanna's mother. Fear caught in her throat. She'd hoped, but never believed there would be a child in her life. She wasn't sure she would know what to do.

No, she'd be fine. Bryce was a wonderful father and would help her in any way she needed. He was nothing like her father. Nothing. She glanced at the other women in the room And she'd be she'd find plenty of help from them as well.

A hand rested on her shoulder and Nightshade leaned close to her ear. "I'm happy for you, honey. I'll miss you at the club."

"Why would you miss me?"

"You won't be dancing anymore, except for your husband. A loss to the rest of the world." He sighed dramatically.

Not dance? She hadn't really considered that. Okay, she had thought about it. About how she was already much older than the other dancers and how she wanted to quit at the peak of her career. Now, she had a perfect reason.

Nightshade whispered to Bryce as well and both men grinned. Sharing some masculine secret she supposed.

Although he smiled at Nightshade's comments, his mind had jerked to a painful halt when he'd heard their friend ask Carrie about dancing. He didn't want her to dance, no other man should see as much of her as was exposed by her diminishing costumes. But how could he ask her to stop dancing? She'd said she loved her job, and truthfully, when he forced himself to admit it, she was damn good at it.

Another, more immediate need made itself known once Jaye finished the family meeting. It wouldn't be long until their joining.

"Nightshade?"

"Yes, honey?"

"Tonight's very important to me."

"I should hope so. I hope you'll forgive me for not introducing you two sooner. I was only doing what Carrie asked."

"I know, Nightshade. You can make it up to me, though."

"How?"

"Stand with me tonight at the joining."

"*Moi?* You want me? What about—"

"No. You're it."

Carrie leaned close. "I think that's a great idea." Her eyes widened. "Do I need someone, too?"

When the family broke into smaller groups to continue discussions, Allyn joined them. Carrie glanced at her, worry filling her expression. "Do I need someone to stand with me at the joining?" Her eyes got wider. "Oh, no? What should I wear?"

"Not well prepared for this, were you?" Allyn chuckled, the low throaty sound made others in the room glance their way.

"I... I guess not." Carrie's face turned pink, and Bryce caught his breath. Although she had been the one to press for an immediate marriage, he had selfishly gone along with her, not even thinking how important the trappings might be for her. Heat filled his face and he prepared to apologize.

"If your intended will allow me?" Allyn wrapped one arm around Carrie's shoulder. "I'll take Carrie to the Otherworld and help her get ready. You, young man, need to get yourself prepared as well. Jaye's rather involved right now, maybe Iain could give you a hand. Hmmm, and Lara will get Breanna ready. Good. All set then?"

Bryce stared at Allyn until she laughed again. "Guess I've been married too long to a party planner, huh? Both of you come with me. We'll gather Iain and Lara and go to Faerie together. We don't have much time before sunset."

"Sunset?" Carrie asked.

"Of course. The time of Faerie joining."

David gasped, slid off the couch, and stood facing a side wall. "It's my angel." He was silent a moment before he nodded. "That's okay. They'll want to see you... Really? Oh, he'll be so happy."

Tommy moved to stand behind David and rested his hands on the boy's shoulders. "Who are you talking to?"

"The angel who told me about you when we were... there. She wants everyone to see her."

Derrik stepped in front of the pair, one arm spread in a protective gesture. David reached out, found the hem of Derrik's shirt, and tugged. "It's okay. She won't hurt us. She especially wants to see you."

Brow furrowed in a deep double wrinkle, Derrik glanced down at the boy. The gathered family inched forward. Beside him, Bryce felt tension emanate from Nightshade but when he looked sideways, the man seemed as relaxed and as carefree as ever. Until he winked at Bryce and gave a fierce grin. Struck again at the enigma of his friend, Bryce turned his attention back to David.

A faint gray haze formed before the boy. The cloud hovered against the wall for a moment, then a figure, cloaked and hooded in a slightly darker gray, formed. It took a single step forward, barely emerging from the surrounding haze. Time paused as the figure slowly lifted its hands, grasped the edges of the hood, and pushed the material away.

THIRTY-SIX

The woman looked around expectantly and a long golden braid fell over her shoulder. When her gaze landed on Derrik, she smiled, soft and sad. "Well met, cousin."

With agonizing slowness, Derrik took a step forward. His hand inched upward, but when he reached to touch the woman, his hand passed through her.

"I am unable to fully exist in this world. Until this day, I wasna even able to do this much. Only in dreams, only speakin' within my charge's mind, was I able to be with any of ye."

Derrik slumped to his knees. "Searlait."

At the sound of the name, Carrie crowded forward and stopped at Derrik's side. Her mouth gaped open. "L... Lottie?"

The woman lifted her gaze from Derrik and smiled. "Aye, child, 'tis me." She glanced at the others around the room. "Though banished for the rightful killin' of Torquil, I found the way to watch o'er ye. To protect this family."

Her eyes widened and she glanced back over her shoulder. "I canna stay. The pull to return to the world between worlds is too strong." She shifted and the cloak parted to reveal a long sword belted to her hip.

Eyes narrowed, Korin moved to Derrik's other side. "You were there. You fought the Bocan, defeated the monster. Saved my life."

"Aye. 'Twas the first time I realized I could briefly enter another plane."

"My thanks will never be enough." Korin bowed low. Searlait returned the action. "'Tis enough." Her shoulders jerked backwards as though pulled by a strong force. "Nay, I dinna wish to leave ye now. I must tell ye, the one ye seek, the one who caused pain to yer family, has disappeared. I canna see him. I dinna believe he will trouble ye fer a length of time, but be wary. I shall keep watch and inform ye when I find him."

Searlait reached out her hand to Carrie. The soft brush of air against Carrie's cheek mimicked the movement of the guardian's hand. "Dear child, ye shall be happy. Dinna concern yerself with the past. Live and love fer yer future. I shall be with ye, though ye no longer need me."

"No. I'll always need your friendship, Lottie. Always."

"Have that ye do, dear child. Go now, prepare fer yer joining. I'll be watchin'." Searlait cast her gaze over the assembled group. "'Tis honored I've been to be allowed to watch o'er ye all. Fear not, fer this is my bound duty within the world between worlds."

Finally she knelt before Derrik. Slowly, he lifted his head and they shared a silent communication. Fat, dull tears trailed from Searlait's eyes. When Tommy stroked his hand down Derrik's hair and clasped his shoulder, Searlait looked up at him. "Aye, I canna wish a better love fer ye." She leaned forward and touched her lips to Derrik's cheek. "Farewell, cousin."

Rising, she pulled the hood to cover her head. Shrouded in gray, she backed into the mist, lifted one hand, and disappeared.

Stunned silence surrounded the family. Carrie chewed on the inside of her cheek. Her imaginary friend and protector was Derrik's cousin? And David's angel? She shook her head slightly. And no doubt Bree's Lottie as well.

A phrase she had once read popped into her head. Suspend belief. She really needed to be able to do that with her chosen family. A slow smile stretched her lips. No, she didn't have to suspend belief. All she had to do was believe and wonderful, remarkable things happened.

She turned to face one of those remarkable, wonderful things and reached up to kiss Bryce. "That answered a lot of questions."

"Aye," Derrik whispered as he rose. "But dinna ye think now there be even more questions?"

"Like how we free Searlait from her banishment?" Jaye nodded. "The deeds she's done to protect this family far outweigh the killing of one who tried to kill Derrik. Derrik, we'll go to the Queen right now and petition her release before we share the news of Feidhlim's return."

"Jaye," Allyn warned.

"Don't worry, darlin'. You just organize this joining. Derrik and I will be there in plenty of time."

Dressed in a pale, cream-colored gown that flowed and draped her body in a material like silken gauze, Carrie felt every bit the bride. And felt every bit of nervousness as she wondered if she was doing the right thing.

::Ah, child. How can ye doubt?::

After Lottie's soft question, Carrie realized she didn't. There was absolutely no doubt within her, no fear, no concern. Only the love she felt for Bryce. Love wasn't enough to sustain a relationship, she realized, but it was a damn good start. They'd work through her past and work together for their future.

She twirled and let the dress settle about her ankles then smiled at Allyn. "It's so beautiful."

"Yes, you are. I think our Bryce is a lucky man."

"Allyn, you've never answered my question."

"Which one was that?"

"Do I need someone to stand with me during the joining?"

"No, not really. But lately, in the rare cases when Faeries join, they have begun that custom. Maybe it's an influence from the increased contact with the human world." Allyn shrugged and spread her hands.

"Would you... be willing to stand with me?"

"Wouldn't you prefer your mother? Or a friend?"

"I don't think Mom would be ready for all this yet. And, my best friend has already agreed to stand with Bryce. You've been so kind and helped me so much these past few days. I can't think of anyone else I'd be honored to have with me."

"Then, of course, I'd be honored as well." Allyn glanced out the window. "It's time. I hope everyone's done their part."

Carrie crossed to the window and hugged Allyn. "Now what have you been planning?"

The smile of a kept secret brightened Allyn's face. "You'll see. Ah, here comes Lara with Breanna."

Carrie rushed from the cottage they'd used for dressing and waited on the wide porch. Lara wore a dress that fell to mid-calf, the deep forest green a perfect foil for her golden curls. Bree skipped in front of her, a short, pink, ruffled dress swinging as she moved. Her white-blonde hair sparkled in the late afternoon sun. When she saw Carrie, she froze, then ran forward with a squeal and launched herself into Carrie's open arms.

"Mommy! See, I told you!"

"Told me what?"

"That you'd be my mommy." She twined her small arms around Carrie's neck. "I love you."

"I love you, too, Breanna."

Bree refused to be set down, so Carrie held her as Allyn shooed them toward the path. A short walk through the forest brought them to Bryce's glen, but Allyn wouldn't let Carrie pass from under the trees.

"Not until it's time," she said with a laugh.

Lara took Bree and, after warm words of welcome, left Carrie and Allyn standing in the cool, dim light. Carrie peeked around a thick tree trunk and gave a soft cry of delight.

Bryce's already beautiful glen had been transformed. An open pavilion, surrounded by panels of lace rippling in the soft breeze stood to one side. A round table, loaded with platters and bowls of food, centered the pavilion. Carrie's gaze followed the sound of soft music to a second pavilion where Korin played a wooden flute. Jaysson joined him and the muted sounds of a small hand drum became a delightful counterpoint.

Blossoms strewn across the already flower-filled grass, lifted and changed position as the breeze blew across them. A sea of flowers. For her.

She tried to find Bryce amidst the people dressed in bright colors. Bree ran across the glen, took David's hand from Tommy, and led him over to join Lara's twins near the musicians, and although David shook his head and stood next to Jaysson, the other three joined hands in a circle dance. Their laughter rose over the soft conversations.

Carrie glanced at Allyn. "Now what?"

"Once the Queen arrives—"

"The... the Queen? Here?"

Allyn chuckled. "As the leader of this clan, she presides over any Faerie joining involving members of her realm. Bryce, by being son of the leader of her Alastriona, is definitely considered one of hers. And, since Jaye is her heir, and Bryce is a chosen relative, he's got a double whammy. Oh."

"What?"

"Jaye has returned, but without the Queen." Allyn sighed. "He's wearing a crown of flowers, so it looks like he'll be presiding. The trouble with Feidhlim and Searlait's appearance must be keeping the Queen away. I'm sorry."

Relief filled Carrie. She wasn't sorry. It was too soon to meet the Faerie Queen. She needed instructions on how to act, how to speak and address Faerie royalty.

Allyn chuckled and clapped her hands softly. "Jaye looks really uncomfortable. He's never appreciated the flower crowns—but I think he's kinda cute."

The music slowed and became a low undercurrent to the sounds of nature. Jaye moved to the center of the glade. The others gathered close, leaving two open paths, one from where Carrie stood, the other from the opposite side of the glen.

"This is it, Carrie." Allyn brushed at Carrie's dress and

smoothed an errant curl that had fallen over her forehead. "Ready?"

"But what do I do?"

"You'll know." Allyn kissed her cheek. "Let's go."

Allyn took her hand and led her from under the trees. The power of every pair of eyes stared at her and she could barely force herself to look anywhere but at the ground at her feet. When she did, only welcoming smiles greeted her. Allyn led her part way across the small glen, stopped and nodded toward the other path.

Nightshade led the way, resplendent in a flowing, wide sleeved shirt and tight pants. But Carrie barely registered his appearance; her whole being focused on the man following him. Dressed in pale ivory matching her dress, his tunic skimmed his hips. Soft trousers flowed over his legs and brushed the grasses.

Nightshade stopped an equal distance from Jaye. When Jaye lifted his hands, Allyn pushed Carrie forward. "Go on, darlin'."

She met Bryce and he took her hand. His gentle smile gave her the courage to continue. The love shining in his eyes, bright as the sun's highlights in his pale hair, took away any doubts daring to remain.

Together they took the final steps and faced Jaye. The circle of family closed around them, even the children were silent.

"You have chosen to be joined in the Faerie way?" Jaye intoned solemnly.

"We have," Bryce answered.

"What promises do you make to the woman you have chosen? What would you say to Carrie?"

Bryce took her hands in his and ran his thumbs over the backs. He stared at their joined hands for a long moment, then lifted his gaze to hers. "Carrie Newcomb, I love you. From the first moment I saw you, I knew you belonged in my life. My heart belongs to you, now and always. Should we live only in the human world, live only human lifetimes, I shall love you until I die. Here, in Faerie, our lives can be longer still. I will love you that long, and longer. Forever, sweetheart, though forever is only a moment in my love for you. Our love is magick.

"All I do, will be to make you happy. All I do, will be to keep you safe from harm. All I do, will be for the love of you.

"You have chosen me, a choice I still can't believe. You have chosen my daughter as well, to share in your life. You have chosen my family as an extension of me.

"All I ask is that you love me in return."

Silence surrounded them. Carrie's numbed mind accepted Bryce's words. He loved her that much?

"Carrie, what promises do you make to the one you have chosen?"

"Bryce, I..." She tried to get the words she didn't know she had past the knot in her throat. Bryce smiled an encouragement. "I can't believe you've chosen me. How could I do any less than promise you as you've promised me? Forever. That's how long I'll love you. And longer, if fate gives me that chance.

"Your daughter, your family, are a part of me now. I love them as I love you.

"My passion I give only to you. My heart and soul are yours. You have saved me, given me hope, shown me a way I never believed existed. I love you. The words are not enough, I love you."

Jaye removed the flower crown from his head and, with a tiny flick of his wrist, turned the circlet into a short rope of flowers. He wrapped the flowers over their joined hands, tucking in the ends so the rope formed flowery handcuffs.

"Rare as soulfire, Faerie joining binds the chosen forever. By the binding of these flowers, by the choices of your hearts, you are so bound. No mortal laws shall bind you so completely. None of Faerie shall break the vows of your hearts."

He stepped back. Carrie couldn't tear her gaze from the intensity in Bryce's eyes. The world could explode around them and she'd never know. The power of the love between them was so strong, so intense she didn't know how she would contain it—or how she could ever live without him.

Jaye touched their bound wrists. "You don't have to, for it's not a part of the Faerie joining, but if you'd like... you can share a kiss now." He laughed and stepped back. A murmur of comment and laughter rounded the circle as she and Bryce stood, only gazing at each other.

Slowly, Bryce blinked and pulled her closer. He wrapped his unbound hand around her waist, held her tight, and touched his lips to hers with infinite tenderness. She cupped his cheek with her free hand. Their bound hands remained crushed between them.

The family's cheer startled the birds in the surrounding trees. The flutter of the rising birds was nothing compared to the wild beating of her heart.

They were joined. He was hers and she was his.

A small hand patted her hip. Somehow keeping the press of their lips joined in the kiss, Bryce bent them enough to lift Breanna. Together, they held the small girl at their sides and she stroked their hair and faces.

And Breanna was theirs.

A Faerie feast followed the joining, complete with games and dancing. Other musicians joined Jaysson and Korin in playing late into the night and the resilient Faerie grasses were trampled flat under dancing feet.

The hour was late, the moon had risen, peaked, and began to set before the family quietly left the glade. The music silent, only one couple remained, dancing to the sounds of the night, oblivious to everything except each other.

"You have to make sure he's here. Nightshade, tie him up and drag him here if you have to."

Nightshade's reply was lost to Carrie in the buzz and crackle of her cell phone. Damn, he was out of the area. She stared and shook her head at her phone, then lay the offending bit of plastic and circuitry carefully on the dressing table.

Nightshade knew what he needed to do, so she didn't need to worry. Ever since she announced to Bryce a week ago, one week after their joining, that she was going to dance tonight, she'd been trying to obtain his promise to be there. She'd even enlisted Bree's help to persuade her father.

The announcement surprised him, and he had remained silent for nearly half a day. But never once had he asked her not to, nor expressed his dismay at her decision. She saw in his eyes and the tight set of his lips how much he hated even the thought of her continuing to dance—to strip. Actually, she hated it as well. But she had to dance tonight.

She and Nightshade had worked frantically to find the right music and create the perfect costume for his seamstress to put together. And finally, to get Bryce there to see her.

Carrie glanced at the pale blue dress hanging from a hook on the wall. Beaded, fringed and heavy, the outfit was the most spectacular she'd ever danced in. She hoped Bryce would understand.

"Honey, I can't be held responsible if you don't go." Bryce glared at Nightshade. "You know how hard it was before. I could barely stay in my seat. I wanted to punch out every man so they couldn't see her. That was before everything we've gone through. Before our joining. I don't think I could stand it now."

"Have you told her that?"

"She knows."

"Have you told her that?"

Couldn't the man let it go? Bryce crossed his arms. "No. I've never said the words. Satisfied?"

"Um hmm. You're going."

"I can't. I don't know what I'd do."

"You're going. I promised Carrie I'd make sure you're there. And, honey, you know I can do it." Nightshade adopted a pose that hinted at his earlier life. Just as quickly the Nightshade he knew returned.

With a reluctant nod, Bryce agreed. Part of him did want to be at The Panther's Back when Carrie danced. If, for no other reason, than to somehow protect her from the leers of other men. He rolled his eyes at his foolish thought. But maybe, after tonight, he'd be able to talk with her about this. Maybe she'd give up stripping. He wanted her to be happy, but just the thought of her dancing tore him apart.

"You're a good man, honey." Nightshade slouched in the chair across Bryce's desk and peered out the wide expanse of his office windows. "How're things going with David? Any luck with the adoption?"

"Pop's had no trouble keeping him out of the social services system and has an attorney checking into what he needs to do. The Relinquishment of Rights was signed and recorded in court in

Ohio just like David said, but nobody seems to know how he ended up with Templeton."

"So nobody's been legally responsible for the boy?" Nightshade leaned forward. "Shoddy legal system."

"I won't argue with that." Bryce pulled a folded newspaper from under a pile of papers and handed it to his friend. "Pop's got to run this ad three times to announce they're looking for David's natural father. If he doesn't show up, then Pop will be free to start the adoption proceedings. If there's any problem there, Carrie and I will petition to adopt David. He's not leaving this family."

"Hmm. Don't think that'll be much of a problem. You'll either have a little brother or a son. Not a bad thing, honey. Oh, I heard the detective's brother will be handing the legalities."

"Yeah. He's been a great help to my folks and to David as well. He knows all the resources around for the visually impaired. And, David's fallen in love with his guide dog."

Nightshade's eyebrows lifted. "Guide dog? A blind attorney? Interesting." He glanced at the wall clock. "Gotta be going, honey. I'll pick you up at..."

"I'll be ready at eight. I don't want to do this Nightshade. Can't—"

"No, honey, I can't. Ta."

Nightshade flowed from the room, his low chuckle grating on Bryce's taut nerves. Maybe watching Carrie dance wouldn't be so bad this time. Maybe he'd be able to block out everything but Carrie. He had to try. If she wanted to continue her exotic dancing he'd have to get himself and his emotions under tight control. Bryce scrubbed his hands over his face and through his hair. He stared out the windows. Somehow...

Bryce sat at the small dark table near the bar. Nightshade positioned himself in the next chair, and Bryce knew if he made even the slightest move to leave before Carrie appeared on stage, he'd be tackled to the ground and forced back to his seat.

His hands tightened around the pilsner glass and the beer shook from the intensity of his emotions. He couldn't sit still much longer.

The lights dimmed, and blue spots highlighted the long, narrow stage. A screech from the sound system made Bryce cringe and clasp his glass tighter. Nightshade patted his shoulder and left his hand there for a few moments. After a long, painful breath, Bryce lifted his gaze to the stage.

The spotlights blinked out, one by one, until the only light in the club came from the neon ads over the bar.

"Now, in a special dance, her farewell performance... it's... Carouselle!"

Farewell performance? Bryce stared through the darkness. What was going on? Where was she?

A single blue spotlight grew from a tiny glow on the floor to light the figure posed on the closest end of the stage. Carrie's back was to him, a long, bare expanse of back exposed by the deep dip in her costume. The blue light glittered in the sparkling beads covering the dress and hanging as fringe nearly to the floor.

It's a kind of magic.

Bryce's head jerked at the music, a song by one of his folks' favorite groups. Magic?

Spellbound by Carrie's sinuous movements, Bryce let himself be taken by the song and her presence. She was speaking to him through her dance, telling him something. But as if his mental processes were taken from him, he couldn't think. Could do nothing but experience the dance.

Carrie moved from one end of the stage to the other, and up the short runway centered down the room. She swayed, twisted, and made facets of blue jump around the bar when the beads caught the light. The costume never changed, was never removed. The elegant dress remained a dress.

The song spoke of flames, of harmonies. Carrie held his gaze, and although there were others in the room, she danced only for him. Only... for... him.

Magic.

Magic. Yes, she was. And she was his. She wasn't stripping; this was her last dance. The tension left Bryce's shoulders and as he relaxed, he barely registered the fact that Nightshade's hand was gone as well.

Magic.

The lights and music faded, then the bar lights came up. Carrie received a wild round of applause from the gathered men, but she waved away the offered tips they held toward her. With a wave and a smile, she sauntered to the end of the stage.

Bryce leapt from his seat and waited at the bottom of the four risers when she stepped from the stage. Before she'd reached the second step, he'd wrapped his arms about her waist, pulled her from the stage, and kissed her fiercely. Vaguely, he acknowledged words from the announcer stating he was the reason for Carrie's final performance. The begrudging applause was little more than white noise in his ears.

Then Nightshade pushed them gently behind the curtain and away from prying eyes. He stepped back and closed the dusty drapery behind him. Bryce glanced around and grinned at the outline of their friend, guarding their privacy.

"Magic, Carrie?"

"You're my magic. I wanted to tell you that. I wanted my last professional dance to be for you. Do you understand what I wanted to say?

The insecurity in her eyes endeared her to him, not that he needed anything else to love her beyond reason.

"I understand, Carrie," he whispered against her cheek. "Our love, it's a perfect kind of magic."

DEAR READER

Thank you for reading this tale. Bringing stories to life is one of my greatest delights and I hope you enjoyed your time in one of my worlds. Readers like you spark the energy needed to tell these tales. Again, thank you.

With today's world of vast reading choices, word of mouth is the best advertising. So please let others know about this book. Tell your friends, relatives, acquaintances, the dog next door (hey, you never know...). And please consider leaving a review at your favorite retailer or review site.

To keep up with new releases, sign up for *Starr Words*. Yes, it's a newsletter, but will appear in your email only occasionally. Your email is safe with me, will never be shared, and you can, of course, unsubscribe at any time. You can find the link on my website www.lizziestarr.com

Next, there's a bit about each of my books. Enjoy the love and discovery! Happy reading!

Lizzie Starr

NEXT IN THE SERIES

Keltic Dreams: *Double Keltic Triad 5*

Passion blazes hotter than the desert sun.
Time alone might bring solutions to Bard's quest. But will unknown danger and the search for knowledge drive a wedge between him and Kaelea? Will they survive a passion that burns hotter than the desert sun?

KELTIC MULTIVERSE: DOUBLE KELTIC TRIAD

By Keltic Design: *Double Keltic Triad 1*

It ain't easy to be fey when you don't believe in fairy tales.

In the fey Otherworld, a half-faerie child is born. To protect him from evil's crusade to ensure the purity of the faerie race, he is abandoned in the human world, never to know of his magical heritage.

Now Jaye Zeroun is a successful businessman, rooted in reality. Fantasy is only something from an undisciplined imagination. Until he meets Celtic artist and friend of Faerie, Allyn Keeley.

Allyn has found the man she can love but fears their age difference and the overwhelming task of helping him realize his destiny will tear them apart. But Allyn knots her way around Jaye's heart and fills his life with a fantasy he refuses to believe.

Until danger threatens their love, forcing him to either accept a deadly battle or lose the very things he never planned for in his life' a family and a love beyond his wildest imaginings.

Fires of a Keltic Moon: Double Keltic Triad 2

Can love find a way through time?

Lara Zeroun needs an adventure, so she opens a portal in time and travels to the ancient Scottish Highlands. She meets two mysterious men but dares not trust her heart with either.

Under a matriarchal line of succession, Iain is unable to claim his father's holdings--his home. With no lands or possessions, he fights the temptation of a golden-haired woman who came to the manor on the arm of a wandering storyteller.

The storyteller's deceptions bring danger in Iain's time and threaten the destruction of Lara's present. Will Lara and Iain defeat the power of this growing evil and find their ways through time to the love they both desire?

Keltic Flight: *Double Keltic Triad 3*

What does she need to believe in love?

Even as a mythical faerie, Nanceen doesn't believe in the legends of tiny winged fey. Until a soft voice compels her to search... for love. She doesn't know what she believes but what she discovers changes everything.

Korin Goodfellow has loved the gentry maid from afar. But showing himself to her is forbidden by the fairy king, until using deceptions hidden by dark plans, the king forces Korin into an agreement with seemingly impossible conditions. Fueled by his pure emotions, Korin appears to Nanceen as a wingless man. One she can see. Touch. Believe in.

The evil fairy king keeps Korin's heritage hidden, warping the conditions to force Korin into battle after battle until he discovers his true place in the fairy world. Will Nanceen stand at his side as he risks everything for love?

Wild Keltic Carouselle: *Double Keltic Triad 4*

Falling in love is easy, the possibilities endless.

After months of searching, Bryce accepts he'll never find the masked dancer who captured his heart. Time to get on with life. But when his darlin' daughter climbs onto the lap of a captivating woman in a coffee shop and calls her Mommy, he certainly wouldn't mind exploring the possibility.

After a lengthy vacation, Carrie dreads returning to the job she once loved. Especially when a blond-haired cherub insists on calling her Mommy. The tiny girl's father is intriguing, and Carrie believes she's ready for a real relationship. But memories of a horrific attack surface making her doubt and fear a happy future.

Although he's human, Bryce's family ties are to the Faerie Otherworld, so when one of his fathers is kidnapped, no one knows if the abduction was of human or fey origins.

Falling in love was easy. Telling Carrie about the Otherworld risks that love. But demons resurfacing from both their pasts and evil-doers intent of destroying the present are intent on tearing them from their newfound love. Will their love survive a world of deception, lies and revenge?

Keltic Dreams: *Double Keltic Triad 5*

Passion blazes hotter than the desert sun.

A spiritual quest throws Bard, naked and alone, from his world to the desert Sahara. In search of answers, each grueling step through the shifting sands only adds to his questions and confusion. What did the seven Guardians mean for him to learn in this strange place?

An ever-present evil continues to stalk her family, so Kaelea researches possible protections at the Fey Library of Alexandria. The appearance of a stranger at the oasis is an unwelcome interruption. Her instant fascination with the man, and the overly possessive actions of a fellow researcher are even more distracting.

Time alone might bring solutions to Bard's quest. But will unknown danger and the search for knowledge drive a wedge between him and Kaelea? Will they survive a passion that burns hotter than the desert sun?

(Author's note: The action of the book *Prince of Dark Ness* takes place between Triad books 5 and 6. While it's not necessary to read *Prince of Dark Ness* here, it does give background into Lucidea's life prior to meeting Jaysson.)

A Faire Keltic Renaissance: *Double Keltic Triad 6*

It ain't easy being fey... and the subject of prophecy

Lucidea had no idea her father wasn't human—until a chance assignment as a forensic artist leads her to Scotland and a family she never knew. With her uncle imprisoned in the World Between Worlds, she's forced to assume leadership of a parallel, underwater world as his half Alfar-Sindhu heir.

Then she meets Jaysson Zeroun who has Otherworldly issues of his own. Once again evil plagues his clan and protecting a newborn child takes priority over personal dreams. When

Lucidea offers to hide the family at her uncle's manor, Jayse accompanies them to Scotland. He's falling for Lucidea, but he fears how she'll react to the fact he's part Faerie.

Three worlds are in peril. A pieced together ancient prophecy might defeat the separate evils, but will it also bring them love?

KELTIC MULTIVERSE: OTHER TALES

Prince of Dark Ness: Keltic Mulitverse

(Author's note: This story takes place between books 5 and 6 of the *Double Keltic Triad* and introduces the heroine of book 6.)

An ill-prepared Alfar-Sindhu prince struggles to protect two worlds from an ancient fire elemental.

Torn between duty and love, Morghan stands alone to protect both his Alfar-Sindhu underwater world and humanity from an ancient fire elemental bent on escaping the World Between Worlds. While he's loved Coralie long upon long, he never acted on his desire.

Raised in the royal household, Coralie has remained steadfast at Morghan's side through long human years. She's hidden her true feeling for him, even from herself.

A forensic artist from America, Lucidea Galvagin travels to Scotland to determine the identity of a skull found on Morghan's land. What she discovers changes her life and possibly the fate of two worlds.

Will Morghan's two worlds be lost if he chooses family and Coralie over battle? Or will his actions doom a multiverse of worlds to fiery destruction?

Blue Keltic Moon: Children of the Triad 1

Love and redemption? Only under the blue Keltic moon.

It's been twenty years since Morghan, leader of the Alfar-Sindhu, was trapped in the desolate World Between Worlds. Now blue moons are aligning in a multitude of worlds, signaling a magical opportunity.

Devoting his life to the Fey library hasn't saved Gowthaman from the agonies of his past, and the long moments he spent in the World Between Worlds. Now, the woman he loves stands ready to lead others into that cursed place. Only he holds the knowledge enabling them to enter. And with luck, safely return with the prince. The risk to his mind doesn't matter, as long as he keeps Breanna from harm.

A competent warrior, Breanna sets aside her personal desires to lead the rescue mission, facing the unknown to bring Morghan home. While she's loved Gowthaman forever, he claims their age difference is too great. But she's seen their soulfire and knows he loves her as well.

Together they must face the World Between Worlds. Can a place filled with despair and loss also be a discovery of love and redemption? Perhaps... only under the blue Keltic moon.

Candy Guy and the Chocolate Brownie: *Keltic Mulitverse*

A short story

Who better to assist a struggling chocolatier than a Brownie?

Candy Guy is in trouble. Winning a design contest will prove his abilities as a chocolatier, but creativity eludes him. An enchanting intruder invades Trace's workspace. She may be real, or she might be a dream. It doesn't matter. Desire consumes him at her lingering touch and the deep chocolate flavor of her kiss.

Deleesi hopes to end the ancient fey curse haunting her family, but the handsome wisher defies her sleep-inducing magic. Something about this human calls to her soul, and, unbelievably, to her heart. The sensual distraction proves impossible to ignore, even while granting his unspoken wish.

By the end of the rainy afternoon, Trace has his inspiration. But will he ever again see the tiny woman who captivated his heart and became his muse?

ASPEN GOLD SERIES

The Aspen Gold Series

The Aspen Gold Series is a multi-author series set in the small, but affluent tourist town of Spenser, Colorado. I'm delighted to join with these six fantastic authors to bring you these tales. Find out more about the entire series at www.aspengoldseries.com.

These are my contributions to the series... so far.

Ryder's Heart: *Aspen Gold Series Book 3*

Ryder discovers an intriguing woman in his bed...

Five celibate years in Hollywood didn't ease Ryder Barlow's guilt over his father's death, and now he's coming home to Spencer with a new purpose—to create a camp specializing in equine therapy. When he discovers a beautiful woman in his bed, his plans aren't exactly derailed, but definitely knocked off kilter.

Escaping her past hasn't been easy for Vianna Harrison, but she thinks she's found a welcoming home in Spencer—as long as she can keep her ability as a psychic medium hidden. Not an easy task when spirits need to speak of forgiveness and joy to so many loved ones. Or when the owner of the exquisite cabin she's been allowed to live in comes home unexpectedly.

Neither can start a new chapter in their lives until they stop rereading the old ones. Will acceptance overcome their secrets and show them their Rocky Mountain path to love?

For Keeps: *Aspen Gold Series Book 4*
Hiding the truth is like denying the sun.
Widow Kate Michaels kept a secret from the man she loves, and from the entire community of Spencer, Colorado. She's content running her bookstore and life is good. But in order to pay for his medical care, she must sell the ranch that was her father's dream, and in doing so disappoint her 8-year-old, horse loving daughter. Madison makes an unlikely friend in someone Kate would rather forget.

Veterinarian Jackson Samuels is intrigued by the charming girl, and occasionally lets her shadow him in his nearby clinic. He's enamored with the child's mother, but her defenses are so sturdy, not even his charm or their shared past can make a dent. When Jack uncovers a family secret, the truth makes him question who he thought he was.

Will two people who once shared a heartfelt love, allow their lonely secrets to consume and define them? Or will they help each other, forgive each other, and build a future together—For Keeps?

*(Author's note: Barbara Gwen was one of the original authors who created the Aspen Gold Series. When I joined the group and planned my own story, we discovered our heroes were best friends. When Barb left this world much too soon, how could I not finish the book of her heart. **For Keeps** is by her and for her.)*

Speechless: *Aspen Gold Series Book 8*

How many peonies does it take to get married?

It's a beautiful day in Spencer, Colorado, and the peonies are in bloom. A perfect day to gather for a wedding, filled with love, traditions, fun, and maybe even a prank or two.

Vianna Harrison and Ryder Barlow would love the honor of your presence as they celebrate their marriage.

Fortunate Cookie: *Aspen Gold Book 11*

This woman. Wearing Frosting. And nothing else...

Cookie Lamont owns a successful cupcake shop in Spencer's trendy tourist center. Life would be perfect if not for the escalating unwanted attention from a self-important town trustee. She has everything she needs—and a man is the last thing on her mind.

Until he walks into her shop.

Treehouse builder and TV personality Anthony Burnham returns to Spencer and finds focus building cabins for a new camp. His passion for treehouses is rekindled as a sweet, sexy new love blooms.

But the past haunts his steps and threatens his growing relationship with the alluring baker.

Some Days are Diamonds, is a short story included in:
Yesterday's Promise: *Aspen Gold Series Book 16*

A high-stakes poker game, first meets, a dog rescue, loves lost and rekindled, and life-altering choices fill the history of Spencer, Colorado. Discover the challenges faced in these heartwarming stories crafted by the multi-author group who brings you romantic fiction at its finest in The Aspen Gold Series.

This collection includes:

The Card Game~~ M.A.Jewell

Some Days Are Diamonds~~ *lizzie starr

Ah, Venice ~~ Debra Hines

First Chance ~~ Donna Kaye

Racing Hearts~~ Bernadette Jones

Rescue Me ~~ Cheryl St.John

FANTASY ROMANCE

Double Moon Destiny

On the night of the Double Moon a
child is born, and the destinies of an
acolyte and a rebel are changed forever.

Jermanah, acolyte of the religious
Compound, has never been given the
opportunity to make her own choices.
Although she accepts her way of life and
yearns to rise higher in the order, she
learns ancient, forbidden healing from the
Seer. On the night of the Double Moons, a
child is born and given into Jermanah's
care until the boy is taken to the king.

Kierigh was born moments before the rising of the Double
Moons, but his twin brother wasn't so lucky. Rumors flow from
the Stronghold—following an ancient prophecy, the king sacri-
fices the baby boys to increase his power. But Kierigh senses that
even after five cycles, his brother still lives.

When Kierigh's rebels attack the procession, he takes the
babe, and Jermanah, to his hidden camp. The captivating acolyte
disrupts Kierigh's ordered and simple life. He opposes her religion

and all the Compound claims to stand for. She's everything he doesn't need in his life. Yet she is everything he desires.

No longer considering herself one of the Compound, Jermanah discovers freedom, and truths she finds difficult to believe. But when the babe is taken from the forest, she will do anything to save the child, including face the leader of the Compound—and the king.

Can a rebel and an acolyte set aside pride and differences to find a lost brother, defeat evil, and discover their prophecy fulfilling destinies?

CONTEMPORARY ROMANCE

Birds Do It!

A search for truth, switched babies, and a threat from the past

Macaws as lovebirds?

An avian expert, Birdie Simons is called to help control a cantankerous hyacinth macaw during a young girl's birthday party. Inexorably drawn to each other, she and single father Garr Logan share an afternoon of joy and bittersweet memories, for Garr's wife died the same day as Birdie's newborn child.

Something about Rachelle makes Birdie wonder if the golden-haired girl is her daughter, switched at birth. Then her child's father returns, dogging her search for understanding and throwing her deeper into fear and confusion.

Ready to move on after his wife's death, Garr wants the intriguing woman, but Birdie keeps the search, threats, and hidden relationships to herself, driving a wedge between them.

Will discovering the truth from nine years ago bring them closer, or forever tear them apart?

SHORT STORIES

Written in Stone: *'Structs in the City 1*

Fantasy Romance

Undercover agent Stone Mason must find a data-link before a demonstration for underground bidders leads to mass destruction. His search of a posh hotel is risky, but time is up.

Monika Linberg returns to her hotel room after her boss dumps her and assumes the striking, robotic sex-struct is her consolation prize.

Stone is no construct, but a living, breathing man whose touch and need for information and assistance turn her world upside down. Will working with the sexy agent to keep the city safe be too dangerous for her heart?

Dead Lily Blooms: *At Death's Gates 1*

Fantasy Romance

For ages uncounted, Master Death has assisted souls in transition. But what happens when love gets in the way?

Someone wants vampyre Lily dead, and a bargain with Death has been struck. Death sends servant Agaar to bring Lily to him, but the task becomes more complicated than either Death or Agaar anticipated.

*This short story originally appeared in the anthology **Tales From The Mist**. This re-release has had minor corrections from the original edition.*

Death and the Dryad: *At Death's Gates 2*

Fantasy Romance

For ages uncounted, Master Death has assisted souls in transition. But what happens when love gets in the way?

What's Death to do when a dryad appears at his gate without her soul? She can't move on, nor go back. Will Death find a place for her--at his side?

*This tale appeared originally in the **Martini Madness** anthology and this re-release has had minor corrections and additions from the original.*

FUN STUFF

*lizzie also enjoys creating journals and guided workbooks for authors and other creatives. Look for them on her website.

www.lizziestarr.com

ABOUT THE AUTHOR

*lizzie always made up games and stories to keep her company. So, a cunning witch lived in Grampa's weather research station and was only held at bay by waving a certain weed. An ancient road grader morphed into a boat carrying wild adventurers to islands filled with fierce lions and dangerous cannibals, which really looked a lot like sheep.

Now filled with fantasy, love, and romance with a sparkling twist, the stories of her imagination swirl their way into the mundane world.

*lizzie recently retired from her more routine life of being *the Lunch Lady* at a private school. According to the kids, she was 'the best cooker!' Yes, she misses the students and teachers, but is delighted now to start her days by telling stories rather than opening cases of chicken nuggets and counting milk cartons.

Her tag line of *Author and lunch lady~~what a combination!* no longer holds true (which makes her sad because she really liked that one).

Now you'll know *lizzie by her tales of...

~~*Romance with a sparkling twist*~~

Want to keep up to date with all of *lizzie's worlds? Sign up for her newsletter on her website.

facebook.com/authorlizziestarr

twitter.com/lizziestarr

instagram.com/lizistarr

amazon.com/*lizzie-starr/e/B003F33Y0W

bookbub.com/profile/lizzie-starr

goodreads.com/lizziestarr

pinterest.com/lizziestarr

tiktok.com/@authorlizziestarr

www.ingramcontent.com/pod-product-compliance
Lightning Source LLC
Chambersburg PA
CBHW031119210626
46816CB00016B/1721